Jaeden felt as if he c... hard work. He'd spent ... off. The Herswick Corpor... ... to put their logos on hi... hats. As an added bonus, they wanted to develop a strategy for the best way to market them. There were still details to be worked out, but this was a big accomplishment for Jaeden. He couldn't wait to share his good news with Alexis.

Knocking on the door to her hotel room, he waited. When she opened it in a short pink nightgown and a matching robe, he swung her into his arms, giving her a deep kiss that nearly made her moan his name. Jaeden walked into the room with her still in his arms, closing the door behind him.

"...ou did it. Herswick accepted your proposal?" Alexis gushed in a high-pitched voice.

"...es," Jaeden shouted, then placed kisses all over Alexis's face.

"...hat didn't take long at all," Alexis said, closing her robe as best she could. "I'm not even dressed yet. I'm so happy for you, honey."

...eden set her on her feet, lifted her chin, and looked into her eyes. "I couldn't have done it without you."

"...le?" She pointed to herself. "I haven't done anything. *You* created the designs, *you* made it happen."

"*You* were there for me."

"That's what friends are for."

"Friend?" Jaeden gathered her close again, "You mean more to me than just a friend. I love you, girl." There, he finally said it. He released Alexis and walked away, waiting for his response.

SEAN D. YOUNG

TOTAL
Bliss

BET Publications, LLC
http://www.bet.com
http://www.arabesquebooks.com

ARABESQUE BOOKS are published by

BET Publications, LLC
c/o BET Books
One BET Plaza
1900 W Place NE
Washington, DC 20018-1211

All Kensington Titles, Imprints, and Distributed Lines are available at special quantity discounts for bulk purchases for sales promotions, premiums, fund-raising, and educational or institutional use. Special book excerpts or customized printings can also be created to fit specific needs. For details, write or phone the office of the Kensington special sales manager: Kensington Publishing Corp., 850 Third Avenue, New York, NY 10022, attn: Special Sales Department, Phone: 1-800-221-2647.

First Printing: June 2005

10 9 8 7 6 5 4 3 2

Printed in the United States of America

To My Daddy
Leon Taylor
1943–1994
For dropping the seed of determination in my spirit.

ACKNOWLEDGMENTS

O give thanks unto the Lord for he *is* good . . . .

The Lord has blessed me with people that have touched my life with their wisdom, kind words, prayers, and just their presence. Without these unselfish and kind hearts, there would be no me:

Gerold Sr.—Your honesty and support helped me make it through. I love you.

Gerold II and Brandon—I am so blessed to have been chosen to bring you into the world.

Mary Taylor—Mommy, you always told me I could do anything I put my mind to. I love you with my whole heart for being with me every step of the way.

Shirlonda—Red, it's always been just the two of us. Thanks for keeping Jeremiah 29:11 in the forefront of my mind. I love you, Jaeden, and Jarius.

Jacquelin Thomas—Thanks for being God's chosen vessel to get me here. Most of all, I want to thank you for your friendship and love. You're a jewel and your kindness will never be forgotten. The Lord will definitely reward you openly.

Rochelle Alers—You told me you can never get anything with a closed fist. The Bible is true when it says give and it shall be given unto you, pressed down, shaken together, and running over. May your cup overflow with God's richest blessings. I can never repay you for your wisdom.

Gloria Blackmon and Josie Martin—What would I do without you? You've always supported my every endeavor. Your belief in my ability humbles me and I'm so grateful to you for your prayers and support. You definitely remind me of the woman in Proverbs 31.

Gwen Osborne—What a wise woman you are and I love you for your spirit and strength.

Pastor Charles M. Morgan, First Lady Francine Morgan, and the entire Galilee M. B. Church family—Thanks for preparing me for my next journey in life. I'll never forget what you've done for me. I love you all.

Michele Robinson and Betty Williams—You were invaluable to me in writing this book. I don't think I could have done it without you. I love you both.

Demetria Lucas—Thank you for this opportunity to share my story with the world. May the blessings of the Lord be upon you.

CHAPTER ONE

"You *are* coming?" Stephanie Redus rolled her eyes and tried to keep from losing her temper. She'd lost count of the number of times she'd asked her best friend the same question.

"I've got so much to do, Stef," Alexis Shire said. "I'm sorry I can't make it this evening." Alexis had just taken a shower and put on her pajamas. Her only plans for the evening were to finish as much schoolwork as she could before she went to bed. It wasn't that she didn't want to go with Stephanie, she couldn't.

"Lexie, you promised me last time you would go to my uncle Tommie's place the next time we had a family get-together."

"I'll go the next time then, Stef, I promise." She tried to sound convincing.

"Uh-huh. Whatever. Look, I'm on my way over, so be ready when I get there."

The next thing Alexis heard was a dial tone. Clearly, Stephanie's patience had run out.

Alexis hung up the telephone and went back to her laptop, glancing over the paragraph she'd written before Stephanie had called. Alexis had been attending Purdue University Calumet on Tuesday and Thursday evenings since last fall. Always focused, she was pursuing a master's degree in order to reach her goal of becoming an administrator at the elementary school level.

She diligently worked on her English paper until the shrill ring of the telephone startled her, causing her to nearly jump off the stool where she sat. Slowly, she slid from her seat and crossed the room. Alexis was in no hurry to answer it because she had a pretty good idea of the caller's identity.

She picked up the phone, pressed the Talk button, and put the phone to her ear without saying a word.

"Let's go," Stephanie demanded.

"What?"

"I told you I was coming to get you." This time, she didn't even try to hide her irritation with her friend.

Alexis moved to the window and pulled back the white damask vertical blinds. She looked down at Stephanie, who was standing under the streetlight in front of her building.

Alexis chuckled into the phone as she waved. "You are so crazy, girl."

"Don't let me have to come up and get you," Stephanie threatened.

Alexis had no doubt Stephanie would try to drag her out. "Oh, Stef, please, girl, not tonight," Alexis pleaded, still staring at her friend.

Stephanie put a determined hand on her hip to let Alexis know she wouldn't take no for an answer. Alexis sighed in defeat. Stephanie could worry a person bald-headed, and at twenty-six, Alexis had no intention of losing any of her long hair.

"Fine, I'll be down in a sec."

"That's better," Stephanie said, walking toward her car. "And, Lexie?"

"Yeah?"

"Don't take all night."

Moving away from the window, Alexis pushed the button to end the call, exhaling in a huff. She clicked the Save button on her computer screen and shut down the laptop before making her way to the walk-in closet in her bedroom.

Alexis liked order in her life, and her closet was no different. All the slacks, blouses, suits, and dresses each had their own section and were arranged by fabric and color. Since she knew she didn't have time to be choosy about an outfit, she pulled out a pair of black slacks and her favorite white pullover blouse. She walked toward the back of the closet where she kept stacks of shoe boxes and grabbed a white box that held a pair of black pumps. As she made her way out of the room, she picked up her black Coach belt from the rack where she kept her accessories.

Quickly, she slipped on her clothes and hurried into the adjoining bathroom to fix her face. To accentuate her delicate features, she applied Victoria's Secret makeup to her honey-colored skin. When she finished, she ran her fingers through her long dark brown hair until the curls lay around her shoulders. She pulled her gold charm bracelet from beneath her blouse, then adjusted her belt and smoothed out the cuffs of her slacks.

Alexis was slipping on her shoes when she heard the blaring sound of Stephanie's car horn.

"She is so impatient," she said aloud, hitting the light switch as she left the bathroom. Alexis moved to the front of the apartment and grabbed her purse from the couch. She swiped her keys off the end of the breakfast bar on her way out the door.

"'Bout time," Stephanie said when Alexis opened the car door and slid into the passenger seat.

"Just drive."

Stephanie looked Alexis up and down, turning her

nose up before she pulled off. "Ms. Lexie, why are you dressed like you're going to brunch? We're only going over to Uncle Tommie's place. Girl, you crack me up."

Alexis ignored her friend's remarks and rolled up her window so her hair wouldn't get blown out of place. Folding her arms over her purse in her lap, she stared outside.

Stephanie shrugged and turned up the volume on the radio when an old-school classic by Cheryl Lynn came on. She began to sway from side to side to the music, turning her head back and forth toward Alexis for effect.

Alexis smiled even though she didn't want to. "You are so silly," she said, shaking her head at Stephanie.

She was familiar with Stephanie's playful antics. Three years earlier, the two women had met after Alexis took a position as a kindergarten teacher at Nobel Elementary School. Stephanie taught first grade across the hall and they'd become fast friends. The tall, deep-brown-skinned young woman had a carefree attitude and always had a good time. No matter where they were, *nothing* ever got her down.

"You'd better watch the road," Alexis warned, holding in her laughter. "Where does your uncle live anyway?"

Stephanie turned onto Bigger Lane. "Down this street."

There were cars parked on both sides of the tree-lined street. Stephanie had told Alexis she had a big family and it seemed everyone showed up for the gathering. Luckily, they found a parking space for Stephanie's Nissan Altima not too far from her uncle's house.

"I didn't know you had relatives that lived over here. This is nowhere from my apartment," Alexis said, checking her watch as they got out of the car.

"Uncle Tommie just had this house built a couple of years ago."

Alexis turned and stared at the white brick two-story

home. This particular area of Taylor, Indiana, had been part of a revitalization project.

"You always late, girl. Where ya been?" a voice behind them called out.

"Minding my business and leaving yours alone," Stephanie yelled back, slamming the car door.

"Who are you talking to?" Alexis asked. Closing the passenger door, she looked around, but didn't see anyone.

"My uncle Toot. He is so nosy." Stephanie twisted her face in mock disgust.

"Where is he?"

A portly, older man with tinted glasses stepped out of a dark green Cadillac that had been parked three cars behind them. He was dressed in a brown suit and matching hat with a long red feather sticking out of it. He smiled, showing off his gold teeth as he strode toward them. He reminded Alexis of a short version of Superfly.

When he took off his hat, Alexis noticed his hair was longer than hers.

"Anthony's the name, but my friends call me Toot." He extended his hand to Alexis. Each finger sported a different ring.

"She is not your friend, Uncle Toot," Stephanie said, walking around him and pulling Alexis along with her before she could shake his hand. "He's always trying to push up on my friends," Stephanie muttered, leaning close to Alexis so her uncle couldn't hear.

Alexis chuckled at how overprotective Stephanie was being. "He was only introducing himself to me, Stef."

"There's no harm in that is there?" Anthony said from behind them.

Alexis hadn't realized he was close enough to crush the backs of her shoes. She quickened her pace.

"Let's go inside and see what's cooking. I'm starving, aren't you?" Stephanie said, leading the way into the large house. "Oh, before I forget, I want to introduce you to my cousin," she added over her shoulder.

"Okay," Alexis responded nonchalantly as she stepped into the house behind Stephanie. She had no idea that her friend was up to something.

The massive structure was beautifully decorated, but there were so many people, Alexis couldn't take in the real beauty of the place. She tried to keep up with Stephanie as they went from room to room.

In the kitchen, Stephanie walked to the stove and hugged a slightly overweight woman who was sprinkling seasoning into a large pot. She had light brown skin and very delicate features. Her dark brown hair was styled in the same short fashion Stephanie wore and a white apron covered her oatmeal-colored slacks and beige blouse. Alexis could see her ivory pearls peeking from underneath the top.

"Aunt Glo, this is my friend, Alexis Shire," Stephanie said, motioning toward Alexis. "Alexis, this is my aunt, Gloria Jefferson."

Gloria's eyes sparkled as she smiled. "Pleased to meet you, Alexis."

"It's a pleasure to meet you, Mrs. Jefferson." Alexis accepted the neatly manicured hand the older woman offered.

"Is Jay here? I didn't see him when we came in," Stephanie said to her aunt.

"Not yet, dear," she replied, reaching into a cabinet for spices. "He called and said he was tied up in a meeting."

Stephanie lifted the lid off one of the pots on the stove to check its contents. "I hope he gets here before we leave."

Gloria sprinkled seasoning salt into another pot, only half paying attention to her niece. "I'm sure he'll try. He never likes to miss these things."

Stephanie turned to Alexis. "Do you see anything you want to eat?"

The food had been presented in a buffet style. Two cloth-covered tables were completely filled with all kinds of scrumptious dishes. Fried and baked chicken, chicken and dumplings, collard greens, black-eyed peas, macaroni and cheese, ham, pot roast, corn on the cob, string beans, mixed vegetables, potatoes, spare ribs, and red beans and rice. They even had a dessert table with pound cake, various chocolate cakes, banana pudding, and sweet potato and chess pie.

"Get whatever you want. There's plenty," Stephanie said when Alexis nodded. She grabbed utensils and began to fill her plate with a chicken leg and macaroni and cheese.

Alexis followed close behind, choosing a small portion of the pot roast, a few new potatoes, and some mixed vegetables. Satisfied with her selections, she took a seat next to Stephanie at the kitchen table.

"Is that all you're going to eat?" Stephanie asked as Alexis put down her plate.

"This is enough for me, thank you," Alexis said kindly. She wasn't that hungry and didn't want to put food on her plate she had no desire to eat.

"Do you want anything to drink? There's beer, soda, iced tea, punch, or water . . ." Stephanie went toward a red cooler sitting on the floor next to the refrigerator.

"Water is fine."

Stephanie picked out a soda for herself and grabbed a bottle of water for Alexis before taking her seat at the table again. Alexis whispered a short prayer and ate quietly. As she took another bite of the tender pot roast, she had to admit the food was delicious. She was enjoying herself, but her mind still kept going back to the paper she wanted to complete before she went to bed.

As she ate, a dark-skinned gentleman approached the table.

"Stef, when did you get here?" he asked.

"I've been here for a while. Where were you?" Stephanie replied as she rose from her seat to hug him.

"Your aunt Sherly and I have been downstairs beating the stank out of Jesse and Katherine in bid whist."

Stephanie laughed. "Uncle Tommie, I want you to meet my friend, Alexis Shire. Alexis, this is my uncle, Tommie Mitchell."

"Alexis," he repeated slowly. "What a pretty name for a beautiful girl."

Alexis wondered if all Stephanie's male relatives were flirts.

"Well, let me get back downstairs and see if I can't whip some more butts before the night is over." Tommie walked to the cooler and pulled out a bottle of Miller Lite.

"Come on down after you finish eating, Stef. And bring your friend with you." He winked at Alexis before he left.

Stephanie waved him off. "Girl, these old men are a trip. Don't pay any attention to Uncle Tommie, he's really a sweetheart, but he's a serious ladies' man."

Alexis giggled. "Don't worry about it. He didn't offend me. My mother's baby brother, Darren, is the same way. He's thirty-four and you should see him. He woos women everywhere he goes."

They both laughed and commenced finishing their meal.

"I'm starving," a booming voice bellowed from the hallway.

Alexis glanced up at the sound and had to do a double take. Her heart quickened as she looked straight into the most intriguing dark brown eyes she'd ever seen. The owner of those eyes was tall and clean shaven with a lean build. His hair was neatly cropped and his skin looked as if it had been kissed by the sun. He smiled, and Alexis thought if she had to sum him up in two words, they'd be devilishly handsome. She tried not to stare and willed her eyes to look away, but they wouldn't obey her command. His powerful presence had immediately filled the room and Alexis wanted—no, needed—to know his name.

She leaned forward to ask Stephanie, but before she could get the words out, Stephanie jumped up and threw her arms around him.

"It's about time you got here," Stephanie exclaimed, pulling her twenty-nine-year-old cousin close.

Alexis sat ramrod straight in her chair, waiting to be introduced. *Is this who Stephanie wanted me to meet?*

"Hey, Stef, I came as soon as I could," the stranger said.

Stephanie kept her arm around him and turned to Alexis. "Jaeden, this is my friend, Alexis Shire. Alexis, this is my cousin, Jaeden Jefferson."

Alexis's heartbeat accelerated. She grabbed her water bottle and put it to her mouth, taking a big gulp. Then she quickly wiped her hands on the paper napkin beside her plate.

"It's nice to meet you, Alexis." He extended his hand.

"Hello." She accepted his open palm and watched as her dainty hand was swallowed by his larger one.

When he didn't release it, Alexis looked up at him and immediately wished she hadn't. Their eyes were transfixed. What was it about this man that made butterflies swarm in her stomach? She hadn't been this nervous since she won the D. G. Lewis Academic Achievement Award in high school.

"We haven't met before, have we?" Jaeden asked after a pregnant pause.

Alexis opened her mouth to speak, but nothing came out. She cleared her throat and tried again. "No, I don't believe we have." *I never would have forgotten if we had,* she thought.

Jaeden slowly released Alexis's hand, but his eyes never moved from hers.

"I thought you were hungry," Stephanie said, breaking the hypnotic stare between them.

"I am." Reluctantly, Jaeden made his way to his mother, who had just filled a plate with food.

"Hey, Mama." He kissed her on the cheek.

"How did things go?" Gloria whispered, nodding toward Alexis.

Jaeden ignored the question and pointed at the plate his mother held. "That mine?"

She pulled the plate toward her chest. "No, I've been fixing plates all evening," she said, pursing her lips. "I'm tired now, so this one's *mine.*" Gloria held on to the plate and left the kitchen before he could argue.

Alexis leaned forward and whispered to Stephanie, "Is Jaeden who you wanted me to meet?"

Stephanie grinned, moving her head up and down. She slid to another chair, leaving the one across from Alexis vacant.

Jaeden walked back with a plate piled high with food. He took the seat Stephanie had just vacated. Bowing his head, he said a quick prayer, then picked up his fork and began to eat.

Alexis couldn't help herself; she watched every move he made. Suddenly, he looked up from his plate. She quickly looked down at hers so he wouldn't catch her staring.

Stephanie chuckled and Alexis gave her an evil look, which made Stephanie laugh even harder.

Jaeden stretched out his long legs, causing them to brush against Alexis's. "So, Alexis, how long have you and Stef been friends?" he asked before taking a bite of fried chicken.

Alexis fingered the rim of her water bottle. "About three years. We work together at Nobel."

Jaeden looked between Alexis and Stephanie. "So, you're a teacher, too?"

"Yes, I teach kindergarten."

"Wow, so you like working with those bad kids?"

Alexis smiled. "Yes, I do and they aren't all bad."

"She spoils them," Stephanie interrupted. "They all love Ms. Shire," she commented, mimicking one of the students.

"I do not spoil my students," Alexis defended.

Jaeden turned to Stephanie. "Are you still tormenting those kids in your class?"

Alexis chuckled.

"I do not torment my children, they love me," Stephanie huffed.

"Yeah, love to get away from you," Jaeden continued, teasing her.

"She's right. The children do love her, because she acts just like them." Alexis giggled. "You should see her with them at the school picnic."

"Ha, ha," Stephanie said sarcastically. "Now both of you got jokes."

"I'm sorry, Stef, I didn't mean any harm, but I couldn't resist." Alexis reached over to pat Stephanie's hand, but she snatched it away.

"Ha, ha," Stephanie said again as she playfully punched Jaeden in his shoulder to stop him from laughing.

"Seriously, though, you should come to the picnic this year," Stephanie suggested to Jaeden.

Jaeden's eyes fused with Alexis's again. "Maybe I'll do just that."

Alexis tried to turn away, but it was something about the way his eyes sparkled that pulled her in.

Finally, Jaeden's eyes left hers. "Is Ronnie here?" he asked Stephanie.

"Yeah, he's downstairs playing cards with Uncle Tommie and Junior, I think."

"Alexis, do you play cards?" Jaeden looked into her eyes once again.

She cleared her throat. "No."

"Maybe I can teach you sometime. That is, if you want lessons."

The undertone of his statement caused Alexis to conjure up several things he could probably teach her and cards wasn't one of them. She smiled, but didn't respond.

Stephanie pushed her chair from the table and stood up. "I'm going to find Aunt Glo to tell her we're leaving."

"Aw, so soon? I just got here," Jaeden said.

"Too bad, we've been here awhile and Alexis has a project to finish. She's in college again."

"So you're in school as well. Hmmm, a teacher, a student, and you're beautiful. I'm impressed." Jaeden rose from his seat so Stephanie could pass by and then sat down again.

"Thank you," Alexis said, blushing. She picked up her napkin and dabbed the corners of her mouth.

"Well, it was nice meeting you, Jaeden." She pushed her chair back and stood.

Always a gentleman, Jaeden stood too. "It was great to meet you, Alexis. Maybe we'll see each other again soon."

"Maybe," Alexis responded just as Stephanie walked back into the kitchen.

Stephanie looked between the two and said, "You ready to go, Lexie?"

Alexis was hoping Jaeden would ask for her number. When he didn't, she followed Stephanie from the room. She was tempted to turn around to see if Jaeden was watching her walk away, but decided against it.

"You still have time to finish your paper, right? I know how you are about your assignments," Stephanie said to Alexis once they were in the car.

Alexis hadn't heard a word Stephanie had said. She stared at Tommie's house, thinking about Jaeden's soulful eyes and sensual lips.

"Lexie!"

"Yes?" Alexis turned her head in Stephanie's direction.

"You didn't hear a word I said, did you?"

"I guess not." She blushed again, embarrassed to have been caught daydreaming.

Stephanie started the car and pulled away from the curb. "Forget it."

"I enjoyed myself, Stef. Thanks for inviting me."

"Is Jaeden the reason you had a good time?" Stephanie's right eyebrow rose up and down.

Alexis laughed as the image of Jaeden strolling into the kitchen replayed over and over in her mind.

"Lexie, you never answered my question."

Alexis grinned. *And I'm not going to.*

The following Saturday, Stephanie insisted Alexis go with her to Whispers Social Club. The sophisticated nightspot with its merlot-colored exterior had served as a hot spot in Taylor for many years. They played music of every kind—from old school to progressive house to hip-hop and urban remixes. Alexis hadn't been to the club since she'd returned home from college several years ago. She was amazed at the throng of people eager to get in.

Inside, the place was jumping, lights flashed, and there were already bunches of people on the floor dancing. There were many more seated at tables in the dimly lit corners. Looking around the crowded room, Alexis suspected some of the people that were still outside wouldn't get in tonight.

She followed Stephanie as they weaved their way through the crowd, trying to find a place to sit down. "I never understood why they called this place Whispers," Alexis yelled over the loud music.

Stephanie spotted an empty booth on the other side of the huge dance floor. She pointed in that direction. "Do you want a drink?" she asked, looking for a server after they had taken their seats.

"A glass of wine would be fine."

When the server came, Stephanie ordered two glasses of White Zinfandel.

Alexis looked around the room and spotted Jaeden. His towering height and lean body seemed to glide toward them as he zigzagged his way through the crowd. He looked better than he did the night she met him.

Without thinking twice, she brushed her navy slacks with her hands, then pulled out her compact to check her hair and makeup. She ran her fingers through her long tendrils to make sure every strand was in place.

As soon as she shut her compact, she found Jaeden in front of their table giving them a bright smile. "Hello, ladies."

Alexis's eyes focused on the way his olive-green shirt clung to his body, molding to the width of his firm chest. The alluring scent of his cologne wafted through the air.

"Hello," the women finally said in unison.

"When we spoke earlier, you didn't tell me you were coming tonight, Stef," Jaeden said.

"I—I guess I forgot to mention it," Stephanie stuttered, clearly lying.

Jaeden chuckled.

Alexis slid from the booth and gently pulled Stephanie's

arm. "Excuse us for a moment, we'll be right back," she said to Jaeden.

"No problem." Jaeden stood next to the table and watched the two walk away.

Alexis gently yanked Stephanie to the side. "What are you doing?"

Stephanie gave her friend a blank look. "What do you mean?"

"Oh, you know what I mean, Stef. You're trying to hook me up with your cousin," Alexis said in a not-so-pleased voice. "You know I'm too busy to date anyone."

Stephanie laughed, but didn't confirm or deny the accusation. "Let's get back to our table." Stephanie turned and walked away, leaving Alexis to stare at her retreating back.

Alexis caught up with her. "It's not going to work, so forget it," she insisted, frowning when Stephanie kept walking without giving a reaction to her statement.

Jaeden was standing right where they'd left him. As they approached, Alexis noticed the delicate features of his face, the smoothness of his skin, and square chin.

"May I join you?" he asked after they were seated.

"Of course, cuz." Stephanie moved down, not looking at the scowl on Alexis's face as Jaeden slid into the booth beside his cousin.

Alexis looked around the dimly lit room at nothing in particular, trying to ignore Jaeden, but still keenly aware of him.

"Hey, there's Chucky." Stephanie pointed in the crowd suddenly. "I've been trying to get in touch with him since last week. Let me out, Jay, so I can catch him."

Jaeden slid from the booth and waited for Stephanie to scoot out. She glanced at Alexis, who glared at her, and said, "I'll be right back," before she rushed into the crowd.

Jaeden sat back down across from Alexis. "Do you know who Chucky is?" he asked, already knowing the answer.

Alexis shook her head. "No, I thought you knew him."

They both laughed at Stephanie's not-so-subtle setup.

"I hope you had a good time the other night. I hate that I was so late."

"I had an enjoyable evening," Alexis said primly.

Jaeden's eyes fell on her lips. "I didn't want it to end so quickly though."

Alexis had to control the urge to squirm under his magnetic gaze. Illuminated by the light from the hurricane lamp on the table, his piercing eyes were mesmerizing. She quickly lost her train of thought.

The music slowed down a bit and several couples headed to the dance floor. The romantic song changed the ambiance in the room, making it seem like Jaeden and Alexis were on a date. She smiled nervously, unable to recall the last time she'd been out with a man. Being in a relationship was even further back in her memory bank.

Though she loved his smile and the way his dark eyes sparkled when he looked at her, the fact of the matter was Alexis didn't have time for a relationship. She had specific goals she needed to meet, and getting involved with someone would only complicate her life and distract her from pursuing her dreams.

As the butterflies in her stomach intensified, she realized she had to do something to keep herself calm. She pulled her Palm Pilot from her purse, hoping maybe Jaeden would think she wasn't interested in him. She sat quietly and turned it on.

"I've been planning to get a Palm, but haven't gotten around to it," Jaeden commented, peering at Alexis.

"I'm lost without mine." Alexis placed it in full view. "I put everything in here. I've had this one forever." She looked up at the screen just as two women passed their table.

"Hey, Jay," the women said in unison, waving as they walked by.

"Ladies," Jaeden responded. His eyes stayed on Alexis.

As soon as they left, another woman stopped by to speak to him. Again he acknowledged her, but never allowed his focus to slip from Alexis.

Alexis frowned. *Player*, she immediately thought after another woman winked and sashayed past the table. After witnessing the parade of women, she was sure Jaeden could have just about any woman he wanted. "Do you know everybody here?" she asked incredulously.

"I don't know you, but I'd like to."

Alexis didn't have a retort for his comment.

Just as another sultry ballad made for getting in the mood for love began to resonate through the room, Jaeden rose from his seat and extended his hand out to her. "Would you like to join me on the dance floor?"

"I don't dance."

Jaeden reached for her hand. "There's nothing to it. Just follow my lead. You'll catch on in no time." She hesitated. "Come on, don't be afraid," he insisted. "I won't let anything happen to you."

Alexis opened her purse and dropped her Palm Pilot inside. Slowly, she reached for Jaeden's hand and grabbed it. The warmth of his touch caused her to lose her footing when she tried to stand. Jaeden held on tightly.

Throwing her purse over her shoulder, she allowed him to hold her hand until they reached the dance floor. He gently pulled her around him and into his solid chest. Alexis's arms automatically stretched around his neck, her body melting into his as he drew her closer.

At first, it seemed she couldn't get close enough to him, then she relaxed and laid her head against his shoulder, allowing herself to get lost in the music, in being in his arms. They began to sway slowly to the beat. Jaeden snuggled against her neck and Alexis thought she would fall to the floor. The intoxicating scent of the woodsy cologne he wore filled her nostrils and she held him even closer.

Jaeden lifted his head and glared deeply into her eyes, but said nothing as they continued to move in sync to the sensual rhythm. Alexis couldn't speak, but she met his stare and held on to him. She imagined his head descending as if he were about to kiss her, but suddenly the music changed to a more upbeat tempo that killed the mood. She moved quickly to step out of his embrace, but Jaeden stopped her.

"See, that wasn't so bad, was it?" His eyes twinkled as his tongue flicked over his lips.

In a daze, Alexis shook her head slowly from side to side.

Gently catching her right hand, Jaeden led her back to the table.

Relief swept through Alexis's slender frame when she saw Stephanie headed in their direction. She'd been so nervous since she and Jaeden had returned to the table, she'd been unable to say a word.

"Lexie, I'm sorry, but I have to take Chucky home," Stephanie spat out. "He's had too much to drink, so I'm the designated driver."

"That's okay. I have a paper to finish at home anyway." Alexis stood and turned to Jaeden to say good-bye.

"Oh no," Stephanie exclaimed, motioning with her right hand for Alexis to sit back down. "You don't have to leave," she insisted. "You two seemed to be having a good time. I wouldn't leave myself, but I really don't want Chucky driving home."

"Bu—" Alexis started.

"Jay, can you make sure my girl gets home safely?" Stephanie cut off Alexis's words before she could get them out of her mouth.

"Sure, you know I will," Jaeden answered before glancing at Alexis. "You don't mind, do you, Alexis?"

Stephanie didn't wait around any longer; she rushed off as she waved her good-bye.

Alexis sighed because she realized Stephanie had been watching them on the dance floor. It looked like the whole evening had been a setup.

"I don't have a choice, do I?" she said, looking at Jaeden.

"I can take you home now if you're ready to go," Jaeden offered.

Although she was enjoying her time with Jaeden, she was mindful that she had another paper waiting for her at home. "I'm ready when you are."

"Come on, let's go." Jaeden slid from the booth and waited for Alexis to do the same. He placed his hand on the small of her back as they made their way through the crowd and out to the parking lot.

Opening the door on his late-model SUV, he grabbed her hand to steady her as she climbed in. "Watch your step," he advised. Closing the door securely, he jogged around to the driver's side, opened his door, and got inside.

"Where do you live?" he asked Alexis, turning the key in the ignition.

She covered her mouth as she failed to suppress a yawn. "Fifteen sixty-five Morton Avenue."

"You aren't far from Uncle Tommie's place. There are some beautiful homes being built in that area," Jaeden said as he drove from the parking lot to the street.

"Yes, there are. They're trying to rebuild it. A strip

mall is supposed to go up not too far from me in the fall," Alexis responded, looking at Jaeden's profile. She studied his full lips and long eyelashes. He was perfect as far as she could tell.

They drove along in comfortable silence the rest of the trip. After a while, Jaeden turned into the parking lot of her apartment complex and Alexis pointed to her building. He pulled his vehicle into one of the open spaces.

"You could have just dropped me off at the door."

"It's better that I walk you up," he insisted.

Alexis unfastened her seat belt and pulled the door handle. "That's really not necessary." She liked Jaeden, but she wasn't ready to let him in her home. Alexis was sure that was his motive in walking her to her door.

"Alexis, wait." He put his hand on her elbow. "You're wasting your breath by telling me not to. My mother raised me to be a gentleman and would kill me if she found out I didn't escort you to your door. Just dropping you off would seem disrespectful on my part, don't you think?"

Alexis realized she was fighting a battle she would lose. She nodded and waited for him to come around to her side. She reminded herself she didn't need distractions in her life and that Jaeden Jefferson with his impeccable manners was becoming a huge one.

Jaeden opened the door and assisted her from the SUV. They walked silently to Building C. She unlocked the main entry door and looked over at him. "I'm safe from here, thanks for bringing me home."

"Why are you in such a hurry for me to leave?" Jaeden asked, moving closer to her.

Alexis inhaled and exhaled quickly. She hadn't realized until then how much Jaeden had affected her. In fact, she'd been fighting it all evening. "You've given me a ride and walked me to my door. I appreciate it." Alexis stood, hoping he would leave. She could tell by the way she was responding to him that he would make her lose track of her goals. She didn't need a man like him in her life right now. She was too busy.

Jaeden looked around the inside hall of the building. "I know you don't live out here."

Alexis wanted to tell him to go, but she couldn't. Instead, she gave him a slight smile and walked up the staircase in front of them. Jaeden followed.

"Well, this *is* me," Alexis said when she reached her apartment door.

Jaeden leaned against the frame of the door. "I was wondering if I could call you sometime. Maybe we could go out and work on your dance moves," he teased. A wide grin spread across his face.

"I—I don't think that's a good idea." Alexis's voice trembled. "I have a very busy schedule with work and school."

"I have a busy schedule myself, but let's see . . ." He looked down at his hand. "There are twenty-four hours in a day. You work at Nobel for seven." He counted on his fingers. "You probably don't go to your night class every day, but that's only three and you sleep for eight. There are still a couple hours left that I'm sure we can use to at least get a bite to eat."

Alexis couldn't help but smile. She opened her purse and pulled out a card and handed it to him.

Jaeden glanced at one side, then turned it over. He looked up at her. "This is your school telephone number and extension."

"I know. If you can't get me at my extension leave a message on my voice mail." *I bet that will fix him. He won't call,* she thought.

"I'll do just that." Jaeden stuck the card in the right pocket of his black slacks and watched as she disengaged the lock on her door and turned the knob.

"Make sure you lock up and I'll talk to you soon," Jaeden said.

"Good night and thanks again," Alexis said before going inside.

Jaeden waited until he heard the lock engage, then jogged back to the parking lot with a smirk on his face.

Alexis dropped her purse in the chair and hurried over to the window. Pulling back the blinds, she watched as Jaeden left the complex. She watched until she couldn't see the red glare from his taillights.

As she permitted the vertical blinds to slip from her fingers, she sighed and headed to the bathroom. After removing her makeup and clothes, Alexis stepped into the shower. As the soothing water beat her body, she admitted to herself that Jaeden was intriguing. She'd *never* allowed herself to relax and lose focus, but for a brief moment tonight, she'd forgotten about her schoolwork.

A smile grew on her face as she remembered being wrapped in Jaeden's arms. The chemistry between them was almost indescribable and she couldn't get close enough to him. Yet she kept telling herself she didn't have time to get tangled in a relationship. She almost regretted giving him her work number. She was sure he wouldn't call her there.

Alexis stepped out of the shower and picked up a fluffy pink towel. Patting herself dry, she thought about Stephanie's impromptu exit. It was too late to call her, she thought, looking at the clock on the nightstand. She'd wait until the next morning to talk to her.

Moisturizing her body with her favorite raspberry-scented lotion, Alexis slipped on a short baby-blue nightgown and walked to the kitchen to get a glass of water. As she pressed the glass against the button on the ice dispenser, she noticed the worn piece of paper being held by her Purdue University magnet. Years ago, she'd made a list of things she wanted to accomplish in her life. She'd sat down at her desk with a piece of notebook paper and a pen right before she left home to make her valedictorian speech at her high school graduation ceremony.

She always wanted to keep the list in full view to help her stay focused, but didn't want anyone else to know what the list meant, so she wrote it in a code only she could decipher. Any time she felt she was getting off track, she'd read over the list to remind herself of her goals. She pulled the piece of paper from under the magnet and reread the list, making a mental note of what she'd accomplished and what she hadn't. When she was finished, assessing her progress, she put the paper back in its place.

Sighing, Alexis drank her water, then placed the glass in the sink and turned out the light. *I've come far, but I still have a long way to go,* she thought.

CHAPTER TWO

Monday afternoon, Alexis sat in her classroom at one of the round tables she used for one-on-one reading enrichment. She graded papers while she ate her lunch.

This morning she had worked with the students on word recognition and vocabulary. All kindergarteners in Indiana were required to recognize letters, words, and sounds before moving on to the first grade. Alexis had been working diligently with her students to ensure that they all met these standards.

Stephanie stuck her head in the door, interrupting her concentration. "Busy?"

Alexis looked up from the paper she was grading. "Where were you yesterday?"

A wide grin grew on Stephanie's face as she strolled into the classroom and pulled out a chair next to Alexis. "I had to help my aunt Sherly clean out her attic. Girl, let me tell you it was a job, too. I don't know why she keeps all that mess anyway. I asked her why she had to choose Sunday of all days to clean it up. I thought Sunday was supposed to be a day of rest."

Stephanie and Alexis both laughed.

"Well, how did it go Saturday after I left?" Stephanie inquired.

Instead of answering her question, Alexis asked one of her own. "How is Chucky?"

Stephanie looked puzzled. "Chucky?"

"You know, the guy you supposedly drove home. He was so drunk you just couldn't leave him." Alexis rolled her eyes dramatically as she waited for Stephanie's response. When she didn't get one, she leaned closer. "You made him up, didn't you?"

Stephanie paused, then said nonchalantly, "No, I didn't make him up. He just wasn't there."

"Stef, why did you lie?" Alexis asked firmly, looking her friend in the eye.

"Lexie, come on now. You know how stuffy you can be. If I had told you I knew of this single guy who would love to take you out, you would have said no."

"That's not true," Alexis protested.

"I'm not going to argue with you about it, because I know I'm right. Anyway, you still didn't tell me what happened between you and Jaeden after I left."

"I knew you were up to something."

"Are you going to tell me or not?"

"It went okay, I guess. We didn't stay long after you left."

"Hmph, when I saw the two of you on the dance floor, it looked like you were getting along pretty well." Stephanie grinned.

"I think he's a nice guy. What else do you want me to say?"

"Did he ask for your number?"

"Why do you keep asking me that?"

"Because I think you two would make a great couple. He's such a fun guy and I think whoever gets him will have a gem."

Alexis waved at her. "He's your cousin. Of course you would think he's a great guy."

"No, that's not true. I have some cousins that I wouldn't introduce my dog to. If I had one."

Alexis chuckled.

"Seriously," Stephanie started. "I love Jaeden and I think he needs to settle down with a good woman. All he thinks about is running his business."

"Stef, that's not a bad thing. If he's set a goal to make his business successful, he has to work hard to do that."

"I'm not hating on him for that, but I think he needs more," Stephanie insisted, sweeping a piece of lint from her skirt.

The phone rang, catching their attention. Alexis crossed the room and picked up the receiver. "Ms. Shire speaking."

"Hello, Alexis." The deep voice boomed on the other end of the line.

The sound of her name coming from his lips gave Alexis the shivers. Her pulse quickened as she recognized the caller's voice. "Jaeden?"

"I guess that just answered my question," Stephanie said knowingly.

"Did I did catch you at a bad time?" Jaeden asked.

"Oh, no, no," Alexis said quickly. She covered the bottom of the receiver with the palm of her right hand. Pressing her forefinger against her lips, she motioned for Stephanie to be quiet.

Stephanie quickly rose from her seat. "I'll talk to you later," she whispered, hoping Jaeden couldn't hear her as she left Alexis to her phone call. She uncovered the receiver. "I'm sorry, Jaeden, someone was just leaving. You were saying?"

"I surprised you, didn't I?"

Alexis paused for a couple of seconds. "Yes, you did."

"You were so sure I wouldn't call you at school," he teased.

"Well, I guess I stand corrected then."

"Listen, how's your schedule for this evening? Oh,

wait, I forgot I have a meeting this evening. What about tomorrow evening?"

"I've got a class," Alexis said in a hurry.

Jaeden stared at his desk calendar. "What time do you get out of class?"

"Around eight o'clock."

"Would you like to meet after?"

"I don't know if that's a good idea. I'm usually tired by the time I get home," Alexis said, twisting the cord around her finger. She'd spent Sunday afternoon working on a portfolio for her English class. She had to illustrate a teacher's curriculum based on the state of Indiana's academic standards. At the very least, it had to include a teacher's lesson plan and a grading scale. She had completed her outline last night, but she still had to create transparencies and handouts for her presentation.

"We can go out for coffee or something." Jaeden really didn't care where they went; he just wanted to see her again.

"I guess it wouldn't hurt," Alexis said, thinking about Stephanie's comment earlier. "I can meet you somewhere."

"I thought maybe I could pick you up at your apartment. To give you time to get back to your place, I'll come by at around eight-thirty?"

"Okay, I'll see you then."

"I'm definitely looking forward to it," Jaeden said before hanging up.

Excitement zipped through Alexis as she waited for him to disconnect the call before she hung up.

She immediately went over to her desk drawer, retrieved her Palm Pilot from her purse, and entered the date she had made with Jaeden in her calendar. As she closed the drawer, a smile grew on her face as she thought about seeing him again.

* * *

Jaeden waited in the parking lot of Alexis's apartment complex on Tuesday evening. As she pulled her silver Maxima into the empty space next to him, he smiled.

Always a gentleman, Jaeden climbed out of his SUV and went to help Alexis out of the car.

"You're early," Alexis said.

"I know, I changed my mind and wanted to be here when you arrived. Let me take that for you," he said, reaching for her book satchel.

"I just need to run up and put my books away," Alexis said, shutting the car door.

As they walked to the building, Jaeden couldn't keep from staring at Alexis's delicate features. He wanted to commit every angle and curve to memory.

"Why are you looking at me that way?" Alexis looked down as she patted herself. "Is there something on my clothes?"

"No, I'm just admiring your beauty in the moonlight."

Alexis blushed. It was something she found she did often around him.

"I really mean it. You are a very attractive woman, Alexis." His eyes ran the length of her body.

"Thank you for the compliment." Alexis shivered under his appreciative gaze.

Jaeden held the door open after she unlocked it and walked into the building behind her.

"I'll wait here," he said. He could tell by her shocked expression that she thought he wanted to follow her into the apartment. This was their first date and he didn't want to push her beyond her comfort zone.

"It will only take me a minute." Alexis took the bag from him and walked up the stairs.

Jaeden watched intently as she climbed the stairs, loving the way her long bouncy hair moved from left to right matching the sway of her hips.

Fifteen minutes later, she returned and Jaeden looked at her curiously. "You didn't have to change clothes. You looked gorgeous in what you had on," Jaeden said, admiring Alexis in her denim jeans, pink pullover shirt, and matching jacket. The fitted jeans accentuated her full hips even further. The wait had been well worth it.

"I figured I'd freshen up a bit."

Jaeden nodded approvingly and opened the large oak door for her. "Ready?"

Again, his eyes followed the sway of her hips as she walked down the stairs.

"I'm surprised it's this warm in April," Jaeden said after he and Alexis were seated in the car. He was just making small talk. Alexis's curves had him so flustered, he couldn't think of anything else to say.

"It is warmer than usual this time of year, but I won't complain." Alexis was flustered too. Jaeden was wearing another shirt that accentuated his chest and she could barely stop herself from staring.

After several moments of silence, Jaeden asked her, "What is your major?"

"I'm working toward a master's in administration," she explained. "I want to eventually become an elementary school principal. My plan is to complete it in the next two years."

"You're going to have to take summer classes then too?"
"Yes."

"Sounds like you've got everything figured out."

"I try to think everything through first."

"Hmm," was Jaeden's only response. He was too busy looking at Alexis's charm bracelet.

"How did your meeting go yesterday?"

"Good, I think I'm progressing." He smiled to himself, pleased that she'd remembered.

Jaeden parked in front of Starbucks and helped Alexis from the vehicle. It was a habit of his that she was slowly growing accustomed to.

"Why don't you find us a table and I'll get us something to drink?" Jaeden suggested after they'd entered the store.

"Sure. I'll have an iced white chocolate mocha."

Jaeden walked to the counter and placed their orders.

Alexis thanked him as he set her drink down in front of her a few minutes later. She lifted the cup and enjoyed a long swallow. "These are a trillion calories, I know, but I like them."

"I only drink regular coffee," Jaeden said as he stirred in cream. "And this cup is going to keep me awake."

"We could have gone some place else, if you wanted."

"No, this is fine. I'm satisfied just to be here with you."

Alexis blushed before taking another sip from her drink and changing the subject. "So, tell me more about your meeting yesterday."

"The Herswick Company holds all the licenses for the NBA and MLB team logos. I've proposed a new line of fitted and adjustable caps for infants and young children," he started.

"I'm impressed. That sounds like a great idea."

"I thought so too, but it's hard to tell what will and will not work in today's society." Jaeden took a sip of his coffee. "I've noticed there's a large market for sports apparel. The hip-hop generation is really into the old NBA throwback jerseys and anything else from back in the day. They're becoming parents earlier in life and their babies are always dressed in the latest fashions and name brands. I realized that included sports apparel, so I thought it would be a great market to tap into."

"How long have you been in business?"

"I started Ova Yo Head Cap a little over two years ago, but I started designing caps for some of my friends and relatives when I graduated from college. Everyone told me I should try to go mainstream and really make some money with it. I thought about it, started doing some research, and here I am."

"What a wonderful idea. You should really be proud of yourself."

"I'll be proud when I see my hats in major chain stores and retail specialty shops.

"Looks like you're on the right track. Keep up the good work," Alexis said.

Jaeden leaned forward in his chair. "Alexis, I have to admit I thought kindergarten teachers only talked about things concerning children."

"It looks to me like we both are interested in children. I love educating them and you want them as clients."

"I guess you're right. I'd never thought of it that way."

They talked for another hour before Jaeden looked at his watch. "Let's get going. It's getting late. I don't want you falling asleep on your students in the morning." Jaeden rose from his seat, picking up their containers and dropping them in the trash on their way out. He caught Alexis's hand as they walked to his SUV.

"When did you discover your love for teaching?" Jaeden asked as he drove back to Alexis's apartment.

Alexis dropped her head. "You'll probably think it's silly."

"No, I won't. Try me," Jaeden said sincerely.

"When I was a little girl, I'd line my dolls up and pretend to be their teacher." She laughed at the memory.

"That wasn't silly at all, Alexis. Are you an only child?"

"Yes, what about you?"

Jaeden looked over at her. "Me too."

After a brief pause, Alexis spoke. "Thanks for asking me out. I would have gone straight home and started working on my schoolwork."

"It was my pleasure."

Outside her apartment door, Jaeden was so close to Alexis it seemed as if he'd taken all the air. "Would you like for me to continue to contact you at work or can I have your number?" he asked, seemingly unaware of the effect his deep voice was having on his date.

Alexis stared as she watched his lips move and felt the caress of his breath on her cheek. Her eyes fluttered because she thought he was about to kiss her. She soon realized Jaeden was still speaking.

"I'm sure you don't trust men very easily, but you don't have to worry about me." He pulled the card she'd given to him from his pocket and handed it to her. "Can you write the number on here? I don't want to lose it."

Alexis wrote her cell phone number on the back of the card and handed it back to him.

"Thanks," Jaeden said, accepting the card. He turned it over and then looked up at her. "Still not going to give me your home number? I see." He smirked. "This is just as good. Now I can contact you wherever you are."

Alexis had decided to take a chance. A little male companionship couldn't hurt, right? Plus, Jaeden gave her the impression that he was a very kind and considerate man.

"It's getting late. I'd better be going." He bent to place a chaste kiss on her cheek before she went into her apartment. "Good night."

CHAPTER THREE

Jaeden stared at the invitation he'd just received. Arnold Herswick had invited him to attend their annual spring dinner party. He hoped Arnold would give him the opportunity to make his presentation to the company. He would try to get them to manufacture, distribute, and market his designs since he didn't have the resources for the area he'd targeted. His company did manufacture a small number of designs that were being sold in mom-and-pop shops around Taylor, but he wanted to expand. If they liked the idea, it could put Ova Yo Head Cap on the map and make the Herwicks a lot of money in the process. In order to reach this major goal, Jaeden had to make sure he was prepared for any questions or concerns about his proposal.

The White Hawk Country Club, where the party would be held, was a ritzy establishment in the next town. The membership fees were the highest in the region. The dinner was a black-tie affair, which meant he couldn't have just anyone accompanying him. He had to have someone special by his side.

"Alexis," he said aloud.

Dropping the folded white card, he propped his elbow on his desk and rested his chin on the heel of his right hand. He wondered if she would agree to go with him. It had been a couple of days since Jaeden had called her because of his hectic schedule. More orders for hats had come pouring in from the shops and he needed time to oversee their completion.

Staring at his desk clock, he noticed the time had slipped by and it was already after seven o'clock. He pulled out his wallet and retrieved the card she'd given him. Hitting the speakerphone button, he dialed her cell number. He hoped she would answer.

"Hello."

Jaeden quickly picked up the receiver. "Alexis, how are you?"

"I'm kind of busy trying to get an assignment completed for my English class. How are things with you?"

"That's the reason for my call. I need a favor."

"What kind of favor?" Alexis moved her hair out of the way so she could hear what he had to say.

"It's not at all what you're thinking. It's business, not pleasure."

"Oh."

"I have to attend a dinner party on Friday and I was wondering if you would accompany me."

"What kind of dinner party?"

"It's an annual event hosted by the company I told you about. I thought it might be a good idea if you went along with me."

"Why didn't you ask someone from your office who is familiar with the project to accompany you?" Alexis asked, wondering if she was the right person to tag along.

"Let's just say I think you are the best choice for this occasion. Will you go with me?"

"Hold on a sec and I'll check my calendar." Alexis held the phone in the lock of her shoulder to free both hands. She picked up her pen and clicked on the screen of her Palm Pilot. She had nothing noted on her calendar for

Friday evening. After a pause, Alexis's husky voice came through the phone line. "Jaeden, you still there?"

"Yes."

"My evening is clear."

"Can you be ready by five o'clock?" Jaeden asked anxiously before she could change her mind. "Cocktails will be served at six-thirty."

"I'll be ready when you arrive. Is there a dress code for this occasion?"

"Black tie."

"No problem. I can handle that. Are you still at work?"

"Yes, I still have some stuff to complete before I go home."

"Well, I guess I'll see you on Friday, then," Alexis said. She would have liked to see him sooner, but she understood he was busy. She was too.

"See you on Friday."

"Don't work too hard," Alexis said before disconnecting the call.

Jaeden hung up the phone. "Yes," he yelled, lifting his arm and jerking it back. He couldn't wait to see Alexis again. Friday couldn't come fast enough.

Jaeden straightened the lapel of his black dinner jacket and rubbed his hands together one last time before he stabbed the doorbell with his forefinger. He hadn't realized his palms were sweating. The last time he was this nervous, he was picking up Sarah Richardson for the prom.

Just as he was about to ring the bell once again, Alexis opened the door.

"Wow," Jaeden exclaimed. His eyes moved slowly down the black satin strapless tea-length dress hugging her breasts and rounded hips. The gown showed off every

curve on her slender frame. Her long beautiful locks
had been pinned on top of her head. Alexis's makeup
was perfectly applied to her honey-colored skin and her
lush lips shimmered with a hint of bronze lip color. She
looked so regal. He tried to imagine what she'd look like
with her hair in disarray after a night of passionate lovemaking. "You look absolutely stunning," he said walking
through the open door.

His eyes continued to roam downward to the sexiest
pair of black strappy sandals he'd ever seen. *She even has
pretty feet,* he said to himself.

"I take it you approve," Alexis said, modeling her outfit.

Jaeden couldn't take his eyes off her.

Alexis looked at her silver bangle watch. "If we don't get
out of here, we're going to be late." She picked up a small
black-beaded clutch and a satin shawl that matched her
dress from the couch. "Ready?" she asked, heading toward
the door.

The desire to pull Alexis back into his arms and kiss
her senseless grew stronger as Jaeden stood behind her.

Instead, he took the shawl from her and laid it around
her arms, leaving her shoulders bare. He placed a light
kiss on her shoulder blade and traced the outline of the
top of the shawl with his finger before stepping away from
her. He was doing his best to behave like a gentleman.

A warm feeling begun to run through Alexis's body.
She wanted to say something, but didn't know what. In
all her twenty-six years, no one had ever touched her
that way before.

"Thanks for agreeing to come with me. You really
do look gorgeous." Jaeden knew he was being forward
by kissing her shoulder, but he couldn't help himself.
Jaeden swung the door open and waited as she strolled
past him, leaving a trail of her hypnotic fragrance. It
was time to leave before he did something he'd regret

later. He pulled the door closed behind him and waited for her to secure it.

As they drove to the country club, Jaeden glanced over at Alexis several times.

Alexis looked over at him. "Are you nervous about tonight?"

"A little," Jaeden responded.

Alexis smiled and reached over and grabbed his hand, interlocking her fingers with his. "Don't be. I think you'll do fine."

Jaeden pulled up to the valet at White Hawk. A scrawny young man in a white tuxedo shirt, black pants, and a bow tie came to the passenger side of the vehicle and assisted Alexis. After Jaeden handed the attendant his extra key and gave his name, he was handed a ticket. Now, they were ready to go inside.

When they entered the elegantly decorated green and gold lobby, they found the marquee that informed them their dinner party would be held in the Tiara Room. Jaeden walked proudly with Alexis on his arm as they leisurely strolled through the lobby area and down the hall.

The Tiara Room was beautifully decorated in mauve and slate blue. There were ceiling-to-floor windows on one side that overlooked the eighteenth hole of the golf course. The crystal chandeliers made the room look even more elegant.

"This is lovely," Alexis commented.

Jaeden spotted Arnold Herswick and guided Alexis in his direction. The two men greeted each other with a strong handshake and introduced their companions. Arnold immediately suggested Jaeden meet the other executives from his company.

While the two men went to talk, Alexis and Arnold's wife, Marian, mingled with the rest of the attendees.

Jaeden tried to keep his focus on the executives' conversation, but his eyes kept roaming in Alexis's direction.

"I really need to work on my golf swing," one man stated.

"All you need to do is move the club back and forth a little before you swing," Arnold responded. "Jaeden, do you golf?"

Glancing in Alexis's direction again, he noticed she'd moved. He scanned the room until he finally spotted her sitting at a table in the back with Marian.

"Jaeden?" Arnold called his name again.

"Did you say something, Arnold? My mind was someplace else," Jaeden said.

"I asked if you played golf," Arnold repeated.

"No, I haven't had the opportunity," Jaeden responded absently. He looked in Alexis's direction once again, thinking of how he liked everything about her—from the way she sat with her back so straight to the way she held her wineglass. All of a sudden, Jaeden wasn't pleased with the idea of Alexis being so far away from him. He wanted her by his side. Placing his heavy crystal tumbler on the nearby table, he quickly excused himself and strolled over to where Alexis sat.

When she looked up, he smiled and winked at her. She smiled back and gave him a quick wave.

"Marian, would you excuse us for a moment, please?" he said, reaching for Alexis's hand. Assisting her from her chair, Jaeden wrapped her arm over his as they sauntered out of the banquet room.

He found an empty Victorian-style sofa in the hallway and offered her a seat. Jaeden enveloped her hand in his as he positioned himself next to her.

"Are you having a good time?" Jaeden asked.

"Did you know Marian Herswick is a retired elementary school teacher?"

Jaeden watched the excitement on Alexis's face as she spoke. "No."

"She's a lovely woman."

Jaeden moved closer to her and whispered, "So are you."

Alexis's cheeks flooded with heat. "Thank you."

Jaeden moved even closer to her ear. "I can't stop saying it, Alexis. You are so beautiful."

Turning her head slightly, Alexis looked into his eyes and placed her hand on his. She saw an emotion in his depths she had not seen prior to that moment. Before she lost herself in his game, she changed the subject. "How did your conversation go with Arnold?"

"They talked about golf and I don't know what else because my mind was on you in that little black dress."

Alexis palmed his chin. "Jaeden, you are so sweet."

The feel of her soft hands created a yearning inside him he couldn't ignore. Jaeden lifted her dainty hand and lightly brushed his lips against the inside of her palm. "I feel like the luckiest man in the world when I'm with you. I know you have a lot of things going on in your life, so do I. But I really want to spend more time with you." He kissed her hand once again.

Alexis looked into his eyes again and saw something more than just lust. She believed he really wanted to know her as a person and not just as a conquest to get in his bed.

"Alexis, I didn't offend you, did I?" Jaeden asked, sensing her hesitancy.

Alexis smiled, placing her hand atop his again. "No, you didn't. I would like to spend more time with you as well."

Jaeden relaxed. He noticed an influx of couples heading

into the room and he checked his watch. "They should be serving dinner shortly."

He pushed himself to his feet and held out his palm for Alexis to take. She accepted and they strolled back into the dining room, hand in hand.

Jaeden removed her chair from under the table so she could sit before he took the empty one next to her.

As the evening progressed, he continued to watch Alexis from time to time. Her smile made his heart happy. He'd never seriously pursued one woman before, but Alexis had that something he didn't even know he'd been looking for.

They dined on seared filet mignon with red wine truffle sauce, garlic whipped potatoes, baby carrots, and asparagus tips.

Alexis leaned into him after she'd eaten everything on her plate. "I am so full. I can't eat another bite," she said as the waiters served lemon sorbet for dessert.

"Maybe we can work some of that off on the dance floor."

"Remember, I don't dance well," she reminded him softly.

"If I remember correctly, you did just fine the other night."

"That's because you were holding me."

"How well I do remember. I would love to hold you again," Jaeden whispered huskily, recalling the feel of her body against his.

The band played modern jazz, rock, blues, and some R&B to entertain the guests. There were several couples already on the parquet-tiled floor and many others were making their way to join them.

When the band played their rendition of Kenny G and

Babyface's "Every Time I Close My Eyes," Jaeden asked her to dance once again. He leaned into her ear and whispered softly, "Come, let me feel you in my arms again."

Alexis gave him a knowing look.

"It's okay, baby, I'll be with you the entire time."

She beamed and took his hand as they walked out to the dance floor.

As Jaeden drove back to Alexis's apartment, she pulled out her Palm Pilot and began writing in the notepad. "I had a good time this evening. Thanks for inviting me, Jaeden," Alexis said without taking her eyes off the screen.

"What are you putting in that thing now?"

"I'm just checking my to-do list."

Jaeden shook his head. "You weren't playing when you said you don't go anywhere without your Palm Pilot."

"Nope, I can't function without it."

Jaeden pulled into her parking lot and parked in an empty space near Alexis's entrance. "Thank you again for joining me. I'd like to see you again. Soon," he added firmly.

"It was really an enjoyable evening," Alexis said as she prepared to get out of the vehicle. "You don't have to walk me up this time," she offered, although she knew Jaeden would argue.

Jaeden turned to her. "Are we going to have this conversation at the end of every evening we spend together? I'm not going to let you walk up to the apartment alone."

He got out of the SUV and walked around to the passenger-side door just as she was about to open it. Jaeden assisted her out and followed her up to the second floor of her building.

As she unlocked the door, Jaeden pulled out a blue

and white business card that had two additional telephone numbers written on it.

"Here's *my* card. It has my office number, my home and cell. Just in case you ever want to talk or need anything, you can reach me."

Alexis took the card, slipping it into her handbag. She turned to face the white door of her apartment and placed her key in the lock. Jaeden stopped her. "One more thing," he said before she could enter the apartment.

Alexis turned to him. "Yes,"

"I've wanted to do this all evening." Tenderly Jaeden captured her face with his hands, tilting it so he could look into her eyes. After he searched for any hesitation on her part and found none, he willed himself to be gentle before tasting her sweet lips. He didn't want to devour them the first time they touched.

Slowly, he lowered his head until his moist mouth met hers. He retreated, then methodically repeated the act.

"Good night, Alexis," he finally whispered a couple of inches from her lips. He reached past her and turned the knob on the unlocked door and stepped aside to allow her to enter. Alexis walked into her apartment and turned back to find Jaeden still standing at the door.

Their eyes met and there was silence, before Jaeden spoke again. "Go on and lock up, I'll talk to you later."

Inch by inch, Alexis closed the door and Jaeden didn't move until he heard the lock engage.

His heart raced as he made his way to his car. He turned and looked back at the building he'd just left, wishing he was there making love to Alexis. He didn't know exactly what was happening between them, but he definitely wanted to pursue something more with her.

He climbed into his SUV and started it. The song playing on the car radio echoed exactly how he felt. As Atlantic Starr crooned "Closer Than Close," he eased out of the parking lot, singing along and hoping the words of the song would come true. He definitely wanted to get closer to Alexis.

Alexis didn't know what to do about Jaeden. His gentleness and kindness made her feel things she'd never felt before. Every time she was near him, she wanted to get closer and closer.

She headed to her bedroom and removed her clothes before making her way to the bathroom. Turning on the hot water, she poured her favorite raspberry-scented bath salt into the water. She cleansed her face while she waited for the tub to fill.

Stepping into the tub, Alexis submerged herself in the water. She lay back on her pink terry cloth bath pillow and let the soothing liquid relax her. As soon as she closed her eyes, the image of Jaeden bare and beautiful in all his splendor entered her mind. He walked into the bathroom taking proud and powerful strides toward her. He knelt beside the tub and she looked into the depths of his brown eyes. He claimed her mouth, kissing her until she was breathless.

Picking up the large bath sheet that was next to him, Jaeden spread it out on the floor and stood to his feet. He reached out, inviting her to take his hand, and helped Alexis from the tub. With water dripping from her body, she took a step forward, moving closer to him until there was no room left between them. Her nipples were aching pebbles against his wide, hard chest.

His touch was electrifying. When he caressed her bottom, she thought she had been struck by lightning. The feel of his body next to hers and his manhood rising with a heartbeat of its own made the butterflies swarm in her stomach.

He kissed her neck and devoured her shoulders as she pulled him closer to her. Jaeden explored her mouth, her neck, her shoulders before he paused at the top of her breast. He sucked her nipples until she cried out with pleasure, and then he pulled away. Without warning, he dropped to his knees to get better access to her nether regions. Alexis moaned softly in anticipation of what was to come. Jaeden stared at the honey-brown satiny skin of her belly and pulled her body toward him as his lips caressed her. The flick of his tongue caused another moan to slip from her lips.

Alexis quickly pulled herself forward, spilling water over the side of the tub. She looked around and realized it had only been a dream.

Climbing out of the tub, she picked up a white towel and secured it around her body. She wiped the steam from the lighted mirror and saw perspiration on her face. She wondered what would have happened next, if she hadn't awakened so fast.

Shaking her head, she opened a drawer, pulled out a tube of creamy raspberry body lotion, and gently rubbed it on her body.

Once she slipped beneath the sheets of her empty queen-sized four-poster bed, her thoughts drifted back to Jaeden. Even though she hadn't known him a significant amount of time, she found that she felt safe when she was with him. She couldn't remember ever feeling so excited about life. The magnetism between them was unquestionable and she wanted to see where it would take her.

CHAPTER FOUR

At lunchtime on Monday, Alexis went to Creative Floral Shop, which was located a couple of blocks from the school. She wanted to surprise Jaeden by sending him flowers, but didn't know what kind he liked.

After looking through several floral catalogs and talking with the florist, she decided on two simple long-stemmed roses. She pulled a card from the metal spindle and scribbled "Thanks, I had a great time" on the front. She signed the card simply with her initial, A. At the last minute, she decided to add her home telephone number to the bottom and placed the card inside the envelope.

She pulled out the business card he'd given her with the address of his company and wrote it down on the delivery form. After paying for her purchase, she headed out and picked up a sandwich on her way back to work. She still had a reading session with one of her students before the end of the school day.

Back at her desk, Alexis pulled out her Palm Pilot and smiled as she checked off all the items she had written on her to-do list for Monday. She had completed two of the four goals she'd set from last week and she wrote a couple of new ones for the upcoming week.

Placing her PDA back in her purse, she grabbed her book satchel as she left her classroom. Peeking in the door across the hall, she saw Stephanie at her desk working.

"How's it going?" Alexis asked as she entered the room.

"Okay, I'm just about finished grading these papers."

Alexis took a seat near her desk. "So what's going on? I haven't talked to you in a long time."

"I hear you and my cousin have been seeing each other," Stephanie said, grinning.

"I wouldn't call going out for coffee and to a business dinner going steady," Alexis replied.

"You know what I mean. Did you have fun?"

"I had a really good time at the dinner party. He got me on the dance floor again. I've never been a great dancer, but I think I did okay."

"Jaeden loves to dance. As a matter of fact, he loves music period. Even when we were teenagers, he always had a lot of music. Still does, he even has forty-fives, LPs, and some eight-tracks."

"Wow, I didn't know he was so into it. I do know he's an excellent dancer."

Stephanie leaned forward. "And he's easy on the eye," she added, raising her finely arched brows.

"Don't start, Stef," Alexis said.

"I'm not just saying that because he's my first cousin. The man is fine. Come on, Lexie, admit it. The man is fine *and* I think he likes you."

Alexis blushed and then looked at Stephanie. "Yes, girl, he is very nice looking," she replied finally, remembering his lips descending on hers.

Stephanie waved her hands in front of Alexis's face.

"Did you hear me talking to you?" she asked, studying her. "You like him, don't you?" Stephanie didn't wait for an answer. "I knew you two would hit it off. I just knew it."

"Whoa." Alexis lifted her hand. "Let's not get carried away. Yes, I've gone out with him a couple of times and I like him, but you're acting like he's proposed marriage or something."

"Anything's possible."

"Let me get out of here, you are really talking crazy now." Alexis rose from her chair and pushed it back under the desk.

"I'm going back to my room, I have to meet with a student."

"Hey, I think we're going to be cousins soon," Stephanie predicted, ignoring Alexis's attempt to change the topic.

Alexis walked out of the classroom, ignoring Stephanie's last statement and leaving her corny laugh behind.

Jaeden stared at the flowers that had arrived earlier that day. He'd been out of the office and when he returned they were sitting on his desk. He asked his secretary if she knew who they were from. She shook her head before saying good night as she left the building.

Jaeden had never received flowers before, so this was definitely a surprise. He was even more amazed when he opened the small envelope attached to them and read the message from Alexis. She'd even given him her home telephone number.

Picking up the small card from the desk, he read it for the fifth time. He lifted a long-stemmed red rose under his nostrils and inhaled its fragrance. It reminded him of Alexis's intoxicating perfume when her body was molded against his on the dance floor. The attraction between them was electric and he didn't want to deny it. Each time he held her, he had to wrestle to take control of his body because it betrayed his mind.

Lifting the receiver, he dialed Alexis's number. The flowers really touched him and he wanted to thank her right away. After the third ring, he motioned to hang up the phone until he heard her voice.

"Hello?"

Jaeden sat upright in his chair. "Alexis, is everything all right?"

"Yes, I was trying to get to the phone before the machine came on," Alexis said breathlessly.

"This is Ja—"

"I know. You must have received my flowers," she said, smiling. She took a seat at the breakfast bar.

"Yes, I did. They were a nice surprise." He fingered the outline of a rosebud.

"You sound like you've never received flowers before," she teased.

"I haven't. I'm supposed to put them in warm water, right?"

"Yes, so they can live longer."

Jaeden paused. "I'm glad you were the first."

His statement was met with silence.

"Alexis?" he called out to her, hoping she hadn't disconnected the line.

"I'm here. I'm just trying to catch my breath," Alexis said, tucking a wisp of hair behind her ear.

There was another pause, but this time Alexis was the one to speak first.

"I really enjoyed myself the other night."

"I had a great time too, but we always have a good time together. Don't you think?" He leaned back in his chair.

"Yes, we do," Alexis admitted.

"If we keep dancing, you'll be a pro."

Alexis released a husky laugh. "I doubt that. Hey, how are things coming along with your proposal to Herswick?"

"I'm making a presentation to Arnold in my office tomorrow."

"Good luck."

"Thanks. Why don't we celebrate tomorrow evening over dinner? I don't know how things will turn out, but I want to celebrate anyway."

"Oh, I'm sorry, I can't. I've got a class."

Jaeden didn't say anything at first. He hated to admit he was disappointed. "I understand, maybe some other time. Hey, I need to prepare for my meeting, so . . ." His voice faded.

"We can go out another time." Alexis offered, sensing the change in his mood.

"Okay, just let me know when you're free. And thanks again, you know, for the flowers."

Jaeden hung up the phone. He couldn't mask his displeasure, but promised himself he'd hold Alexis again soon.

Arnold Herswick hadn't informed Jaeden of the number of people who would accompany him to the presentation, so Jaeden had Marie, his secretary, prepare for at least five people.

The gray-haired older woman had been a great help to him. He'd known her since his childhood and appreciated her willingness to keep the office—and him—in order.

Everything had been prepared in the small conference room by the time Marie escorted Arnold to Jaeden's office. She announced his arrival from the doorway and then left, closing the door behind her.

Jaeden laid the manila folder with the file he had been reading down. He rose from his seat and walked around the desk to greet Arnold.

"Mr. Herswick, great to see you again." He extended his open palm to him.

"How are you, Jaeden?" Arnold responded, firmly shaking his hand.

"I'm doing well."

"Are we ready to get started?"

Jaeden nodded and led him toward the conference room. As they got closer, a bout of nervousness hit Jaeden, but he told himself everything would be all right. Placing his hand on the doorknob, he inhaled deeply before opening the door.

"You can have a seat anywhere you'd like, Mr. Herswick."

"Jaeden, we don't have to be so formal, you can call me Arnold."

"Would you like something to drink, Arnold?"

"Water would be fine."

Jaeden walked over to the small table in the corner that had bottled water, juice, and soda. He grabbed two bottles of water and handed one to Arnold.

Walking over to the light panel, Jaeden turned the knob, dimming the lights before pressing the button on his laptop computer to begin his slide presentation.

Jaeden could see Arnold's facial expressions change as he spoke and he couldn't determine if that was a good sign or not. He explained in full detail his plans for the children's head-wear line.

After the two men had gone through each aspect of the proposal, Arnold rose from his seat. "I'm impressed. I like your ideas. Let me take this with me." Arnold held up the folder he'd been given. "I'll try to get back to you by the end of the week. If you don't hear from me by then, don't panic." Arnold smiled as he reached to shake Jaeden's hand.

"Thank you, sir, I look forward to your call." Jaeden said, rising from his seat to escort Arnold to the reception area where they said their good-byes.

The nervousness had vanished and was replaced with excitement. Jaeden understood how business was done;

he knew Herswick wouldn't okay his proposal until the company's marketing team reassured him the product would be a success.

As Jaeden drove down Broadway Avenue, he looked around at the other businesses on the strip. Broadway was the main thoroughfare in the city of Taylor. Most big businesses were located here.

Jaeden had been delighted when his father told him about a small building that would be a great starting place for his hat business. It had taken him the whole time he'd been on the corner of Sixth and Broadway to afford the sign that had been placed on the building.

Turning right onto Lincoln Street, he drove to his parents' house. Donald and Gloria Jefferson lived in a modest tudor-style home on Adams Street. It was a very quaint place with beautiful rosebushes and landscaping that looked like something out of a magazine.

He pulled into the driveway just as his father was getting out of his car.

"Hey, Pop," Jaeden said, stepping from his SUV.

"This is a surprise. I didn't know you were coming by. Come on in. I'm sure your mother will be delighted to see you."

Inside the house, Jaeden looked for his mother, but Gloria wasn't in her usual place in the kitchen. Jaeden continued through the house, looking for her. In the family room, he found his mother sitting on the couch with her feet up as she read a novel.

The room was very spacious. On one side, the walls were a nutmeg color filled with photos of Jaeden as well as other family members. There were also plaques earned from his high school accomplishments.

"Look who I found outside, Glo," Donald said.

Gloria looked over her reading glasses and a wide smile grew on her face. Placing a bookmark in the mystery novel she'd been reading, she slid the book on to the coffee table.

"How was your big meeting?" she said as she got up from the leather sofa.

"Okay, I guess. I'm keeping my fingers crossed," Jaeden replied. Gloria stared at Jaeden. "I'm praying," Jaeden corrected.

"Much better. If it's the Lord's will, everything will work out in your favor."

"You staying for dinner?" Donald asked.

"Of course," Jaeden said, smiling.

"I'm going to wash up and I'll be back," Donald said before he left the room.

"Come on into the kitchen with me, Jaeden," Gloria beckoned. "You can tell me all about your meeting while I get my steak out of the oven."

"Didn't you work today?" Jaeden asked, following her.

"I met with the team that's going to work with me on the Making Strides campaign."

"You've decided to have a team for the breast cancer walk again this year?"

"Yes, we're trying to encourage others to join. The money we raise helps so much."

"I think it's great. I'll write you a check to sponsor your walker."

"I appreciate that. Now how did you feel after the presentation?"

"I felt good. Arnold's remarks were encouraging. I guess I'm just going to have to wait and see what happens next."

"You just keep praying and I'll be praying also." Gloria busied herself placing the succulent meat and its gravy in a large serving dish. "Pull out two white serving bowls and pour the string beans from that pot on the stove in it," she directed. "The rice is in the other pot. Bring those to the table for me, will you?"

Donald had returned and taken a seat at the head of the table when Jaeden walked into the dining room. Gloria brought the dinner salad and rolls to the table and took her seat across from her husband.

"Jaeden, would you ask God's blessing on this meal?" his father asked.

With his head bowed, Jaeden thanked God for the food, his parents, and his new business venture. Everyone gave a hearty amen and they began to eat.

Everyone was quiet until Gloria interrupted, "So you and Alexis are seeing each other now?"

Jaeden gave her a quizzical glance. He laughed when he realized where his mother got her information.

"Stef has a big mouth."

"Who is Alexis? Do I know her?" Donald asked.

"The young lady Stephanie brought to family day earlier this month," Gloria explained before Jaeden could.

"I think I remember. There's always so many people at those things. Was she the light-skinned woman with the long hair?"

"Yeah, Pop, that's her," Jaeden said, picking up the bowl of string beans. He placed a helping on his plate and passed the dish to his mother.

"You're going out with her?"

"Depends on what you mean by going out."

"Hmm," Donald said, cutting into his steak.

No one said anything else about Alexis, but each time Jaeden would look up at his mother, she'd smile knowingly. Jaeden wondered what she was up to.

After dinner, Jaeden helped Gloria clear the table. His father went into the family room, sat in his recliner, and read the newspaper.

"Mom, why are you so quiet all of a sudden?" Jaeden

asked as he loaded the dishwasher. It was confirmed. She was definitely up to something.

"Let's talk," she said, wiping her hand with the dishcloth. Gloria stopped Jaeden from his task and invited him over to the kitchen table. He sat and she took the chair next to him.

"Are you and Alexis serious?"

Jaeden was silent, wondering how to answer her question without revealing too much information.

"If I'm prying, tell me to butt out and I will," Gloria said when her son didn't answer.

"No, you're not," he lied. "I'm not sure how to explain our relationship. I like Alexis a lot. She's beautiful, smart, very focused, goal oriented . . ." He smiled, thinking about her. "But we both are so busy with our everyday lives, we can't seem to get into a steady rhythm of seeing one another. And I'm not sure if she's as interested in me as I am in her."

Gloria had listened and watched her son's reactions. He didn't have to tell her he was in love for her to *know* it. "Why don't you take the time to find out?" she advised. "You're twenty-nine years old. You both are healthy, so why not give it a try?" She shrugged as if to say "It can't hurt."

Jaeden nodded. "After I complete this deal, I'm going to do just that."

"Sometimes we have to make sacrifices to be happy," Gloria said wisely.

"I hear ya." Jaeden got up and kissed his mother on the cheek. He appreciated his mother's advice, but he wanted to figure out his relationship with Alexis on his own.

After loading the dishwasher, he went into the family room so he could talk to his father, but he'd fallen asleep in his recliner.

Jaeden went back to the kitchen to tell his mother he was leaving and headed to his apartment.

* * *

That evening, Alexis was thankful she'd been able to turn in her portfolio on time. She hadn't worked as diligently as she thought she should have on the assignment, but was happy with its outcome.

As she performed her nightly beauty ritual, she couldn't help but think about the disappointment she heard in Jaeden's voice when she declined his dinner invitation. Alexis pulled her long hair back into a ponytail and retrieved her Palm Pilot from her purse. She scrolled through the address book and pulled up Jaeden's information. Nervously, she sat on the side of her bed and picked up the phone to call him.

"Hello."

He sounded like he was asleep. Had she called too late? She didn't call men on a regular basis so she didn't know the protocol. "W-were you busy?"

"No, I was just listening to some music." Jaeden smiled. He was happy to hear from her.

Alexis remembered Stephanie telling her how much he loved music. "What are you listening to?"

"The O'Jays' 'Sunshine'."

"I like their music, too. How did everything go today?"

"I think they're going to accept."

"I'm so excited for you." Alexis picked up one of her throw pillows from the bed and held it in her lap.

There was a long pause before both Jaeden and Alexis spoke at the same time. "I—"

"You go first," Jaeden suggested. He was anxious to hear what she had to say.

"I'm sorry I couldn't go out with you tonight," she said softly. "We were covering difficult material and I knew I'd be worn out afterward."

"I understand, but we can still celebrate."

"How?" Her stomach fluttered and she willed herself to calm down.

"I'd like to take you to dinner Saturday night. Are you busy then?"

"No." Alexis squeezed her pillow.

"Good, why don't we make an evening of it?"

"Sure, what time should I be ready?" she asked enthusiastically. Alexis could no longer deny the fact she enjoyed his company.

"I'll be there around five o'clock."

"Why so early?"

"Just wait and see." Jaeden said, still smiling. He could hardly wait to see her again.

"Well, call me if you hear something from Herswick before Saturday," Alexis said.

"I will. Take care of yourself until then."

Alexis hung up the phone and squeezed the pillow tightly against her chest again. She smiled dreamily at the thought of going out with Jaeden.

She typed the date into her Palm Pilot and went into the kitchen to drop her PDA into its cradle. Alexis wanted to make sure her data would be backed up on her computer. She sighed contently as she shut off the light and made her way to the bathroom to take a hot bath.

CHAPTER FIVE

Jaeden wanted the evening to be special. He'd chosen Vivere, one of three restaurants in downtown Chicago's Italian village that came highly recommended. It was the perfect place for a memorable evening.

As they walked into the restaurant hand in hand, the design and décor captured Alexis's attention. There were copper-clad curls, a chandelier cut from a boiler head, spiral lamps and columns, stained-glass lights, and a mosaic tile entryway, which gave the restaurant a distinct Italian feel.

The maître d' escorted them to their table and pulled out a regal red velvet chair for Alexis. He opened the menu, placed it in front of her, and presented a menu and wine list to Jaeden.

"How did you find out about this place?" Alexis whispered, looking up from her menu.

"My cousin Greg told me about it a couple times, but I never had the time to experience the food and atmosphere for myself. This place has been around a long time and Greg said the food is excellent."

"They have so many items to choose from, I'm not sure what to order," Alexis said, perusing her menu in awe.

"You do like Italian food, don't you?"

"Yes, although I don't eat it often enough. I think I'm

going to try the lobster-filled tomato pasta with a light cream sauce. What are you going to have?"

"I'm not sure yet, I'm considering the veal," Jaeden answered.

When the server returned, Jaeden ordered a bottle of Chardonnay and gave their orders. The server quickly came back to the table with the wine and filled their glasses.

"I'd like to propose a toast," Alexis said, lifting her glass. She waited until Jaeden held his up before she continued. "Here's to you, Jaeden, may all your dreams come true."

They clinked their glasses together before taking a sip.

Jaeden raised his glass again. "Now I'd like to propose a toast. To us, may we find the time to explore our friendship and find the treasure that lies within."

Alexis's eyes sparkled. "That was beautiful, Jaeden."

Jaeden looked at her carefully for a moment. "You are so stunning."

Alexis's face turned a shade of crimson.

"I hope you like surprises," Jaeden said, quickly changing the subject when he sensed her embarrassment.

"It depends on what kind of surprise it is."

Jaeden pulled two tickets out of the pocket of his dinner jacket and handed them to her.

Alexis's eyes widened. "The *Lion King* musical?" she exclaimed.

Jaeden had no idea if she even liked musical stage plays. But he took a chance and watching her reaction brought a genuine smile to his lips.

"I've wanted to see this play, but haven't had the time," Alexis said, studying the front row tickets. "You are so sweet. I've never met anyone like you before," she remarked, handing the tickets back to him.

"Believe me, sweetie, you never will. God broke the mold when he made me," he said playfully.

Alexis chuckled. "Oh no, I think your head is growing," she teased.

"If only you knew," Jaeden mumbled under his breath.

After dinner, they'd walked across the street to the Shubert Theatre to see the show. Alexis had kept her eyes riveted to the stage during the performance and had thanked Jaeden profusely for her gift.

Now Jaeden was driving Alexis back to her apartment after a wonderful evening. Alexis had been quiet most of the ride back to Taylor and when Jaeden came within blocks of her building he looked over at her. She lay back against the headrest with her eyes closed.

His eyes roamed over her body with admiration. *Stunning,* he thought. Bringing his concentration back to the road, he cleared his throat as he turned onto her street. "We're almost there," he announced.

"I'm not asleep, just resting my eyes," Alexis mumbled.

Jaeden grinned. "Yeah, okay, whatever you say."

He slowly pulled into a parking spot and turned to Alexis. They both chuckled because each knew what the other was about to say.

After he assisted her from the vehicle, they walked to the building.

"Jaeden, I really had a fantastic time. The performance was awesome and the costumes were amazing. Thanks again for inviting me to celebrate with you."

"I wouldn't have wanted it any other way," Jaeden said as Alexis unlocked the door to her apartment.

"Would you like to come in?"

The invitation surprised him. "Sure," Jaeden said, trying not to sound too eager as he followed her inside.

Jaeden admired her roomy apartment for the first time. Alexis had a spacious living room, which was connected to a good-sized dining area. The apartment was neatly decorated and everything was in its place. There were beautiful paintings on the ivory-colored walls that matched her contemporary furniture.

"You have a nice place," Jaeden commented.

"Thank you. Why don't you have a seat?" Alexis offered.

Jaeden looked down as she slipped her shoes off. He noticed her fire-engine-red toenails through her panty hose. *Very sexy,* he thought.

"I have some bottled water and iced tea in the fridge. Help yourself. I'll be back in a minute." Alexis walked to her bedroom so she could change into something more comfortable.

Jaeden watched her as she walked away, enjoying the view of her curvaceous bottom in her burgundy tank dress.

His feelings for Alexis had escalated over the last few weeks and for a moment he thought maybe being alone with her wasn't a good idea. If he hadn't already tasted the sweetness of her lips, maybe he could have left without having any regrets. He knew if he stayed any longer, he'd want to taste more than just her lips. But there was no way he would seduce her. Getting her to trust him was too important to their relationship.

Jaeden walked over to the refrigerator and noticed a torn piece of notebook paper held up by two magnets. He didn't know if the letters written on it were acronyms or in code. Some letters had even been scratched out. He stood in front of the refrigerator trying to decipher the letters until Alexis returned

"The water is in the door," Alexis said from behind him.

Jaeden turned to find she had changed into a pair of

pink jogging pants and a white T-shirt. *Even in sweats, the woman is fine,* he thought.

She smiled from the sparkle in his eyes, knowing what he was thinking.

Suddenly, he gave her a puzzled look. "What does OTP, GBD, and OMD2Y mean?" he asked, pointing to the scrap of paper.

Alexis laughed. "I see you found my list."

"Are they organizations you belong to or something?"

"No, they're my goals for life," Alexis said as she removed the magnets and peeled the paper off.

"Why would you keep it here?"

"It keeps me focused. Each time I open the refrigerator door, I read it." She looked down at the worn piece of paper.

"I've heard of keeping a grocery list on the fridge, but this is a first."

"I also keep the list in my Palm Pilot."

Jaeden moved toward her. She'd taken her hair down and now he wanted to run his fingers through the long, loose strands. "I should have known. Now, explain to me what these letters mean, or is this just for you?"

He was so close. Too close. Alexis swallowed hard before she could respond. "It's just for me, but I don't mind explaining them to you." She pointed at each line. "GBD means get bachelor's degree and OTP means obtain teaching position."

"I think I get it, let me try one." He took the paper from her and studied it for a moment. "Does GMD2Y mean get married December second? I don't know what the last letter would be." He looked into her eyes as he spoke.

Alexis took a step back. He was much too close; she could hardly control herself. "No, it means get master's degree in two years. Marriage isn't on this list at all."

Jaeden felt as if he had been punched in the stomach.

He knew Alexis was a goal-oriented woman and he liked the fact she was organized and detailed. But he didn't know she wasn't interested in getting married. Why did that bother him?

He filled the space Alexis had created between them. "You don't want to get married?" He sounded disappointed.

"Of course I do, *when* the right person comes along." She stared at his parted lips.

"How will you know when the right person has come?" he asked seductively.

"I'm sure I'll know." Alexis responded quickly, turning away from him. She didn't want to see him lick his lips again. She wouldn't be responsible for what she did afterward. "Go on and have a seat, I'll get us something to drink," she offered nervously.

Jaeden went to the sofa in the living room and waited for her to join him. A few moments later, Alexis handed him a bottle of water. Then she walked over to the entertainment center and pressed the power button on the stereo. The distinctive sounds of the Isley Brothers' "Don't Say Good Night" boldly filled the room.

Jaeden set his bottle on the table near the sofa and walked toward her with purposeful strides. "This is a great song to practice your dance moves. Come here." Jaeden stretched out his arms to her.

Alexis walked slowly into his arms and laid her head against his shoulder as they swayed to the music. The night had gone well and Jaeden hoped it would continue.

"I could stay like this forever," Jaeden whispered in her ear.

Alexis held on to him tighter. She had never allowed herself to be in a relationship before, and to realize he felt the same way she did made her feel wonderful.

Jaeden sensuously caressed her back as they moved to

the music. The feel of her body, the softness of her breasts against him nearly made him lose control. Afraid he would push Alexis further than she was ready to go, he slowly released her and walked over to the sofa.

Jaeden looked up at Alexis, who was still standing in the middle of the floor. "Is everything okay, Jaeden?" Alexis asked, wondering if she had done something wrong.

"Why don't you come over here and *sit* with me?" Jaeden patted the empty space next to him.

Alexis filled the empty spot, making sure she kept a careful distance from him.

"Come closer, I won't bite, I promise." He made the sign of the cross over his chest before saying, "Not unless you ask me to."

"You are so crazy." Alexis hit his thigh as she moved closer. She was shocked by the firm muscles she felt there.

"You better be careful with those little hands of yours," Jaeden warned, looking into her eyes.

A shiver ran through Alexis when she saw the intent in his eyes. She motioned to get up and change the music, but Jaeden caught her hand.

"Where are you going so fast?" He gently pulled her onto his lap. He wrapped his arms around her and whispered, "I would never harm you." She shifted her body and he lifted her chin. "Ever," he said before his lips softly touched hers.

Alexis's eyes fluttered. "I know that," she said against his mouth.

The Isley Brothers' song had ended and now Atlantic Starr sang of being in a dream and having love for a lifetime. The combination of the music and the softness of Alexis's bottom against his manhood caused his palms to sweat and his shaft to rise. He was sure Alexis could feel him stiffening against her body.

Her facial expression changed and he expected her to

move or break their connection as she always did when he became too intimate with her. But this time, she relaxed against him and put her arm around his neck. It made him want her even more.

"I think I should be going, it's getting late," he said suddenly. Jaeden unfolded his arms from around her. He wanted to make love to her in the worst way, but he didn't want Alexis to think he only wanted her for her body.

Though disappointed, she nodded, stood, and escorted him to the door. As she walked, Jaeden came up behind her, wrapping his arms around her middle and gently pulling her back against his hard body. He wanted her to know the affect she had on him. "You smell so good," he said, burying his face in her hair, and pressing her soft bottom against him.

Alexis was stunned by the power she felt there. Slowly, she turned around to face him, and palmed the side of his face. The feel of her soft hands on his skin was more than he could bear and his lips immediately swooped down on hers.

Alexis wrapped her arms around his neck. She'd intended to give him a brief kiss, but when their lips touched, she deepened it, bringing her body as close to his as she could. They both lost all thought of anything but each other.

Jaeden felt something close to electricity go through him. He wanted Alexis Shire in a bad way. He could no longer deny himself the very thing he'd wanted all night: to have her legs wrapped securely around his waist as he buried himself inside her. That would be the next step if he didn't get out of her apartment.

Jaeden reluctantly broke the kiss. Stepping back, he wiped her lipstick from his bottom lip with the tips of his fingers. "I better go, Alexis."

Lost in the moment, Alexis moved forward to kiss him one last time.

Jaeden stopped her, though he knew he'd regret doing so. "We've got to stop now, before we end up in your bed," he groaned.

Alexis felt two emotions come over her: lust and admiration. She wanted him just as much as he wanted her, she respected him for his self-control. She grabbed his hand and squeezed it.

He brought it to his lips and kissed the back of her hand. "I'll call you later. Sweet dreams," he said, kissing her forehead lightly.

Jaeden left and all the way to the parking lot he thought about how badly he wanted Alexis Shire.

The next day, Jaeden stopped at Gus's Flowerama to purchase four long-stemmed pink roses for Alexis. Even though he hadn't asked her, he figured pink was her favorite color.

He handed the clerk several bills and proceeded to the Nobel school, which was located on the east side of town. He'd decided to surprise her and take the flowers to the school himself instead of having them delivered.

Jaeden stopped in the school office to sign the visitors' book and get a pass. He followed the directions the secretary gave him and soon found himself at Alexis's classroom.

Watching her from outside the door, he could see the children surrounding her in a circle. She had large posterlike cards with pictures and letters on them. The children were calling out the letters in unison. She hugged several of them and for the first time in his life, Jaeden thought about having a beautiful daughter with dazzling brown eyes like Alexis's and a son who would carry his name. Just seeing the way she interacted with the children, he could tell she loved them.

"What are you doing out here?"

Jaeden jerked in the direction of the familiar voice. "Hey, cuz," he responded, walking across the hall to embrace Stephanie.

"Why don't you just go on in?" Stephanie walked over to Alexis's door and peered through the glass.

"She's busy," he said, following her.

"That's okay." Stephanie opened the door and walked into the room, beckoning for Jaeden to follow her. "Ms. Shire, you have a visitor," Stephanie announced with a wide grin.

Jaeden entered the room and walked over to Alexis, who was getting up from her chair. "These are for you," he said, handing the flowers to her.

"This is a surprise," Alexis said, taking the roses and giving them a sniff.

"Oooh, Ms. Shire, you got a boyfriend," one of her students blurted.

"My daddy gives my mama flowers when she's mad at him," another little boy said loudly. The chubby child walked over to Alexis. "Ms. Shire, you mad at him?" he asked, pointing to Jaeden.

"No, sweetie." Alexis lifted his chin so she could look him in the eye. "And you shouldn't tell others about things that happen at home, okay?"

"Okay." He ran back to his space on the carpet.

"Class," Alexis began, "I'd like to introduce you to a friend of mine, Mr. Jaeden Jefferson. Let's welcome him."

"Good morning, Mr. Jef-fer-son," the children yelled in unison.

Jaeden chuckled. "Good morning." Turning to Alexis he said softly, "I don't want to take you away from your lesson."

"We were just finishing up. It's time for them to go to art class. Children, let's line up," she instructed.

Jaeden noticed when they formed the single-file line there was a tiny caramel-colored girl with doe eyes and long braids staring at him.

Stephanie leaned closer to Jaeden. "Alexis better watch out. I think she likes you." She nodded in the little girl's direction. "Lexie, my class is in the gym, so I can take them to Mrs. Martin's room."

"Thanks, Stef," Alexis said, grinning at her visitor.

"No problem." Stephanie winked at Jaeden before leading the children out of the classroom.

"I'm not going to keep you," Jaeden said when they were alone. "I was headed to work and thought I'd stop by. I wanted to deliver the roses myself."

Alexis pulled the wrapper down to get a better look at them. "These are so lovely. How did you know pink was my favorite color?"

"I guessed," he said, staring at her light pink blouse. "Are you in some kind of sorority?"

"No, I just think pink is very feminine." Alexis went to the cabinet and pulled out a vase.

Jaeden watched the way her trousers hugged her hips as she walked away. "I'm going to get to the office," he said quickly.

Without a word, Alexis moved to the door and closed it. She walked back to Jaeden and reached up to brush his lower lip with her thumb. Kissing her lightly, Jaeden slowly pulled her into his arms and held her.

"The real reason I came is I couldn't go to work without seeing your face," Jaeden whispered before capturing her lips in a kiss again.

"Thank you so much for bringing the flowers," Alexis said when their brief kiss ended. She looked into his eyes as she spoke.

"I'll call you later." Jaeden leaned in to kiss her again, but remembering where they were, he redirected his lips to her forehead.

She took his hand and walked him to the door. Alexis stood in the doorway, watching Jaeden walk down the hall. He turned around to see if she was still there and she waved at him before stepping back into the room.

By the time he reached his car, there was no doubt in his mind that he was in love with Alexis Shire.

Several minutes later, Alexis was sitting at her desk writing grades in her student record book when Stephanie walked into her classroom.

"Oh my, girlfriend, it looks like you're in deep," Stephanie said.

"You are always trying to start something, Stef." Alexis frowned at her friend, rose from her seat, and walked to the window.

Stephanie hunched her shoulders. "Start what? I wish I had a video camera so you could see your face when Jaeden walked into this room. It reminded me of a MasterCard commercial. It was priceless!" She looked around the room and saw the flowers on the table. "So he brought you roses, huh?"

Alexis had forgotten to put the flowers in the vase she'd pulled out. She quickly went over and picked them up. When she lifted one of the long stems from the package, a small envelope fell to the floor.

Stephanie scooped it up and handed it to Alexis. "Open it and see what it says," she said eagerly.

"You are so nosy," Alexis said, grinning at her friend.

"So I'm nosy, who isn't? Stop stalling and open the envelope," Stephanie ordered.

Alexis laughed at her friend. She took her time arranging the flowers in the vase and filling it with enough water to hydrate the roses.

"What are you waiting for? I've got things to do, girl," Stephanie said loudly. "Let's see what the card says before I have to leave."

Alexis took the vase to her desk, placing it on the corner before she picked up the card and opened it. In red ink, Jaeden had written "You've touched my heart," and he had drawn a heart with an arrow running through it.

"Aww, how sweet," Stephanie said, peeking over Alexis's shoulder. "I've got one question though. Why did he only give you four roses instead of a dozen? I *know* he can afford it."

"After we went to the dinner party, I sent him two long-stemmed red roses."

"Ahh, so he sends you four in your favorite color."

Alexis smiled. "Exactly."

"The boy is good, I tell you. Don't I know how to pick 'em?"

"Did you get any of the prizes for the picnic?" Alexis asked, moving to another topic.

Stephanie knew what she was up to, but didn't protest. "No, but I did get the jump ropes and hula hoops for the girls."

"Great, I still have to get the volleyball net out of my parents' garage though."

"I've got to get back to my room," Stephanie said, looking at the clock on Alexis's desk. "I'll talk to you later." Stephanie turned to walk out of the room, but stopped. "Lexie, I'm happy for you and Jaeden," she said, turning around. Stephanie walked toward her friend and hugged her, then left the room.

Alexis stared at the card for a while and kept thinking how Jaeden was unlike any man she'd met before. She hadn't wanted to admit to herself, but she couldn't deny the truth any longer. She was falling in love with Jaeden Jefferson.

Jaeden sat in his office staring at the blank computer screen. He couldn't stop thinking about his visit to Alexis's classroom earlier that day. She was definitely adding richness to his life.

"Mr. Jefferson." Marie's voice came through the intercom.

Jaeden picked up the phone. "Yes."

"Mr. Herswick is on line three-zero."

"Thanks, Marie." Jaeden pressed the button of the blinking red light. "Arnold, great to hear from you," he said into the phone.

"I've got some good news," Arnold responded.

Jaeden's heartbeat increased. So he rested his head on the back of his chair and waited for Arnold to continue.

"I would like you to make a presentation to my staff in the New York office. I've told them about your idea and they love it. I want them to see your full layout, so they can get a better feel for the product. If all goes well, we will be able to negotiate on marketing the product as well."

Jaeden sat up straight in his chair. "That would be great!" His excitement was evident. His dream was finally coming true.

"Do you think you can come to New York in two weeks?"

"Yes, sir, I'll be there. Will you be joining me?"

"Yes, I'll be there. And don't be nervous. Just present your plan to the group and everything will work out."

"I will," Jaeden said enthusiastically.

"My secretary will call with the arrangements. I think we're on to something."

"Thank you very much. I'll see you in New York."

"Good luck."

Jaeden hung up the phone, then immediately pressed the intercom to have Marie call an emergency meeting. He wanted to share the good news with his small staff. He thought about calling Alexis, but decided he'd tell her in person.

Every year since Alexis had been teaching at Nobel Elementary, they'd had an annual end-of-school-year picnic for the students and their families at Marquette Park. It was a beautiful place for picnics and outdoor weddings, and it had become a very popular spot for lovers as well. The school had secured a large indoor shelter so they could have use of a kitchen and hold their awards ceremony.

Alexis and Stephanie were responsible for the games and the prize table for the kindergarten and first grade classes. Stephanie even made play money for the children to redeem their prizes each time their team won.

Alexis was busy setting up the prize table when Jaeden approached carrying a large box. She figured Stephanie had asked him to help with the event. "I didn't know you were coming," Alexis said.

"Stef invited me a month ago. Remember? I knew you'd be here, so I decided to come." He placed the box on the ground and leaned over the table, placing a light kiss on Alexis's lips.

"I thought you would be working at the office today."

"No, I wanted to be here with you."

"You are so sweet. Has Stef got you hauling her stuff for her?"

"No, *this* is for the kids though," he said, pointing toward the box.

Alexis bent over and opened it. Looking inside, she

pulled out a small white hat. It had a baby panther, the school mascot, stitched on the back in blue and red.

She turned it around and saw that it had one of her student's names embroidered on the front. She pulled out another one with another student's name on the front, but the stitching was pink. Alexis looked up at Jaeden. "You had one made for each of my students?"

Jaeden slowly moved his head up and down. "I have one for each of Stef's students, too."

"How did you know their names?"

"Stef gave them to me."

"She is something else," Alexis said. "This is soo cute." She turned the hat over again. "Let me go and get the kids. They're inside and will be so excited."

Placing the hat back inside the box, Jaeden pushed it underneath the table. They walked hand in hand inside the building.

All of the students and their families were finishing their lunch. Alexis told the children she had a big surprise for them and to follow her to the prize table outside.

Once they were all present, Alexis called each child's name and gave each one a cap.

After the little girl with a crush on Jaeden received her gift, she walked over to him and stared. Chuckling, he kneeled until he was her height and hugged her.

"What are we going to say to Mr. Jefferson?" Alexis asked the children after she had distributed all the hats.

"Thank you, Mr. Jefferson," they all said in harmony. They ran over to him, knocking him to the ground. The adults laughed as the children played with him.

"You are quite welcome," Jaeden said as he stood, brushing off his blue jeans. He walked over to Alexis. "I have one more present," he told her quietly.

She looked up at him curiously. Jaeden pulled a small box from his pocket and handed it to her.

"What is it, Lexie?" Stef asked excitedly before Alexis could open the box.

"Hold on a minute!" Alexis snapped, taken aback by Jaeden's gesture. The only man that had ever given her a gift had been her father.

"Girl, you know I love presents. I wouldn't be as calm as you are if a man gave me a gift. I'd be tearing the paper off, just like one of these kids at Christmas," Stephanie babbled.

Alexis stood in a frozen like state.

"If you don't hurry up and open that box, we're never going to know."

Once Alexis tore the pretty paper off the package, she knew from the shape and size of the box it could only be a piece of jewelry. The small blue satin square box had a monogrammed letter on top. She lifted the lid and found another box made of blue velvet. Alexis opened the lid on the second box and gasped.

With a low whistle Stephanie said, "Oh my, girlfriend."

There on a bed of blue velvet was a fourteen-karat gold charm in the shape of a red apple. The stem had been filled with pave diamonds.

"I noticed your charm bracelet the other night at dinner, so I decided to buy an apple for my favorite teacher," Jaeden said.

Alexis looked up into Jaeden's eyes with tears brimming in her own. "This is so beautiful," she said, lifting the charm from the box. "My mother gave me the bracelet for my birthday last September."

She couldn't believe Jaeden had casually given her such a special gift. A tear ran down her face. Jaeden moved over to her and kissed her tearstained face when he thought no one else was looking.

"Yuk," a little boy said, sticking his finger in his mouth.

Some of the other children had also seen Jaeden kiss Alexis and were laughing, so he kissed her again.

"Ugh, that's nasty."

"My daddy kisses my mama like that, too," the child added in a louder voice. He pointed to his mother standing beside him.

"Carl," his mother said firmly, trying to silence him.

"Doesn't your dad kiss your mama?" he asked his classmate.

"Carl," his mother called again, grabbing him and covering his mouth. "Stop that," she whispered in his ear.

"Who's ready to play some games?" Stephanie yelled, attempting to get the children to focus their attention elsewhere. "I'll get Mrs. Martin to help me with the games while you talk to Jaeden," Stephanie said to Alexis. Turning to Jaeden, she added, "You are too much."

He hugged her.

"Let's go to that tree over there so we can get our teams together." Stephanie walked swiftly in front of the children, but looked back at Alexis and Jaeden and smiled.

Walking to a nearby bench, Alexis sat while Jaeden hunched down in front of her, pulling her hand in his.

"Alexis, you are so special. The gift is just a small token." He lifted her hand to his lips. "I hope you aren't upset by it," he said, staring at her eyes filled with unshed tears.

"Oh no, how could I be angry about something so special?" she asked softly. "You were kind to the children as well. Stef said you were an awesome guy. I just didn't realize the magnitude. Thank you so much for my gift." She leaned forward, kissing him on the lips with tears spilling from her eyes.

He wiped her face with the pad of his thumb. "I want you to know that I would do anything for you. You are such a special lady."

Alexis captured his face in her hands. "You're pretty special yourself." She playfully pinched his cheek.

Jaeden pulled himself up, grabbing her hand to help her from the bench as well. "I think they're getting ready to start the potato sack race. Let's go." He could hear the squeals of laughter from the children.

She smiled up at him and they started to walk over.

"Wait." Jaeden stopped. "One more thing, I have to go to New York in two weeks. I've been asked to make my presentation at Herswick's corporate office."

Alexis hugged him. "That's a good sign, baby."

"I want you to come with me," Jaeden said, pulling back from her and watching her excitement turn to discomfort. "We can have adjoining suites if you want," he added. "I just don't want to take this trip without you."

"I've got—"

Jaeden placed his finger over her lips. "Your night class is over and you won't have to teach after next week."

"But, I—"

"Your summer class won't start until after we return from New York. Please, say yes."

Alexis had never done anything without planning ahead of time, but she decided to take a chance. "Yes, I'll go with you to New York."

"I can't wait and I promise, no strings attached." Jaeden kissed her one last time before they joined the others.

CHAPTER SIX

Jaeden was very impressed with the hotel accommodations Arnold had provided for him at the Plaza Hotel. And he loved the expression on Alexis's face when he'd handed her the key card to the adjoining suite he'd paid for. His presentation would take place the next morning, so he planned to spend his entire free day with Alexis.

He knocked on the connecting door and waited. Alexis opened it wearing white linen pants and a black off-the-shoulder shirt with a fold over the collar.

"I thought we'd go to the museum after breakfast or we can just sightsee for a while," Jaeden said as he walked into her suite. "I want to come back later and go over my presentation for tomorrow."

"That's fine with me. Remember, I'm only here for moral support," Alexis said, reaching for her sunglasses on the dresser.

"Yes, and a sexy supporter at that," Jaeden said, pulling her into his arms. He kissed her slowly, exploring every crevice of her mouth. "I appreciate you coming with me," he said after he pulled away. She wiped her smudged lipstick from his mouth. "These next three days are going to be special, I can feel it in here." He pointed to the middle of his chest. "You ready to go?"

"Yes, let me get my bag." Alexis walked over to the coffee table and picked up her white Coach clutch purse.

***

Several hours later they returned exhausted. They had gone to more places than they had planned to. After breakfast they had gone to a museum, then Radio City Music Hall, before deciding to walk down Fifth Avenue to check out the shops.

"I'm going to take a shower and rest for a while," Alexis announced as she set her shopping bags next to the armchair.

"Do you want some company?" Jaeden lifted his left brow.

Alexis put her hands on her hips, then smiled. "You are so silly," she said, rolling her eyes playfully.

Jaeden backed up toward the connecting door. "Just kidding, I'm going to my room. I'll call you later so we can go to dinner," he said, opening the door and closing it behind him.

Jaeden felt as if he could fly. After all the time and hard work he'd spent on his proposal, it had finally paid off. The Herswick Corporation agreed to put their logos on his hats. As an added bonus, they wanted to develop a strategy for the best way to market them. There were still details to be worked out, but this was a big accomplishment for Jaeden. He couldn't wait to get back to the hotel to share his good news with Alexis.

Knocking on her door, he waited. When she opened it in a short pink nightgown and a matching robe, he swung her into his arms, giving her a deep kiss that almost made her moan his name. Jaeden walked into the room with her still in his arms, closing the door behind him.

"You did it. Herswick accepted your proposal?" Alexis guessed.

"Yes," Jaeden shouted, then placed kisses all over Alexis's face.

"That didn't take long at all," Alexis said, trying to close her robe. "I'm not even dressed yet. I'm so happy for you, honey."

Jaeden set her on her feet, lifted her chin, and looked into her eyes. "I couldn't have done it without you."

"Me?" She pointed to herself. "I haven't done anything. You created the designs, *you* made it happen."

"*You* were there for me."

"That's what friends are for."

"Friend?" Jaeden gathered her close again, "You mean more to me than just a friend. I love you, girl." There, he finally said it. He released Alexis and waited for her response.

Alexis's eyes grew larger. "What did you say?"

Jaeden quickly moved closer to her, gently grasping her hands in his. "I've been pondering it, holding it in my heart, but what's the use if you don't know how I feel? So I'm telling you right now . . . I love you, Alexis."

The sparkle in his eyes as he spoke caused her to inhale several breaths in quick succession.

Jaeden cupped her face and moved even closer to her until their lips were inches apart, until he lightly brushed his mouth against hers. The contact was so electrifying that he consumed her mouth.

Jaeden ran his fingers through her hair, causing Alexis's head to fall back. He began to rain kisses on her neck. She moaned, adding to his already burning desire. Knowing all she wore beneath her robe was her skimpy nightgown didn't help any.

Jaeden pulled the knot loose on the satin belt that held her robe together. When it fell open, he pushed one side off her shoulders and watched as it slid down her body to the floor. Her nipples puckered underneath the fabric as he reached out to touch her breasts.

Capturing her lips in a hypnotic trance, he lightly stroked her tongue with his while he continued to caress her body.

Breaking the kiss, Jaeden glared at her swollen lips and then her passion-filled brown eyes. He ran his hands down the sides of her gown before his breathing grew heavy and he lifted the silky fabric up her body.

Alexis raised her arms so he could remove it.

Dropping the garment to the floor, he stood spellbound at her nearly naked figure. "You are so beautiful, but I always knew you would be," he whispered huskily. He stared approvingly at Alexis, who wore only her skimpy white thong.

Alexis was a bundle of nerves; the time had come. Her heartbeat quickened at the thought of the pleasure ahead.

Jaeden began to undo his tie and Alexis quickly assisted with removing it and his shirt. When she reached for his belt, he covered her hand with his.

"Baby, if you have any doubts about making love to me, I'd like to hear them now. If my pants hit the floor there's no turning back," Jaeden said in a raspy voice.

He took a step forward, closing all the space between them. Her nipples ached as his hands began to caress her back and moved to her rounded bottom.

"I want you to make love to me," Alexis said boldly. She looked up at him with desire in her eyes.

Jaeden scooped her up and carried her further into the room. Laying her on the unmade bed, he stood back and assessed the exquisite woman he'd fallen in love with.

"I've wanted you since the night I held you in my arms at Whispers," he said as he stretched out beside her.

Kissing her passionately, he slipped his tongue inside

her mouth. The feel of her hot body against his already burning skin was almost overpowering.

He placed kisses on her neck and shoulder, continuing his journey until he captured one dark-pointed peak in his mouth and teased it with his tongue. The friction of her nipple running through his teeth almost made Alexis leap from the bed. She squirmed with pleasure, then whimpered as he continued his sweet torture, paying as much attention to the other breast.

Jaeden skimmed over her rib cage with his fingertips as he moved down to her thighs. His fingers touched the dark curls that hid her essence. As he stroked the delicate folds of flesh, her thighs immediately closed, trapping his hand.

He kissed the tip of her nipple and then her swollen lips. "It's okay, baby, relax," he said hoarsely as he pulled the scrap of material down and off of her.

Jaeden brushed his fingertips along her wet, sensitive nub and watched as Alexis's body jerked in the throes of passion. He continued to pleasure her and she began to shift her body against the rhythm his fingers.

Jaeden thought he would lose control. He got up from the bed and Alexis moved toward him on her knees. She unzipped his pants and was about to reach inside them and touch his throbbing sex, but he grabbed her hand.

"Are you sure you're ready for this?" His voice was heavy with need.

She nodded, unable to speak.

Jaeden removed several foil packets from his back pocket and tossed them on a table near the bed before pushing his pants and underwear down.

Alexis watched nervously as he stepped out of his pants and revealed his curving sex. He positioned her across the bed and eased his arm around her waist. Caressing his back, she moaned from the circular motions he made on her bottom and the feel of his thick manhood against her thigh.

Jaeden dipped his head and captured one of her chocolate nipples in his mouth again.

"Jaeden," she cried out.

"I know, baby." Jaeden moved from her nipple and spread her legs, finally settling his face between her thighs.

Alexis thought she would explode when he kissed the inside of her thigh. He continued to place kisses there until he moved to her core. When he flicked his tongue, touching her clitoris, Alexis cried out again. Involuntarily, her legs locked his head between her thighs.

Jaeden stroked the outside of her legs. "Relax, baby. Let me love you," he whispered.

Slowly, she unclamped her legs and allowed Jaeden to take her higher and higher. Soon, Alexis's legs fell wider, giving him full access to her body.

When she was ready, he reached for the foil packet on the bedside table, opened it, and secured it over his aching sex. Moving over her, he slid between her thighs, supporting his weight with his elbows, and began to lower his body.

Jaeden looked down and saw Alexis's eyes were closed tightly. He hadn't tried to enter her yet and she was already bracing herself? He stopped suddenly. *No, she can't be,* he said to himself, but decided to make sure. If it was her first time, he wanted to make it a memorable experience.

Jaeden eased himself into the entrance of her body. The contact of her essence on the tip of his sex made him tremble. Slowly, he moved against her, pressing into her tight heat. He kissed her lips.

"Alexis, are you a virgin?" he asked nervously.

"Yes."

Jaeden claimed her mouth in another soulful kiss. "Relax, I'll take care of you."

"I want you to be the first," Alexis said, moving her body beneath his to claim his sex.

"I'll be your first and *only*," Jaeden said with assurance.

Taking his time, he slowly pressed forward until he felt her thin barrier give way. He willed himself to keep still until her body could adjust.

"Are you okay, baby?" He kissed her closed eyelids and then her mouth. He could barely speak, trying not to spill his contents before giving her the pleasure he knew she deserved.

Alexis smiled, reveling in the moment.

"Open your eyes," Jaeden said as he sank deeper and deeper inside her wet heat; her body wrapped around his member like a fitted glove.

The intensity of the sensations caused his thrusting to become more frequent. He lifted Alexis's buttocks and she met him stroke for wonderful stroke.

"I love you too, Jaeden, with my whole heart," Alexis confessed.

Hearing her words caused his movements to become more frenzied. Alexis's moans grew louder and Jaeden knew she was near completion. He continued his rhythm and suddenly spasms began to hit them both and continued until the last one quieted.

Jaeden gathered her in his arms beside him when they were finished.

"You are so amazing," he said as he kissed Alexis on the forehead.

Alexis snuggled closer to him. "I had no idea."

"I hope you don't regret making love to me."

"No, never, it was the best experience I've ever had." Alexis grazed his muscular chest with her fingertips.

"Alexis, why didn't you tell me you were a virgin?"

"The subject never came up," she said shyly.

"I love you, more and more each day." He turned toward her, lifting her chin. "I want you to understand I didn't bring you to New York to bed you, we could have done this at home."

Alexis moved closer to his lips. "I believe you. I wanted to share my body with you, this felt so right." She placed one kiss after the other on his luscious mouth.

"You're playing with fire. Be careful or you might get burned," he said, cupping her round bottom.

Alexis chuckled and continued rubbing his chest. "I'm not afraid," she said huskily.

"Oh, baby, I don't want you to be afraid." Jaeden let a long tendril of her hair slide through his fingers. "Making love is beautiful when it's between two people who really love and care for each other."

Jaeden grabbed another condom from the nightstand and sheathed his thickening sex. He moved between Alexis's legs again, he wrapped them around his waist and entered her. He had so much to teach her about lovemaking and she was a willing student. With deep thrusts, he made love to Alexis, stroking her very core.

"You feel sooo good, baby," he moaned.

Alexis tried to keep up with his strokes. She reveled in the pleasure of having him inside her. For the rest of her life, she would treasure this experience.

Jaeden suddenly rolled over, bringing Alexis on top of him. She gasped as he maneuvered his sex deep within her. He held her hips firmly and stroked Alexis until he sent her over the edge.

She screamed out his name and began to rotate her hips to her own rhythm. Jaeden caught on and continued his thrusts while lightly brushing her nipples with his fingers.

Soon, Alexis quivered, feeling another release coming forth.

"Let's come together," Jaeden moaned. He quickened the pace of their lovemaking and soon they both were spent.

He gently laid a dazed Alexis beside him and kissed her mouth just as she was about to declare her love for him once more.

Alexis's eyes fluttered closed as she lay in his arms and fell fast asleep.

Jaeden watched Alexis sleep and wondered what his life would be like without her. Even the thought of her not being there made him uncomfortable. He didn't want to ever be without her and he knew exactly what to do to make sure he wouldn't.

Jaeden kissed Alexis's mouth several hours later. "Wake up, sleepyhead."

Alexis squirmed and slowly opened her eyes. "What time is it?"

"It's six o'clock."

She yawned, sitting upright. "I'm sorry I fell asleep on you."

"How do you feel?"

"Marvelous," Alexis said as she stretched, causing the sheet to slip.

Jaeden's gaze went to her exposed breasts. He bent to kiss her nipple.

Savoring the feel of his lips on her skin, she moaned and then gently pushed him away, giggling. "I'd better take a bath so we can go out. There are still a couple of places I want to visit before we leave tomorrow."

Jaeden planted kisses on her neck. "You sure you want to go out?"

Alexis closed her eyes, enjoying the sensation before playfully pushing him away. "If we don't we'll be in bed the rest of the night."

"Not a bad idea, I wish I'd thought of it."

Alexis caressed his face. "I really do want to go out," she pleaded.

Jaeden rolled to the other side of the king-sized bed. "Okay."

He watched as Alexis left the bed, dragging the sheet with her. "Baby, you can leave the sheet, I've seen all your assets. And may I say, they are the most beautiful I've ever seen."

Jaeden got out of bed with no thought to his own nakedness and walked over to where she stood. He lifted his hand carefully, placing his forefinger and thumb on the top of the sheet where she held it. Looking into her eyes, he gently pulled the sheet away, letting it fall to the floor.

"Woman, you are driving me crazy," he said, staring at her naked body. Even after making love all afternoon, he still wanted her so bad, his hands trembled.

Jaeden started to kiss her neck to gauge her response to him. He devoured her shoulders as she pulled him closer to her. Suddenly, he dropped to his knees again.

She moaned her response since she could barely speak.

Jaeden pulled her hot body and pressed it to his face. "I want to love you," he promised.

Another moan slipped from Alexis's lips. Jaeden retreated from her most sensitive spot only to return once again.

She was getting weaker and her moans louder. "Jaeden, please," Alexis murmured. Her hands caressed his head as he explored her. "Please," she begged.

Jaeden willed himself to stop. He knew if he continued they'd end up in the bed once again.

"Go take your bath, baby," he said, pushing himself from the floor. "Holla if you want company." He tapped her on the buttocks.

"Knowing you, we'd never get out of the tub," Alexis said, giving him a deviant look.

"Hmmm, I like that idea. You are brilliant, you know that? Beautiful and brilliant." He winked at her.

Alexis chuckled as she went to the bathroom. Jaeden was very tempted to follow her, but decided against it. They'd made love all afternoon and he didn't want her body to become sore.

As he watched Alexis disappear behind the bathroom door, he made a vow to himself to have her permanently in his life.

Alexis stood in the middle of the bathroom floor, her body pulsing. She walked to the tub and flicked the handle to fill it. Grabbing her bubble bath, she poured a cap full of the potent organza fragrance into the tub.

She twisted the cap back on and slowly walked toward the large lighted mirror. Her legs trembled as images of Jaeden making love to her played over and over again in her mind. She couldn't describe the way he made her feel when they became one. She'd been hesitant at first, but once he touched her, she let all her inhibitions go.

Happy she'd saved herself for the right man, she never imagined anything like what she'd experienced with Jaeden. Now she had fallen in love with him and wondered what would happen next.

The running water caught Alexis's attention and she quickly twisted the handles to stop it before the tub overflowed. She stepped into the tub and leaned against the back of it, willing her body to relax as the warm water comforted her aching muscles. She didn't mind though;

it was the sweetest ache she'd ever experienced. This time, she could close her eyes and not have to *wonder* what it would be like for Jaeden to make love to her.

Stepping out of the tub twenty minutes later, Alexis felt like a new woman. She rubbed a creamy, scented lotion on her body, then she slipped into a lacy pink demi bra and panty set.

Pulling on her robe, she went back into the bedroom and found Jaeden sprawled over the bed. Alexis moved over to the other side of the huge bed and watched the man she'd fallen in love with sleep. He had forever changed her life, and now she couldn't imagine her life without him in it.

Later that evening, Jaeden kept his word. They left the hotel room to do some more sightseeing after he showered and changed.

They returned to the hotel to change before they went out for a late dinner.

Jaeden knocked on the connecting door before opening it.

"I don't know why you paid for an extra room, it was a waste of money," Alexis said as she stood before the mirror, smoothing her dress.

Jaeden stood behind her. "No, it wasn't. I hadn't planned on making love to you, but I'm glad I did."

"Speaking of making love . . ." Jaeden moved closer, snuggling against her neck.

"Jaeden, don't start," she pleaded, trying not to moan. "We're going to go out and have a good time this evening."

"We could have a good time right here."

Alexis laughed as she picked up her diamond earring

from the dresser and placed it in her right earlobe. "We've done that already," she whined halfheartedly.

"I've got something for you." Jaeden pulled out a small box and watched in the mirror as he set it on the dresser.

Alexis looked down to pick up her other earring and saw it. She looked at the box, then in the mirror at him. She slowly turned to him and lifted her arms around his neck.

"You didn't have to get me anything," she said as she placed a soft kiss on his lips.

"You didn't have to give me the best gift I've ever received."

"What are you talking about?"

"Your innocence. It's the most precious gift a man could ever receive from a woman and I'm honored." Jaeden picked up the box and handed it to her. "Aren't you going to open it?" Jaeden asked as he wiped away a tear from Alexis's cheek.

"You are too good to me, you know that?" she said, taking the box from him.

"My queen, you're *supposed* to be showered with lovely gifts."

"Stop, you're going to make me completely ruin my makeup," Alexis said, trying to keep any more tears of happiness from spilling down her face.

Alexis dabbed the corners of her eyes with her right hand before lifting the lid on the red box. She pulled out another red velvet one and handed the empty box to Jaeden. Opening the smaller box, she found two charms for her bracelet. This time it was a shoe and a purse. "This is so lovely," she said, fingering the delicate jewelry. "When did you get it?"

"I went back to the jewelry store after I left you in that store where you bought a gazillion pairs of shoes."

"I did very well, thank you. I only bought three pairs," Alexis said playfully in her defense.

"I hope you have enough room to get all of them in your luggage."

"Trust me, I'll find a way. Hey, is that why you chose a shoe?"

"Every time we go out or you change your outfit you have matching shoes and purses."

"This is so darling. Look, the shoe is pink with diamonds in the heel and the purse matches," she squealed. "Oh, Jaeden, I love it." Alexis kissed him passionately again.

"Wait, baby," he said, stepping back. "If you still want to go out, we'd better stop right now."

"Can we get my charms—"

Jaeden interrupted her before she could finish her thought.

"Our flight doesn't leave until tomorrow afternoon, so we can go down to the jeweler and have him add them to your bracelet."

"Let me get dressed so we can go." Alexis handed him the box and went over to the closet. She pulled out a pair of shoes and slipped them on.

Jaeden waited patiently as she dressed and thought about the conversation he'd had with his mother. He was glad he took the time to see where their relationship was headed. He had found the perfect woman and now all he had to do was keep what they had alive forever. *How hard could that be?*

CHAPTER SEVEN

Alexis drove to her parents' house after she returned from New York. She pulled her silver Maxima around the back of the house and parked it in front of the twin garage beside her mother's car.

Stepping out of her vehicle, she spotted her mother on her knees digging in the ground with a small shovel.

"Hey, Mom," Alexis yelled, waving as she walked through the gate.

Josephine Shire flipped the front of the wide-brim hat up so she could see. "Hey, sweetie." She waved at her only child. "How are you?" she asked, pulling herself to her feet.

Alexis hugged her mother. "Good."

Josephine pulled off her dirty gardening gloves and big floppy hat. Alexis ran her hands through her mother's short silvery bob-styled haircut and watched every strand fall back in place. "You're working hard today."

"I planted my dahlias, gladiolas, and lilies last month, so I was just tending to them."

"I don't know why you love digging in the ground in the hot sun."

"Helps clear the mind. You should try it sometime. Come on inside, I was just finishing up." Josephine motioned to her daughter as she walked up the path to the house.

Alexis followed her mother into the kitchen. She took a seat at the table. Josephine went over to the sink, turned on the hot water, and squeezed a dollop of antibacterial soap on her hands. "Would you like some iced tea?" Josephine asked, pulling out a large pitcher of brown liquid with sliced lemons floating through it.

Setting it on the counter, she removed two glasses from the cupboard and filled them with ice. She poured the refreshing drink in the tall glasses and placed one in front of Alexis.

"This is gorgeous." Josephine had spotted Alexis's charm bracelet. She picked up her right arm to examine it. "I see you've added more charms."

Alexis didn't respond right away. "They were a gift from a friend."

"A friend?" Josephine looked up at her daughter, then back down at the bracelet. "Are these real diamonds, Alexis?"

"I would hope so. Aren't they beautiful?" Her expression lit up the room.

Josephine lifted her daughter's chin. "A friend, huh? Do I know him?"

"Not yet, but I want you and Daddy to meet him. His name is Jaeden Jefferson."

"Where did you meet him?" Josephine wanted to know.

"He's Stef's cousin."

"Lord, help us. That Stephanie is a character," Josephine said. "You took time away from your studies to go out with someone? I'm surprised."

"Mom, he's such a great guy. I didn't want to go out with him at first, but I'm glad I did."

"So, you really like him?"

"Yes, he's so caring and loving." Alexis's eyes glistened as she spoke. "I can't wait to hear his voice when I get up in the morning."

"So, *he* gave you the charms?"

Alexis nodded. "Yes, all three of them," she said, turning her wrist back and forth.

"Alexis, this is not a casual gift," Josephine said, lifting her arm again and carefully inspecting the bracelet. "The man gave you *diamonds*. I think he's more than just a friend, honey."

"I can't wait for you to meet him, Mom."

"From the day you were born, all I've ever wanted for you is peace, joy, and happiness," Josephine told her. "As long as he provides that, I'm happy for you."

"I've never been this happy in my entire life. Don't get me wrong, I'm proud of the things I've accomplished, but none of them can compare to how I feel about Jaeden," Alexis replied.

"This is sudden, but I'm glad you've found a nice guy."

"I know it's short notice, but can you make dinner for us tomorrow evening? I'll have to check with Jaeden to confirm the time."

"I'd love to. Is there anything in particular you want me to prepare?"

Alexis kissed her mother's cheek. "No, anything you make will be great."

Josephine lifted her finger. "One more question. Are you in love with Jaeden?"

"Yes," Alexis said boldly.

"That's what I thought." Josephine pulled her daughter into a strong embrace.

"Where's Daddy? I wanted to talk to him," Alexis said, stepping back from her.

"He's at the bowling alley with Mr. Blackmon."

"Oh," she said, slightly disappointed. "Well, I'll call you later to confirm everything for tomorrow."

"That's fine, sweetie. I'll talk to your father when he comes in later this evening."

Alexis stood and picked up her handbag. She kissed her mother before walking out of the house.

As soon as Alexis got in her car, she called Jaeden to invite him to her parents' house for dinner. After he accepted, she prayed her parents would approve of him.

Jaeden was nervous about meeting Alexis's parents, but she kept reassuring him there wasn't anything to worry about. Still, he'd left thirty minutes early to pick her up to make sure they would be on time for dinner.

As he pulled up in front of the large brown two-story brick home, he glanced over at Alexis. "Did I tell you how gorgeous you look tonight?"

"Yes, you did, several times."

Jaeden leaned over and Alexis met his kiss. As he withdrew, he looked deeply into her eyes for reassurance.

"Everything will be fine. Come on, let's go inside," Alexis said as she pulled the handle on the door. Jaeden quickly climbed out of the vehicle and went around to the other side to assist her.

Following Alexis up the cement walkway that led to the back of the house, he stepped with her inside the patio. There were potted plants by the windows along with a round glass patio table and two chairs with green-and-tan-striped fabric.

"It will be okay, I promise," she reassured him once more before twisting the knob on the door that led to the kitchen.

Jaeden followed her inside the immaculate eggshell-colored kitchen with natural maple cabinets that had cherry inlays. Some of them had frosted glass as fronts. The countertops were made of granite and there was an island cook top.

"Mom, we're here," Alexis announced, looking around for her.

Josephine walked into the kitchen and embraced Alexis. "I was in the dining room setting things up. I'm glad you two made it. Your father says he's starving."

"That's what he always says," Alexis replied, laughing. "Mom, I'd like you to meet Jaeden Jefferson. Jaeden, this is my mother, Josephine Shire."

Jaeden extended his hand. "Pleasure to meet you, Mrs. Shire."

"I'm so glad to meet you too, Jaeden." Josephine accepted his hand as she carefully looked him over.

The doe-eyed woman's features reminded him of Alexis's. Her salt-and-pepper hair was expertly styled.

A tall, distinguished-looking man with sprinkles of gray throughout his hair walked into the kitchen. The uncertainty in the man's eyes caused Jaeden's nervousness to heighten. Jaeden knew this was Alexis's father, Robert Shire.

"Hi, Daddy." Alexis walked quickly over and planted a kiss on her father's cheek.

"How's my baby girl?"

"I'm good, I'd like you to meet someone," she said, waving for Jaeden to join them. "Jaeden, this is my father, Robert Shire."

"Pleased to meet you, sir," Jaeden said as he offered his hand to him.

Robert paused before firmly shaking it. "Why don't we have a seat in the family room while the ladies finish getting the food on the table?" He gave his wife a meaningful look.

"We'll have everything ready in a minute, Robert," Josephine said in response to his expression.

"She only calls me Robert when I've annoyed her,"

he said to Jaeden as they walked through the dining area to the family room.

The large dark wood-paneled room had tall ceilings and recessed lighting. With all the photos and awards, it reminded Jaeden of his parents' family room.

He sat on the brown leather sofa while Robert sat in the matching leather recliner next to it.

"Jaeden, what do you do?" Robert asked.

"I own a hat company."

"What kind of hats?"

"I design baseball caps."

"You have the building on the corner of Sixth and Broadway?"

"Yes, sir, that's me. We've only been there a little under two years."

Jaeden looked away from Robert and spotted Alexis taking a platter of food to the table. She smiled at him and disappeared into the kitchen again.

"Let's cut to the chase, son. What are your intentions toward my daughter?" Robert asked, bringing Jaeden's attention back to him. Alexis had never brought a man home to meet him before so he knew she must be serious about him.

Jaeden placed his right hand on the end of the sofa, pulling himself forward. He looked directly into Robert's eyes. "My intention is to make your daughter my wife," he said honestly.

Robert raised his brow, pulled himself to the edge of his chair too, and placed his elbows on his knees. He locked his fingers together under his chin.

"How long have you two known each other?"

"Since the beginning of April, sir."

"You've only known Alexis two months, and now you want to marry her?" Robert said harshly. "Why so quickly? Marriage isn't something you take lightly, you know."

"Yes, sir, I am aware of that," Jaeden said evenly. "But I love your daughter and I can't see my life without her in it."

"Is that a fact?" Robert said, continuing to scrutinize him. "Have you shared this information with Alexis?"

"She knows I love her, but I wanted to ask you for her hand in marriage before asking her."

"Are you asking me now?"

"Yes, sir, I am," Jaeden said confidently.

Rubbing his hand over his close-cut silver locks, Robert observed Jaeden without saying another word. After a long pause that seemed like forever to Jaeden, he stood. Jaeden did the same.

Robert extended his hand. "If Alexis agrees to marry you, I will give you my blessing."

Jaeden accepted the offered hand, breathing a sigh of relief. "Thank you, sir, I promise to take good care of her." He hadn't planned on asking Robert tonight, but found it the ideal opportunity.

Just as Jaeden was about to withdraw his hand, Robert pulled it back and applied more pressure. Staring into the deep brown depths of eyes reminiscent of Alexis's, he watched Robert's lips move.

"Let's get one thing straight, I only want my baby's happiness, so if you hurt her in any way, look for me, 'cause I'm coming. Do we understand each other?"

"Perfectly," Jaeden said, nodding.

Robert released his hand. "Josie, is dinner ready yet? I'm starving," he yelled.

"Yes, go on and have a seat. I'm waiting for my rolls to brown on top," Josephine yelled back.

Jaeden followed Alexis's father to the dining room and took the seat on his left.

He admired the way the table had been decorated. The dark cherry-wood table was covered with an ivory tablecloth and gold damask place mats with ivory candles nestled in crystal holders.

Alexis brought the salad, then took a seat next to Jaeden. Josephine entered the room next with a basket filled with hot rolls. She sat on her husband's right.

Robert bowed his head and gave thanks to God for their meal.

"Daddy, how did you do at the bowling alley last night?" Alexis asked when the prayer ended. She reached for a platter and placed a thin slice of meat loaf on her plate.

"I bowled a two hundred, but Blackmon did two twenty, and of course I had to hear about it all the way home. He wanted a rematch this evening, but I told him we had dinner plans."

"Mr. Blackmon is the neighbor next door," she explained to Jaeden. "He and Daddy have always competed against each other. Daddy, don't you think both of you are getting a little too old for that?"

"A little competition is good for the soul, baby girl."

"I agree with Mr. Shire," Jaeden chimed in. "Friendly rivalry never hurt anybody."

Alexis shook her head. "Whatever."

"Jaeden, do you have any siblings?" Josephine asked.

"No, but I have a huge extended family."

"I couldn't believe the number of people that were at their last family gathering," Alexis added before taking a sip from her water glass.

"Is that where you two met?" Josephine asked.

"Yes. By the way, Mrs. Shire, the food is delicious."

"As always," Robert said, winking at his wife.

After everyone had finished their meal, Jaeden stood and began to help clear the table.

"Let me have those, honey," Josephine Shire said, taking the empty plate from him. "You're a guest in this house. I think we can handle things. Alexis, would you please help me clear the table?"

Alexis gathered the serving dishes and took them into the kitchen.

"Jaeden, why don't we go into the family room while you wait for Alexis to finish up? She can show you the house after she's done helping her mother," Robert suggested.

"I have an old photo album with lots of pictures of Alexis when she was a baby," Josephine said, clearing the water glasses.

"Mom, we are not pulling out those old pictures," Alexis protested as she cleared the rest of the items from the table.

"Why not? I'd love to see what you looked like as a baby." Jaeden wondered if their first child would have his features and coloring or Alexis's as he walked behind Robert.

Alexis followed them into the room.

"I thought you were helping your mother in the kitchen," Robert said accusingly.

"She's going to load the dishwasher," Alexis replied, sitting next to Jaeden.

"You're not leaving right away, are you?" Robert asked.

"I hope not, I still haven't seen Alexis's baby pictures," Jaeden teased, leaning close to her.

Alexis playfully pushed him away. "And you're not going to see them either. I've hidden that book in a good place; my mom doesn't even know where I put it."

"Alexis has never liked those pictures, I thought she was a beautiful baby," Josephine commented as she wiped the dining room table.

"Why don't the two of you go for a walk while I help your mother finish up the kitchen?" Robert suggested.

"I think that's a great idea," Jaeden said.

"What's up?" Alexis asked, looking between the two men. "Why are you trying to get us out of the house so fast, Daddy? You want us out of the way so you can make up with Mom for the way you acted earlier?"

"Yes, that's it," Robert said in a hurry. "Now go on and come back a little later." He laughed, then looked at Jaeden.

"Gleason Park is down the street," Alexis said.

"Sounds good to me," Jaeden said, walking to the threshold of the door.

"Daddy, we'll be back."

"All right, we'll be here," Robert said with a smirk on his face.

Alexis caught Jaeden's arm and laid her head against him as they walked slowly up the street toward the park.

"It really feels good out here tonight," Alexis said, feeling a light breeze against her face. "I haven't done this since I was a teenager." She looked up at him. "I told you everything would be fine."

He kissed her forehead. "That you did."

"What did my father say to you?"

Jaeden pretended to wipe sweat from his brow. "Boy, your father doesn't beat around the bush."

"What did he say, Jaeden?" Alexis pushed.

"Nothing I couldn't answer," Jaeden replied, knowing she wanted more of an explanation.

"That's not telling me anything," Alexis said, playfully punching him in the arm.

"Seriously, he asked what my intentions were toward you and I told him."

"I'm not up for riddles. Are you going to tell me what you said or is this some kind of game you're playing?"

They took a seat on a nearby bench. Jaeden moved so close to Alexis, the heat from his body made her shiver. He nibbled at her ear, then kissed her on the neck.

"Jaeden," she squealed, leaning in the opposite direction of him. "What did you say to my dad?"

"I told him if I have my way, I'm gonna make you my wife."

Alexis's eyes grew large in disbelief. "Huh? Why did you say such a thing to him? He probably took you seriously. I've never brought a man home to meet my parents before. You shouldn't have gotten my dad's hopes up."

"I *am* serious. We are supposed to follow our hearts." Jaeden gradually dropped down on one knee and pulled Alexis's left hand to his face, lightly kissing her knuckles. "I know we've only known each other a short time, but every morning when I wake up and find you're not beside me, I can't wait to hear your voice or look into your brown eyes to tell you just how much I love you." He laid his head in her lap and then slowly lifted it to look into her eyes to gauge her reaction. The illumination of the light from the lamppost created a soft glow surround her.

"I'm asking you tonight, Alexis Shire, right here in Gleason Park, to make my soul happy and agree to be my wife."

Alexis couldn't believe the words coming from Jaeden's mouth. She bent over and caressed his face with her hands, looking deeply into his eyes. She wanted to pinch herself. Would she wake up tomorrow and find out she was only dreaming? Quiet tears began to slip from her eyes.

Jaeden pulled himself up from the ground, dusted his gray slacks, and sat on the bench again. He pulled her onto his lap. "I know you weren't expecting a marriage proposal," Jaeden whispered softly while grazing her neck with his lips. "Especially on a park bench. And I wasn't prepared to give one. I don't even have a ring."

Alexis lifted her head. Jaeden wiped the tears from her face and dipped to taste her sweet lips. "I want to share my love, heart, and soul with you," he whispered hoarsely as he placed her hand on his chest, so she could feel his rapid heartbeat. "I knew I couldn't spend another night without knowing you'd be mine forever."

Alexis hadn't said a word since he proposed. "You're quiet, sweetheart." Jaeden nervously kissed her temple. "Please don't tell me you're going to bruise my heart by saying no."

Alexis stared into his dark eyes. Finally, she spoke. "I find myself thinking some of the same thoughts as you. When I go to bed at night, I look for you and when I awake in the morning, I long to see your face, feel your body close to mine," she said as she ran her fingers over his close-cropped hair. "Yes, Jaeden, I will be honored to be Mrs. Jaeden Jefferson."

Jaeden kissed her with such passion it left them both gasping. Then, he kissed her neck and began to move down even farther.

Alexis pushed back from him, giggling. "We'd better get back before we cause a scene in the park." She giggled again. "We don't want to get arrested for being obscene in a public place."

She rose from his lap and waited for him to join her. They walked hand in hand back to her parents' home.

"We'll go tomorrow to look for a ring," Jaeden promised, hugging her to his side as they strolled.

The couple walked in silence back to the house. Once there, they searched for Alexis's parents. When they approached the family room, they could hear Josephine on the telephone, laughing.

"Yes, my baby is getting married," they heard her saying. With her back to them, Josephine had no idea Jaeden and Alexis were standing on the threshold of the door listening to her conversation. "He's a handsome devil, too," Josephine said, laughing.

Alexis didn't understand how her mother knew about the engagement already.

"I'll tell her, Stella."

"Tell me what?" Alexis interrupted.

Robert looked up from his computer toward the door and cleared his throat loudly. Josephine found Alexis standing behind her when she turned around. "I'll call you ladies back later, the happy couple just walked in," she said before hanging up the phone.

She walked toward Alexis and gave her an enthusiast hug. "I'm so happy for you, baby."

"How did you know Jaeden asked me to marry him?"

Josephine looked over at her husband, who in turn looked at Jaeden.

Jaeden caught Alexis by the hand. "Baby, earlier I asked your father to give us his blessing."

"I thought you said . . ." Alexis stopped before completing her sentence. "Forget it."

Josephine squeezed Alexis a second time. "This is the best news I've heard in a long time," she squealed.

Alexis looked at her father still sitting at his computer. "Daddy?" Alexis looked at him curiously. "What do you have to say?"

Slowly, Robert moved from his desk chair and stretched his arms open, waiting for Alexis to fill them. "If you're happy, then I'm happy," he said, hugging her to him. "Are you?" he asked, looking down at her.

Alexis stared into the eyes of the only man she'd ever trusted—until now. "Yes, Daddy, extremely. I've never been so excited in my entire life," she said honestly.

Jaeden stood back watching the exchange between Alexis and her father. "Baby, I want to tell my parents tonight as well."

"Okay," Alexis said, with a nod.

"Alexis, *we've* got to start planning," Josephine shouted excitedly. "I'm so pleased," Josephine said, crossing the room to hug her daughter once more.

"You never told me what Aunt Stella said," Alexis reminded her, pulling away.

"All your aunts said congratulations."

Alexis smiled and then looked at her watch. "I think we should get going. It's almost eight o'clock and we need to tell Jaeden's parents too." She walked over to him and caught his hand and led him to the door.

Alexis blew a kiss to her parents, who stood in the driveway to watch as they departed.

"What are you thinking about?" Jaeden asked, patting Alexis's thigh as he drove to his parents' home.

"My mother was on the phone with her cackling sisters, which means everybody in the family will know about our engagement by tomorrow."

"Everyone's going to find out anyway, so what's the big deal? Why would we keep it a secret?"

"Sometimes my aunts can be overbearing." Alexis placed her hand on top of his before lifting it to her left cheek. "You'll see what I mean," she said, kissing his palm.

"Well, let's go inside and tell my parents," Jaeden said, pulling up to the curb in front of his parents' home a few minutes later. He shut off the ignition and got out of the vehicle.

Alexis opened her car door and swung her legs around to get out, but stopped. "How do you think your parents will react?" she asked Jaeden.

"Probably the same way yours did." Jaeden held the door open.

Alexis followed him up the walkway. Jaeden pressed the doorbell on the side of the door and they waited for someone to answer.

"Hey," Gloria said once she saw who her visitors were. "Why didn't you use your key?" she asked Jaeden as she held the screen door open.

"I didn't want to scare you by walking in the house at this time of night and you didn't know I was coming."

"What brings you by?" Gloria asked, closing the door behind her.

Jaeden gave her a kiss.

"Good evening, Mrs. Jefferson," Alexis said.

"Great to see you again, Alexis," Gloria said, smiling at the couple.

"Come on in, Donald and I were just sitting around watching television." Gloria led them into the family room.

"Who was at the door, Glo?" Donald asked when his wife returned.

"Jaeden. And Alexis is with him."

Donald looked away from the TV just as Jaeden appeared in the opening of the room.

"What's up, Pop?" Jaeden said as he escorted Alexis into the room.

"Nothing much," Donald replied, looking at the couple carefully.

"Alexis, I don't think you met my husband, Donald," Gloria said.

"Nice to meet you, Mr. Jefferson." Alexis shook his hand and then took a seat on the couch.

"We came by to give you some good news." Jaeden sat on the edge of the couch next to Alexis.

"You closed your deal," Gloria blurted out excitedly before he could finish.

"No, that's not it, but I'm confident I will soon."

"There's nothing wrong with you, is there?" Gloria jumped up and went over to pat his face.

"No, Mama, I said we have good news," he chuckled, squeezing his mother's hand.

"Boy, spit it out, you're going to give me a heart attack," Gloria made her way over to the arm of the chair her husband sat in.

"Alexis and I are getting married," Jaeden announced before his mother interrupted him again.

Donald sat up so quickly, the motion nearly knocked Gloria off the arm of the chair. "Did I hear you correctly? You're marrying this beautiful young woman?"

"I asked her tonight and she said yes."

Gloria laced her hands together, shaking them in front of her. "Thank you, Jesus."

Donald got out of the chair and went to the couple. "I'm so happy for you, son."

"Thanks, Pop," Jaeden rose to hug him.

"Come here, daughter," Donald said to Alexis with open arms. She accepted his brief embrace.

They were so excited, no one noticed Gloria sitting quietly in her own chair. Soon Jaeden realized she hadn't said anything in a long while. Gloria Jefferson always had something to say, but tonight she was as quiet as a church mouse. He looked over at her bowed head and went to her. "What's the matter, Mama?" he asked as he rubbed her back.

Gloria looked up at her son with tears streaming down her face.

"What is it? Aren't you happy for us? Mama, please say something, you're going to make Alexis nervous."

At last, Gloria opened her mouth to speak, but then closed it and bowed her head again.

Donald moved closer to her and helped her to her feet. "Please excuse us for one minute? She's just overjoyed.

We'll be back in a minute." Donald escorted her to the bathroom down the hall, leaving Jaeden and Alexis alone.

Jaeden rushed to Alexis, who sat on the couch staring straight ahead. "I don't think your mother likes me."

"Yes, she does. She knew we were dating because Stef told her before I could."

"Oh, I'd better call her." Alexis remembered. She pulled out her cell phone, and began to dial her girl-friend's number.

"Stef," she said when she answered.

"Hey, girl, what's up?"

"Whatcha doing?" Alexis asked casually.

"Chucky and I were leaving to go to Whispers. What's up?" Stephanie fastened a gold bracelet around her wrist while she held the phone to her left ear with her shoulder.

Alexis laughed. "Chucky, huh?"

"Don't even start, girl."

"Okay, I'm going to hold you to that promise. I just wanted to tell you that your cousin asked me to marry him tonight."

"I knew it! I knew it! I knew it!" Stephanie screamed into the phone.

Alexis had to move the small instrument from her ear.

"I told you, you'd be my cousin. I just didn't think it would be this soon. I'm so excited for you. Let me know if you need me to help you with the wedding."

"I don't think your aunt is too happy, though."

"Why? What would make you say that?" she asked, worry seeping into her voice.

"Your uncle had to take her out of the room, she was crying so hard."

"Oh, don't worry about that, Aunt Glo is the senti-mental one in the family. She will cry at anything."

"I'm so glad you said that because I thought it was me."

"No, honey, that's just the way she is. Don't take it personal."

"Thanks. You know I want you to be my maid of honor, right?"

"You sure? You have so many cousins . . ."

"That doesn't matter; I want you to stand next to me."

"Cool. I'd be honored to do it," Stephanie said proudly.

"Ooh, they're coming back. I'll chat with you later."

Alexis quickly pressed the red button to disconnect the call and sat holding her cell phone in her lap.

"Alexis, come and give Mama a hug," Gloria said, standing in the middle of the floor with her arms spread.

Dropping her cell phone in her purse, Alexis raised herself from the sofa and walked into Gloria's arms.

"I'm so glad you accepted Jaeden's proposal. I've never had a daughter and now I'll have one."

Alexis stepped out of her embrace, but took Gloria's hand. "For a minute, I thought you were upset."

"I know, I'm sorry for scaring you that way. Since Jaeden was a little boy I prayed he'd find someone that would share his life and make him happy, but I never thought I'd react this way."

"It's quite all right," Alexis reassured her.

"Have you guys decided when you're going to get married?"

"No," they both said.

Alexis picked up her purse and retrieved her Palm Pilot.

"I don't want a long engagement. I'd like to get married in the next couple of months," Jaeden said, looking at Alexis to see her reaction.

"Fine with me," she said, pulling up her calendar.

"How can we plan a wedding in that short amount of time?" Gloria asked hurriedly.

"Today is the first Saturday in June, so let's set the wedding for August," Alexis suggested.

"What date?" Gloria asked.

"How about the last Saturday? It will give us the rest of this month, all of July, and most of August to pull it off." Alexis made the notation in her Palm Pilot.

"That's a little better, but planning a wedding does take a fair amount of time," Gloria advised. "I would like to speak with your mother about hosting an engagement party for you two, as well."

"I'm sure she'd like that," Alexis replied.

"Would you give me her number?" Gloria went over to the table and picked up her tablet and a pen.

Alexis recited the information, amazed at Gloria's quickness to dial her parents' number. She and Jaeden smiled at each other on hearing the excitement in his mother's voice as she spoke to the mother of her future daughter-in-law.

"Your mother and I are meeting Monday for lunch to discuss plans for the engagement party," Gloria said after speaking to Josephine.

"That was fast, but okay," Alexis replied.

"Well, I'm going to get Alexis home."

"Jaeden," his mother called out to him.

"Yeah?"

"Baby, where is Alexis's engagement ring? I didn't see one."

"We're going shopping for one tomorrow."

"That's good. I'm so happy for you two." Gloria squeezed them both tightly.

"Ma, don't start crying again," Jaeden said as he watched the tears well in Gloria's eyes and begin to slip down her brown cheeks.

"I'm fine." Gloria continued to hold both of them to each side.

Jaeden kissed his mother on the cheek again. "We

hate to have to run, but we need to get going." He wanted to have Alexis to himself.

Gloria finally released them. "Alexis, we'll talk later about wedding plans?

"I'll call you next week," Alexis promised.

After they got into the car, Jaeden and Alexis both released a sigh of relief.

"My family was worse than yours," Jaeden said, shaking his head. "I forgot how weepy my mother can be. You should have seen her when I graduated from college." Alexis chuckled. "She's really going to be bad when we have our first child." Jaeden reached over and planted a soft kiss on Alexis's lips. "Oh, we are going to have some beautiful children. Let's go practice."

Alexis giggled. "You are shameless."

He kissed her again before starting the vehicle, peeling from the curb, and heading to Alexis's apartment.

CHAPTER EIGHT

The next day, Jaeden took Alexis to Sterling Jewelers on Village Court. The family-owned business had been in Taylor since 1965. The store was elegantly decorated with white columns, cherry-wood display cases, and plush burgundy carpeting.

An older distinguished gentleman with a thin gray mustache greeted them as they entered the store. "Good afternoon, my name is Lawrence, how can I be of service?"

"We would like to look at engagement rings," Jaeden said, catching Alexis's hand in his own.

"Do you have a certain style in mind, sir?"

"I'm not sure what we're looking for exactly, but show us your *best* selection."

Pulling out the stool from under the display case, Jaeden patted the pillow top, offering Alexis a seat.

"When is the big day?"

"The last Saturday in August," Jaeden answered.

"That's a couple of months from now," Lawrence said, moving down to the next display case. Unlocking the wooden door, he slid it back and retrieved a white velvet tray filled with sparkling diamond rings and brought it to them. "These are only the mountings. You have to purchase the center stone separately," he informed.

Lawrence pulled a diamond out of its socket. Holding

a tiny magnifying glass, he inspected the diamond before handing it to Jaeden.

"Hmm, I don't know," Jaeden said, looking at it carefully.

"It's one carat," Lawrence offered.

"Baby, do you like this one." Jaeden continued to examine it before giving it to Alexis.

"I think they're all gorgeous," Alexis commented, giving the ring back to the salesman. She glanced at the rest
in the tray.

Lawrence presented several other styles, but after an
hour, they still hadn't decided on a ring. He went to the
back of the store and returned with two velvet burgundy
trays filled with rings. "These are from the Kirk Kara Col-
lection," he explained, placing the trays on the glass.

"These are stunning." Alexis pointed to a ring and
Lawrence pulled it out of its holder. "This is simply gorgeous." Alexis slipped it on her finger. Holding her arm
out, she studied how it looked on her hand. "It's beautiful," she said as she twisted the platinum ring on her finger. "This is the one." Alexis flicked her hand in front of
Jaeden. "Don't you like it, honey? Please, say you love it."

Jaeden kissed her softly. "It's gorgeous, just like you."

"It has one carat of diamonds on each side," Lawrence
informed them.

"Can you size the ring to fit her finger when the center stone is set?" Jaeden asked.

Lawrence gave his best happy expression. "Yes, sir, we
can make it perfect for your bride.

"If I may suggest, a round, heart, or emerald cut
would look lovely in this mounting," Lawrence commented as he slid the ring off Alexis's finger, placing it
on his pinky.

Strolling over to another section of the store, he

brought back a tray of loose stones. They were all in little plastic bags with serial numbers taped on each one.

"They all look the same to me, honey," Alexis said. "You choose."

Jaeden had Lawrence show him several before he decided on a flawless two-carat round stone.

They watched as Lawrence used a utensil that looked like a long tweezer to pick up the stone and place it between the prongs of the ring, giving them the illusion of the finished product.

Alexis's eyes began to water and Jaeden pulled her to his side. "Happy?" he asked, kissing her temple.

"More than I've ever been in my life."

"Will this be acceptable, sir?" Lawrence asked, showing him the model.

Jaeden looked at Alexis and she nodded.

"Yes, this will be fine," Jaeden answered.

"Wonderful choice, sir, you must love your fiancée very much."

Jaeden's eyes were filled with raw emotion as he looked over at Alexis. She got up from the stool and hugged her future husband. "My ring is so beautiful," she whispered.

Jaeden lifted her chin and kissed her softly. "I'm glad you're pleased, baby."

Lawrence pulled out something that looked like a large key ring that had lots of steel round circles attached. He slipped several of them on Alexis's finger until she was comfortable with the fit of the circle. He looked at the outside of it and wrote the size down on a form.

"Would you like to look at matching bands?" Lawrence inquired.

Jaeden kissed Alexis on the temple once again. "Yes, we would."

For their wedding bands, they chose smooth platinum, Alexis's a much thinner version of Jaeden's.

"How long will this take to get done?" she asked.

"We can probably have everything ready in an hour and a half," Lawrence said, looking at the gold clock on the wall.

"Do you want to maybe have lunch? We can have the jeweler get started right away," Jaeden asked Alexis.

"Fine with me. I'm with you."

"We'll return at five o'clock. That should give you plenty of time to get things just right," Jaeden told Lawrence.

"It's been a pleasure serving you today, Mr. Jefferson. You're a very lucky man." Lawrence shook Jaeden's hand. "Ms. Shire, congratulations, you are going to make a beautiful bride, may I say?"

As they walked out of the store, Alexis weaved her hand with Jaeden's. "I'm going to be so spoiled," she said, leaning her head against the top of his shoulder.

Jaeden smiled. "Isn't that what I'm supposed to do?"

Gloria had left instructions with the hostess to bring Josephine to her table when she arrived at Teibels Restaurant on Monday afternoon.

"Gloria?" Josephine asked a regal-looking woman sitting with her hands folded on the table.

Gloria got up from her seat to hug the petite woman. "You must be Josephine."

"Please call me Josie, all my friends and family do."

"My family calls me Glo, so I guess you should too."

Both women laughed.

"I'm so glad we could meet so soon. My husband, Donald, and I were so happy when Jaeden and Alexis told us about the engagement."

"I've always wanted my daughter to be happy. I used to worry about Alexis's social life. She was always more focused on school and her career, so when this happened it made me feel doubly blessed," Josephine revealed.

"I know what you mean. Even though Jaeden went out on dates and things, he never seemed interested in one woman. He was always talking about his company and the meetings he had to attend. I had to remind him, from time to time, that he'd need a family of his own someday. So when my niece, Stephanie, told me he was dating Alexis, I could see a change was about to occur."

They both stopped talking to look at their menus and gave the waitress their orders when she stopped by.

"Did the kids give you the wedding date?" Gloria asked, handing her menu to the waitress.

Josephine frowned. "Yes, Alexis called and told me. Two and a half months from now isn't a lot of time to plan a wedding." She shook her head in dismay.

"I said the same thing. I thought maybe *we* should get a head start on things."

Josephine nodded in agreement. "My daughter's very particular and I know she's not going to be any different about her wedding. Let's talk about the engagement party. Hopefully, she won't object to what we choose." There was a comfortable silence as the women remembered their own weddings.

"What a wonderful moment in their lives." Josephine said, breaking the silence. She put her straw into the soda glass the server placed on the table. "Don't you remember when you were young and in love?"

Gloria waved her hands. "Girl, yes, I was just plain foolish."

"You know, back then they didn't have all the fancy stuff they have today. Donald and I didn't have a formal wedding. We got married in my sister Bettye's house."

"Robert and I married at City Hall," Josephine admitted.

"Well, how many guests do you plan to invite to the engagement party?" Gloria placed her notepad on the table.

"We have a large family and this is the first wedding in a long time. I imagine there will be a lot of people. Then there's the church family and other friends."

"Same here, which means we'll need a large hall."

"I think we're probably looking at three hundred people for the engagement party." Gloria took the top off her blue pen and began to scribble a list of relatives.

"That sounds about right. When should we have it?"

"I really don't know. Everything is going to be back to back since it's such short notice," she huffed.

When their meals were served, the women continued to make plans for the engagement party. Josephine agreed to find a place and Gloria would find a caterer. They promised to meet again and would present their plans to Jaeden and Alexis then.

"I've got to run to a meeting," Josephine said, wiping her mouth with her napkin and pulling several bills from her wallet.

Gloria waved her hand to stop her. "Don't worry about the bill, I'll take care of it. My treat."

"Bless you," Josephine said. "Why don't we have our next meeting at my house Saturday night and we can all have dinner together?"

"I'll call you and confirm," Gloria said, scooting out of the booth to hug Josephine before she left.

Settling back down, Gloria continued to add names to her invite list until the server returned with her bill.

Jaeden and Alexis had dinner with both of their parents at the Shires' home on Saturday. It was the first family dinner and the official start of the wedding planning.

Alexis kept holding out her hand, watching as the

light reflected against her engagement ring. She'd barely been able to concentrate since Jaeden had bought the ring. Each time the glimmer of her two-carat diamond caught her eye, it made her think of Jaeden.

Taking her eyes from her ring, she watched the families interact. She was relieved both their mothers hit it off at the first meeting and her dad and Jaeden's father seemed to get along well too.

"Baby, what's the matter?" Jaeden asked, jarring Alexis out of her deep thought as they were waiting to be seated at the dinner table.

"What?"

"Are you okay?" Jaeden sat down beside her on the sofa. He placed his arm around her and hugged her to his side.

"I'm fine."

"Sure you're okay?"

"Yes." She looked up and kissed him. "Why?"

"Hey," Robert yelled, interrupting before Alexis could answer. "We're starving in here."

Josephine came to stand in the doorway of the family room. "We were just about to call everyone to the table," she said to her fussy husband.

"Good, because I thought you had to go and kill a cow or something."

Josephine looked at Gloria, who had her hands full with the ham platter. "Don't pay Robert any attention, he's always like that when he's hungry."

Josephine laughed.

Soon they all took their seats around the dinner table. Donald gave the blessing and everyone bowed their heads before they feasted on ham, baked chicken, tossed salad, macaroni and cheese, sweet potatoes, and corn.

"Have you ladies decided when the engagement party will take place?" Jaeden asked, looking at his mother. He reached for the salad dressing and liberally poured it on his greens.

"I'm still looking for a place to have it," Josephine replied.

"Because this is being done at the last minute," Gloria added, "every place she's called so far is either booked or not the kind of facility we're looking for."

"Mom, we don't want anything too extravagant," Alexis said, spooning a helping of macaroni and cheese on her plate. "I think it should be small and intimate. We could have it here or at the Jeffersons'."

"Alexis, you can't just shut people out like that," Josephine insisted, surprised by her daughter's poor manners. "Which reminds me with all this running around, I forgot to tell you your aunt Stella wants to make your wedding gown as a gift."

Alexis almost choked on her sparkling cider.

"You okay?" Jaeden took the glass away and patted her on the back as she coughed.

Alexis grabbed her napkin, pressing it against her mouth as she tried to clear her throat. She nodded she was okay.

Finally she said, "Mom, why would I want her to make my wedding gown?" Alexis coughed again. "Aunt Stella never finishes anything she starts. Thanks, but no, thanks," she added, reaching for a glass of water.

Robert rose from his chair and announced, "Donald and I are going out to the garage; I want to show him my new weed whacker." He sensed trouble brewing and knew he had to get out of the room before he was drawn into the mix.

Donald shook his head, then patted Jaeden on the back as he followed Robert from the room.

Josephine gave Alexis an unpleasant look. "That's not nice, Alexis," she scolded. "All of your aunts have offered to help you. Florence volunteered to do the flowers and she wants both Cherise and Brianna to be bridesmaids."

Alexis dropped her fork with a loud clank. Sitting up straight in her chair, she tried to control her temper. "Mother," she said sternly. "Just because Aunt Florence made the flowers for her neighbor's daughter's wedding three years ago doesn't mean she's a floral designer." Alexis took a deep breath to calm herself down. "And Cherise and Brianna don't even like me, so why would they be bridesmaids in *my* wedding?"

"Well, maybe I should chime in here, because I've been talking to our family as well," Gloria said. "My sister Katherine told me *she* could save us some money by making the wedding cake for you."

Jaeden moaned and all eyes were on him.

"What's the matter, honey?" Alexis asked, rubbing his back.

"Mama, Aunt Katherine is a horrible cook. You said it yourself when she brought that red velvet cake to Christmas dinner last year."

"Well . . ." Gloria's voice trailed off. Jaeden was right about that. "Anyway," she started again, "I want your uncle Leon's twins, Kim and Kendra, and his son Xavier to be a part of the wedding." Gloria watched Jaeden's facial expression change. "And don't give me that look, Jaeden. These are my deceased brother's children and I want them to be a part of your wedding," she insisted.

Jaeden gave his mother a pleading look. "Mama, please, I loved Uncle Leon, too, and I'm not saying they can't be in the wedding, but we have to discuss some things first."

"I agree with Jaeden," Josephine said. "We have a big family as well and I've been getting calls from them. They all want to participate or help in some way. I think since both families are large, we should ask two people from each of our siblings' families to participate."

Alexis sat silently trying to concentrate on something other than the conversation at the table. She never had any idea planning a wedding would get so chaotic so soon.

Finally, she opened her mouth to speak. "All I want is a small and intimate affair, okay?" she said with a calm she didn't really feel.

Josephine and Gloria both sighed.

Gloria closed her eyes and prayed for the Lord to give her strength. "You two have not gotten the point yet."

"She's right," Josephine said, nodding. "We don't want to insult or overlook anyone. Weddings are a family affair whether you two realize it or not."

Alexis began to stare into space again.

Jaeden tapped her on the shoulder. "Why don't we go out for some ice cream?"

"Let's." Alexis quickly pushed her chair back and threw her linen napkin in her plate, leaving the table.

"Are you two just going to walk out like this?" Gloria asked in disbelief.

"We'll be back in a little while, Mama, okay?" Jaeden said sincerely.

They walked out of the house and got into Jaeden's SUV. Alexis sat with her right elbow on the ledge of the door, her hand covering her forehead.

Jaeden slid into the driver's seat. He sat silently at first, and then he looked over at his bride-to-be. He moved as close as he could to her and tenderly stroked the side of her face with the back of his hand. "Baby, don't be upset, you know they're only trying to help. Let's go down to Bressler's and think about something else."

Alexis offered him a sad smile and nodded before putting her head back against the headrest. She knew in her heart tonight was the beginning of a roller-coaster ride to the altar.

CHAPTER NINE

Bressler's Ice Cream Parlor was located about ten minutes from the Shires' house. Jaeden found a small table by the window and had Alexis sit while he placed their orders. He returned with a cup of butter pecan ice cream for her and a banana split for himself.

"Here you go," he said, sliding the container in front of her and taking his seat.

Alexis stared past him out the window.

"Baby, I ordered what you told me you wanted. What's wrong?"

Alexis pulled out her Palm Pilot and turned it on. "Our wedding is going to be a circus. I can feel it already," she complained miserably.

"That's not true because I won't let it. I can talk to my mother and you can talk to yours."

"Didn't we just try that a few minutes ago, Jaeden?"

"No, I mean really talk to them, baby." He reached across the table and took her hand.

"We have so many things to do it's ridiculous. I made a list of the things I could think of and I'm sure it probably doesn't even scratch the surface," she said. "The wedding is in a little over two months and there is no possible way we can get all of it done." Alexis's eyes started to water with worry.

Jaeden reached across the table and grabbed her other hand. "Baby, you've got to calm yourself."

"I haven't even looked for a wedding gown. I can't concentrate in class and I definitely need to pass it." Alexis let go of one hand and wiped her eyes.

"Why don't you call Stef and ask her to help you out? I'm sure she'd be more than happy to take some of the stress off you," Jaeden suggested. He lifted her chin, so she could look into his eyes. "Okay?"

Alexis tried to hold back the tears that threatened to fall. She loved Jaeden so much and she was glad he had a level head because she felt as if she had lost hers.

"Okay," she managed to squeak out.

"That's my girl." Jaeden leaned over the table and kissed Alexis on the lips. "Now, eat your ice cream, it's starting to melt."

Alexis placed her Palm Pilot back in her purse, gave Jaeden half of a smile, and dug into her ice cream.

When they returned to Alexis's parents' home, they found their mothers sitting at the dining room table. A million pieces of paper almost totally covered its large surface.

"We're back," Jaeden announced as they walked into the room.

Alexis hugged her mother. "I'm sorry for snapping at you earlier, Mom."

"It's okay, sweetheart, no harm done," Josephine replied, patting her daughter's back.

Alexis apoligized to Jaeden's mother as well.

Gloria gave Alexis several pats on the back. "All brides are jittery when they're planning for their big day."

"I'm going to find my dad," Jaeden said. He kissed

Alexis on the lips, winked, and walked away, leaving her alone with her mother and Gloria.

Alexis pointed to the many pieces of papers on the table. "What's all of this?"

"Some ideas we had for the engagement party. Gloria and I were comparing notes," Josephine explained.

Oh my God, no! Alexis's mind screamed.

"Here," Gloria said, pushing a pile in front of her. "Read it and let us know what you think."

Alexis didn't dare glance at anything because she was afraid it would only upset her more. "It's not necessary, I trust you two. . . ." She cringed as the words came out of her mouth.

"I'm glad you've finally realized we know what we're doing, sweetie," Josephine said, giving her daughter a wide smile.

Alexis gave her one in return, but it didn't quite reach her eyes. She hoped Jaeden would return to rescue her, but he was nowhere in sight.

"Now," Gloria said, sitting up straight and folding her perfectly manicured hands in a praying position. "Have you chosen a theme or colors for the wedding?"

Don't answer that, Alexis's mind told her.

For a brief moment there was silence, then Alexis saw two sets of eyes focused totally on her and she knew she couldn't get around it. Before she could finish moving her head from side to side in response to the question, she was hit with a barrage of suggestions.

"That's important, sweetie," Josephine insisted. "Red is a bold color and it looks pretty in photographs. As for the theme, I would say we should use two hearts that beat as one—"

Gloria couldn't wait for Josephine to finish. "I've heard this new green color is becoming popular," she began. "It's summertime and the color is light. If I could suggest a theme it would be endless love."

As the two women continued throwing out suggestions, Alexis retrieved her Palm Pilot and made notes.

"Lord, help me," she whispered to herself, sinking into her chair.

A few days later, Alexis sat at her desk reading over the syllabus for the Teaching and Learning in the Digital Age course she was taking and wondered if the class would be more added stress. Even though she would complete the course before her wedding day, she wasn't confident she could devote the time that was necessary to achieve the grade she desired.

They would have two papers to write along with one presentation before the class ended the first week of July. But instead of her working on her assignments, she knew she would always be working on to-do lists for the wedding. Alexis had to focus more on her school projects or she would never reach her goal.

She made more notes in her Palm Pilot, then waited for her professor to dismiss the class.

She walked to her car and just as she pulled on the handle of her Maxima, she heard the ring tone of Jill Scott's "He Loves Me" signaling she had a phone call. Sliding into the driver's seat, she sifted through her Coach sack purse, pulling out her cell phone. She glanced at the screen before pressing the button to answer.

"Hi, Mom, how are you?" Alexis tried to sound as pleasant as she possibly could.

"I'm fine, sweetie. Did you decide on how many bridesmaids you'd have for the wedding?" Gloria wasted no time getting to the point.

Alexis looked heavenward. "Remember, I said, *I'd* call *you*."

"Well, Tiffany is home from college and your aunt Theresa wants her to be a bridesmaid."

Alexis rolled her eyes because she'd been over the list of potential bridesmaids four times already and still didn't know what to do. She only wanted four, but to pacify her mother she considered one or two more. She huffed. "No, Mom, I haven't decided yet."

"Alexis, what are you waiting on?" Josephine scolded. "Have you even chosen a dress for them?"

"Mom," Alexis said loudly in the phone. "Mom?" She held the phone from her ear. "You're breaking up," she lied, waving it back and forth from her ear. "Hello? Hello?" She pressed the button to end the call. She hated hanging up on her mother, but she couldn't take her tongue-lashing right then.

"I've definitely got to find someone to help me," she said aloud. Alexis pressed the speed-dial number for Stephanie, but she wasn't home, so she tried her cell.

"What's up, girlie?" Stephanie answered on the fourth ring.

"Help me, please," Alexis pleaded dramatically.

"What's the matter?" Stephanie said in a mild panic.

"My mother and your auntie."

"They're taking over?" Stephanie guessed.

"In a big way. Like you wouldn't believe."

Alexis heard a beep. "Hold on," she said before looking at the screen on her phone.

"It's her now."

"Who? Your mother or Aunt Glo?"

"My mother. I just hung up on her right before I called you. I've never disliked my mother before, but she is getting on my nerves."

Stephanie giggled. "I'm sorry, I know it's not funny. Aren't you going to answer it?"

"No, she's only going to ask me the same question about the bridesmaids again."

"Didn't I warn you about how Aunt Glo can be?"

"Yeah, you did. Somebody should've warned me about my own mother."

"Let me see what I can do," Stephanie said.

"Okay, Stef, but don't disappointment me."

"Have I ever? I'll call you in a day or two, just chill out for a minute, will you?"

Alexis smiled. "Thanks, girl, I knew I could count on you."

Alexis lay across her queen-sized bed glancing through some bridal magazines. She still hadn't made any progress with her first paper for her class, which was due in two weeks. She'd hoped Stephanie could help her get organized, but it had already been a couple of days since they spoke.

The telephone rang and Alexis laid the magazine on the bed.

"Hello."

"Got a pen?"

"Good morning to you too, Stef." Alexis chuckled. "It's about time you called me. Do you have anything?"

"Ready?"

"Yeah, what am I writing down?"

"Meet me at this address in two hours. One seventy-six Bridlewood Lane."

"Where is this?"

Stephanie gave Alexis directions. "Hopefully, we're going to get the help you need. It's called Hearts and Flowers."

"Okay, maybe I'll call my mom so she can come along."

"No, you and I will check it out before we bring any-one else in to wreck these nice people's lives."

Alexis laughed. "Why didn't you tell me about them before?"

"You didn't ask. Actually, I just ran into an old friend and she told me about it."

"I'll meet you over there."

"Lexie, don't keep me waiting. They've cleared some time for you."

"I'll be there, I promise."

"Bring all the stuff you've torn out. I know I don't have to tell you to bring your Palm Pilot."

Alexis chuckled. "Thanks, Stef, I'll see you shortly."

Alexis followed the directions Stephanie had given her and found that Bridlewood Lane was a secluded road. Once she drove through the wrought-iron gates decorated with a heart and a bouquet of flowers on them, she was already impressed. She admired the tow-ering trees and lush lawn as she continued up the road until she spotted a massive gothic-styled mansion.

"What are you getting me into, Stef?" Alexis said aloud as she rolled her car into the empty space next to Steph-anie's vehicle.

"You're late, Lexie," Stephanie said, glancing at her watch as Alexis pulled up.

"Sorry, I thought I was on the wrong street. Would you look at this place," Alexis replied as she retrieved her magazines from the backseat.

"Isn't it gorgeous?" Stephanie looked around. "I heard about the ring, let's see it."

Alexis held out her dainty hand.

"Whoa." Stephanie threw her hand up to her face, covering her eyes. "Girl, you're blinding me."

They both laughed.

"It's so gorgeous, Lexie." Stephanie lifted Alexis's hand to get a closer look.

Alexis's eyes sparkled. "I still can't believe I'm getting married. Now, only if I could get my mother and your aunt to back off a bit."

"I think we're going to remedy that today," Stephanie said, wrapping her arm around Alexis's shoulders.

They walked to the front where three graceful arches covered the entry to the double doors.

"Have you ever been here before?" Alexis asked, tempted to reach out and brush her fingers over the company crest etched into one of the glass doors.

"Lili Hart and I went to high school together. I hadn't seen her in some years and we ran into each other at the mall the other day. She told me to bring you on over, so here we are."

Stephanie pressed the white button on the navy blue box beside the door.

They heard a soft voice coming from the intercom box. "Hearts and Flowers, how can we help you?"

"Stephanie Redus and Alexis Shire here to see Lili Hart," Stephanie said, holding down the button while she spoke.

They heard a slight buzzing sound and Stephanie pulled open the gold door handle.

"Wow, Stef, this is an elegant place," Alexis said as they stepped into the navy blue and gold stone foyer. "They're probably very expensive." She stepped back closer to Stephanie.

"It *is* pretty," Stephanie said, examining the paintings on the wall. "When Lili told me she and her sisters had gone into business together, she wasn't playing."

"Are you sure I'm going to be able to afford them?" Alexis asked, staring at the crest on the marble floor.

"I guess we'll just have to wait and see."

As they continued to admire the décor, they moved past the fluted columns to the receptionist's desk.

A skinny young woman smiled, showing her metal-filled mouth. "Good morning, ladies. You can have a seat in the Crown Room. Lili will be with you in just a minute."

She escorted them to the room decorated in the same blue and gold color scheme as the foyer. There were several Victorian-styled chairs, a sofa, and a coffee table filled with an assortment of bridal magazines.

"I didn't need to bring these," Alexis said, looking down at the stack in her arms.

"I guess not, but hold on to them, you never know. Check out the television." Stephanie pointed to the small flat-panel TV hanging on the wall. It ran a continuous infomercial of the company planning actual weddings.

Stephanie and Alexis sat on the sofa and watched closely as images of wedding cakes, floral bouquets, custom invitations, wedding gowns, and photos of wedded couples played on the screen.

"This is really wonderful," Alexis said excitedly. "Did you see that last wedding cake?"

"What did it look like? There were so many."

Alexis quickly described the four-tier cake and Stephanie nodded as she recalled seeing it. "I'm hoping they have some sort of print portfolio for me to see too," Alexis said, looking around at the décor once more. "This is awesome. I can't wait to meet Lili."

"You won't have to wait any longer, I'm here," a small voice said from the door.

Alexis and Stephanie turned around quickly and saw a petite young woman glide into the room. The fair-skinned beauty had reddish streaks in her dark brown hair. She was dressed in black slacks and a royal blue shirt with the Hearts and Flowers crest embroidered in gold on the left side and the initial L on the right.

"Hi, Stef, I'm glad you found the place," Lili said as she hugged Stephanie.

"Your directions were great," Stephanie replied. "This is my friend Alexis Shire. Alexis, this is Lili Hart."

Lili embraced Alexis too. "It's so nice to meet you, Alexis. You'll make a beautiful bride."

"I sure hope you and your sisters can help me," Alexis said anxiously.

"We try to do our best." Lili took a seat in the chair on the other side of the coffee table. "I've asked my sisters to come down to meet you, Alexis, then we'll get started."

"Good morning, everyone." A trio of voices came from the doorway.

"Here they are now." Lili got up from her seat as three women, who all wore the same outfit, walked into the room. "These are my sisters Ivy, Violet, and Rose Hart," Lili introduced. "Ivy is our consultant/coordinator and all-around wedding guru. Violet handles the bridal salon, and Rose is our floral designer."

Each woman came forward to greet Alexis and Stephanie.

"Lili, these nice ladies should come with me so I can find out what they're interested in," Ivy said. "Once I've given you an overview of our products and services, I'll evaluate your needs so we can better assist you," she said to Alexis and Stephanie.

Alexis and Stephanie followed Ivy down the hall into another section of the mansion.

"This sure is a fancy place," Stephanie said to Ivy as she spotted a huge crystal chandelier hanging from the ceiling.

"Thanks. We wanted to create a beautiful place our brides would enjoy. We've been here for three years."

"How did you find the property?" Alexis asked.

"We inherited the mansion," Ivy replied succinctly, revealing few details.

"I wish somebody would give me one," Stephanie commented, elbowing Alexis in her side.

"I never knew there was a bridal mansion here in Taylor. How unique," Alexis said as they continued to walk down the long hall.

"There wasn't. My father has been a wedding photographer for over twenty-five years and we've been exposed to weddings most of our lives," she said, referring to herself and her siblings. "As we grew older each of us fell in love with some aspect of the wedding business. So after we got the mansion, we decided to do something with it. We had the place renovated and turned into a one-stop shopping mecca for brides."

"You can supply everything I need right here?" Alexis asked, unable to hide how impressed she was.

"Everything except for the tuxedos. We're working on staffing that division." Ivy stopped in front of a glass door. "Here we are." She opened the door and held it as Alexis and Stephanie entered the room. "Through here," she directed, leading them through an elaborate sitting room into another a much larger room.

Alexis and Stephanie took a seat in front of a huge mahogany desk while Ivy sat in a leather chair behind it.

Ivy smiled at them before she spoke. "Now, what can I do for you?"

"Alexis is stressed because both her mother and mother-in-law to-be are trying to push her to do her wedding *their* way," Stephanie explained.

"That's understandable. Weddings can be stressful for everyone involved and even though mothers mean no harm, they often try to make their daughter's wedding the one they didn't have." Ivy pulled out a notebook. "When is your wedding?"

"The last Saturday in August."

"Sounds wonderful, but that's not too far off. The sooner we begin planning, the smoother things will go," Ivy said, rising from her chair. "Why don't I show you around the estate now, so you can get a better feel of what we do, and after that you can make another appointment if you decide to use our services?"

They walked slowly behind the tall and graceful woman as she took them on a tour of the mansion. Their first stop was the floral shop down the hall. A full-figured woman sat behind the counter creating a floral arrangement. She smiled at the threesome as they entered.

"Hello again," Rose said cheerfully.

"We're taking the tour," Ivy explained to her sister before turning to them. "Rose will take care of all your floral needs. If you have any ideas on floral designs for the church, hall, or table centerpieces she can help you with them."

Alexis watched as Rose created a beautiful floral centerpiece with red roses, peonies, and hydrangeas in an extremely tall glass vase. "How lovely," Alexis commented.

"This one is for a wedding reception this evening at Avalon Manor."

"The Avalon is a gorgeous place for a reception," Stephanie said.

"How many do you have to make?" Alexis wanted to know.

"Thirty. I've completed twenty-two."

"Wow," Alexis said, looking at Stephanie.

"Let's go to the next area. On the main floor we have the catering department." Ivy walked out of the room with the women trailing her and turned down another long hallway. They followed Ivy into a sitting room with tons of books and magazines about cakes. They continued to walk until they reached a display room where there were several cakes on exhibit.

"Are all these cakes real?" Alexis asked, wanting to touch them.

"No, they're just for display," Ivy responded with a chuckle. All of her clients asked that question.

Lili came out wiping her hands on a towel. "Finding everything okay?" she asked.

"I love everything I've seen so far," Alexis responded.

"Great. Would you like to see the cake I'm decorating for the wedding reception this evening?"

"Could we?" Alexis asked excitedly as they followed Lili into the kitchen area. It had all the amenities of a professional kitchen, complete with stainless steel countertops. On a smaller worktable was a cake with a weave pattern made of icing.

Alexis stepped forward. "This is going to be beautiful. How many layers will it have?"

"It's a small wedding, so there will only be three. They each have a stand of their own. I'll add flowers to decorate the top of each layer."

"You are really good, Lili," Stephanie said. Alexis nodded in agreement.

"I have a sample cake, if you want to taste it." Lili walked over to the stainless steel refrigerator and pulled out a beautifully decorated cake.

"We don't want to take away from your other customers," Alexis insisted.

"It's quite all right; it will give you an idea of the texture and flavor of my cakes." Lili picked up two small plates from a stack, cut two slices, and handed them to Alexis and Stephanie along with forks.

"Hmm," Alexis said, savoring her delicious first bite of the raspberry-filled cake. "This is sooo good."

"I offer over twenty-seven different flavors and fillings," Lili added, watching them eat.

"We have a couple more stops to make on our tour," Ivy reminded them gently.

Overwhelmed by all she saw, Alexis didn't need to continue the tour. She was certain she wanted the staff of Hearts and Flowers to plan her wedding. "I've already made up my mind. I definitely want to use your services," Alexis said. "Can you give me another appointment so I can bring my fiancé and our mothers?"

"Of course, let's go back to my office and the next time you come, we can check out the bridal salon on the second floor."

Back in her office, Ivy pulled up the calendar for the rest of the month on her computer. Then she wrote down a date and time for Alexis's next appointment.

Alexis plugged the meeting into her Palm Pilot, then thanked Ivy profusely before leaving with Stephanie.

Alexis hugged Stephanie once they were outside the mansion.

"What was that for?" Stephanie asked.

"Girl, I don't know what I'd do without you," Alexis said as they walked to the parking area. "I'm so glad you found them. I liked the way they conducted business. It seemed more like we were part of their family than just paying customers."

"I thought so too. They'll be able to take away the pressure you've been having trying to juggle your schoolwork, the wedding, and the family."

"We'll see about that, *after* they meet the mothers,"

Alexis said, wiggling her fingers and mimicking the theme from *The Twilight Zone*!

Stephanie laughed.

"Do you have other plans for this afternoon?" Alexis asked.

"No, why?"

"I wanted to break the news to everyone together. Will you come to my mother's house with me?"

"You need me as backup, right?"

Alexis chuckled. This was part of the reason she and Stephanie were best friends. She never had to over-examine anything. "Yes, if you don't mind."

"Anything you need, remember?" Stephanie hugged her again.

Alexis pulled out her cell phone and called her mother, then Gloria, and finally, Jaeden.

"Great, everyone can be there by two o'clock," Alexis said, pushing the end button on her last call. She checked her watch. "I didn't realize we'd been inside for so long. We'd better go."

"Great, I'll meet you there," Stephanie said before they both headed toward their cars.

Gloria had already arrived by the time Alexis and Stephanie drove up to Josephine's house. The two older women were sitting in the family room talking when they walked in.

"Hey, Mom," Alexis said, giving her mother a kiss.

"Hi, sweetie," Josephine responded, lifting her cheek.

"Mrs. Jefferson, how are you today?" Alexis said, kissing her on the cheek as well.

"I'm doing fine, Alexis," Gloria said.

Stephanie greeted both women and sat across from them in the leather recliner.

"You've finally decided on the bridesmaids," Josephine said enthusiastically.

"Not exactly, but when Jaeden gets here, I'll tell all of you why we gathered today."

"He's coming now," Stephanie announced as Jaeden walked into the room.

"Hey, baby," Jaeden said, strolling over to Alexis and giving her a soft kiss on the lips before speaking to everyone else. "What's up?"

"Stephanie and I just came from the most elegant wedding facility I've ever seen," Alexis said, watching her mother's facial expression carefully.

"Where is this place?" Jaeden asked.

"It's a bridal estate on Bridlewood Lane called Hearts and Flowers," Alexis replied, unable to stem the excitement in her voice.

"Jay, do you remember Lili Hart from high school?" Stephanie asked.

"Vaguely."

"She and her sisters own it."

"They do everything, wedding coordination, dresses, invitations, flowers, and cakes." Alexis said with her eyes sparkling with happiness. "I loved the presentation they made today and I want to use them to plan our wedding."

"That's fine with me, baby. You didn't need me to come over here for that. Whatever you decide is fine with me," Jaeden said.

"Why didn't you call me when you went over there this morning, Alexis?" Josephine asked, slightly disappointed that her daughter had not invited her to go along. "I would have loved to see the place for myself."

Alexis hated lying to her mother, but she did it anyway. "Stef got the appointment for me at the last minute, so there was no time."

"But your mother and I had already started getting things together," Gloria said, looking at her notepad.

"I know and we're grateful to both of you for helping out," Alexis said sincerely. She patted her mother's hand in a comforting gesture. "We still need your help, there are decisions to be made and your opinions are important to us. It's just that Ivy Hart and her staff will execute all of *our* ideas and make them a reality." Alexis looked intently at the two women, trying to read their faces.

"Mama, I think if Alexis has found professionals that can take the stress off all of us, we should go for it," Jaeden said supportively.

"Please say you understand," Alexis said, hoping the mothers would agree with her decision. In order to keep her sanity she had to do things this way.

"We didn't get an opportunity to see everything they offered because Alexis wanted to bring all of you back," Stephanie interjected, trying to ease the tension.

Neither Josephine nor Gloria said a word. They stared at each other and back at Alexis.

"That's fine with me, sweetie," Josephine finally said, giving Alexis a slight smile that didn't reach her eyes.

Gloria agreed as well; her smile matched Josephine's.

"I'm so glad you understand," Alexis said, clasping her hands together as relief flooded through her. "Now clear your calendars, we have an appointment next Saturday at nine in the morning."

"Didn't they have an opening one day this coming week?" Josephine asked, trying to remain calm. Her daughter's lack of consideration bothered her more than she let on. "We're going to lose a whole week waiting until next Saturday."

"No, this was the earliest appointment they could give me," Alexis replied firmly. "I would like for us all to go over together."

"What's the address of this place, just in case I have to meet you there?" Gloria asked.

As Alexis gave her the address, she still got the feeling neither mother was happy about the new plans. But she was sure she'd made the best decision concerning her wedding ever since she'd said yes to Jaeden's proposal.

"Well, I need to get going, Lexie," Stephanie said, sensing that the storm was over. She stood, motioning for Alexis to walk her out. "Auntie, I'll talk to you later," Stephanie said to Gloria.

"See you later, baby," Gloria responded.

"Thanks for everything, Stephanie," Josephine said.

Stephanie waved as she walked to the door with Alexis following her. "That wasn't *too* bad," she said when they arrived at her car.

"It was bad enough," Alexis replied. "I thought they were going to spit fire, girl." She blew out a ragged breath she didn't know she'd been holding.

"Well, the bottom line is they agreed, so do your thing." Stephanie hit the button on her keyless entry to unlock her car door. "Now you should be able to relax and let the professionals do everything. I'll call you tomorrow." Stephanie slipped behind the wheel, started her car, and drove away.

Alexis stood outside for a while silently praying her wedding plans would come together quickly with minimal hassle from the mothers. But, after watching their reaction to telling them someone else would be planning the wedding, her gut feeling told her she was headed for more trouble. She turned and walked back into the house, hoping for the best.

CHAPTER TEN

By the time everyone piled into Alexis's Maxima, Jaeden still hadn't shown up. Even after they'd been sitting in the parking lot of the bridal estate for more than fifteen minutes, there still was no sign of him.

"Alexis, let's just go on in, honey," Josephine suggested from the backseat.

"He'll show. Don't worry," Gloria said confidently.

Alexis looked over at Stephanie, who nodded in agreement. "Okay, let me try his cell one last time, before we get out." Alexis picked up her phone, which was sitting in the cup holder, and pressed the preprogrammed button. His voice mail immediately initiated, so she called his office to see if by any chance he'd stopped in, but only got the answering service.

Stephanie nudged her before opening the car door. "Come on."

Alexis stepped out of the car, her disappointment apparent.

"Sweetie, don't be discouraged. Men don't usually take part in a lot of the planning anyway," Josephine said, putting her arm around her daughter.

"He was the one who wanted a short engagement. We have some important decisions to make today and I wanted him to be here to help," Alexis said, glancing at her watch again.

"I understand. We will just have to do our best without him. Okay?" Josephine said, trying to reassure her.

The women walked together in pairs from the parking lot to the front door of the estate.

"This *is* a beautiful place," Gloria said, looking at the pristinely manicured lawn and the waterfall display in the middle of the circular driveway.

Alexis pushed the button on the intercom box and announced their arrival. When the door buzzed, Stephanie pulled on the door and allowed the older women and Alexis to enter before her.

Ivy greeted them in the foyer. "Good to see you again, Alexis," she said, shaking her hand.

"I appreciate you taking the time out to see us," Alexis said kindly, before stepping aside to make introductions. "Ivy, I'd like you to meet my mother, Josephine Shire, and my mother-in-law, Gloria Jefferson."

"Pleased to meet you ladies," Ivy greeted the ladies warmly.

"You already know Stephanie."

"Yes, I remember her from your last visit." Ivy shook Stephanie's hand as well.

"Jaeden, my fiancé, is running a little late," she explained nervously. "But he should be here shortly." Alexis hoped her statement was true.

Ivy nodded. "If we're ready to get started, follow me, please." She turned and led them down a long hall.

In the office, there were three chairs lined in front of the huge mahogany desk. Alexis, Josephine, and Gloria took those and Stephanie sat on the sofa not too far from them. Ivy walked around her desk and gave them a pleasant expression as she took her seat. She pulled up a new-client contract screen on her computer.

"Alexis, I'll need some personal information from you for our files," Ivy said as she began typing on her keyboard.

Alexis answered each question Ivy asked and signed the printed contract. Josephine wrote the check for full payment of the consulting and coordination fee.

"You didn't have to do that, Mom," Alexis said, placing a kiss on her mother's cheek.

Josephine smiled, handing Ivy the check. "Your father wanted to take care of it."

"Thank you, Mrs. Shire." Ivy opened the desk drawer and placed it inside before handing her the printed receipt.

"Now, where will the wedding take place?" Ivy asked.

"Pilgrim Branch, of course," Josephine said, glancing at Gloria and Alexis.

Gloria frowned, shaking her head from side to side. "Pilgrim Branch is way too small. We should have the ceremony at Mt. Zion," she said adamantly. "It's much larger than your church, Josie."

"That shouldn't matter, the wedding is always at the bride's church," Josephine shot back testily.

Alexis felt an argument brewing, which was why she wanted Jaeden to be there with her. He could at least talk to his mother and she could talk to hers. Without him, she was stuck in the middle of their bickering by herself.

Not wanting their first meeting with Ivy to turn out like the last gathering at her mother's house, Alexis scooted to the edge of her seat and calmly said, "Ivy, the location hasn't been decided on at this time."

Ivy stopped typing and laced her hands together on her desk. "It's very important we get this settled as soon as possible," she told the group before her. "Most churches have guidelines and fees that we have to adhere to and more importantly, you need to be sure the church is available."

Ivy glanced at her calendar. "Today is the third Saturday in June. You only have two weeks to get invitations ordered, addressed, *and* mailed. You would want your responses back from your guests by the second Saturday in August."

Ivy hesitated, almost afraid to ask her next question. "Have you budgeted how much money you want to spend for your wedding?"

"No," Alexis answered, then looked at her mother and Gloria.

Josephine spoke up. "My husband and I decided a long time ago that we would be prepared, whatever the cost."

"Oh yes, we're prepared to help, too," Gloria added, not wanting to be outdone.

"That's great." Ivy relaxed the breath she was holding and pushed her chair back. She sauntered over to the bookshelf and pulled out a navy blue three-ring binder. Handing the book to Alexis, she took her seat again. "This book will be your bible of sorts for the next couple of months. You'll keep everything in here regarding your wedding. It will be a great help in keeping up with all copies of contracts, et cetera."

"I usually keep everything in my Palm Pilot," Alexis said, opening her purse, pulling it out, and showing Ivy.

"That's fine too, I still want you to keep the planner," Ivy insisted, nodding toward the book.

"Okay." Alexis rubbed her fingers across the company crest and the words "Our Wedding" printed on the front.

"Let's start by completing a wedding budget. Even though both parents are prepared to help you financially, Alexis you need to know approximately how much things are going to cost." Ivy scrolled to another part of the document on her computer. "Okay, tell me about your dream wedding. What kind of feeling do you want your guests to come away with after the ceremony and reception are over?"

"I want them to be able to feel the romance and see the elegance," she answered confidently before describing the details.

Ivy typed Alexis's list into her computer and took a moment to total an estimated cost to meet her needs. She printed an itemized list of Alexis's requests and pushed it across the desk to Gloria and Josephine.

"Remember, these are only estimates, we may go under and even over these figures depending on the items you choose," she explained, seeing the shocked look on the mothers' faces.

"I had no idea weddings had gotten so expensive," Josephine said, staring at the grand total on the bottom of the page in disbelief.

Ivy shook her head. "I'm afraid they *have* become increasingly expensive each year—especially for one of the magnitude your daughter is dreaming about."

Gloria swallowed hard and tried to maintain her composure. The price tag had alarmed her as well. "From the figures you've given us, it seems the wedding reception is the biggest cost."

"Yes, but it all depends on how extravagant your meal is. Most banquet halls include the rental of the building and a four-hour open bar in with the cost of the meal. You can cut some of that by not having a bar at all, particularly if you or your fiancé don't drink," she said to Alexis.

"Or we can have a cash bar like Megan Crenshaw had at her reception last summer," Alexis suggested cheerfully. She hadn't looked at the price, but she could tell from the mothers' reaction that it was way higher than they'd anticipated. She was trying to keep the mood light.

"It's insulting to your guests to ask them to pay for a drink at your celebration," Josephine said quickly.

"But you can always serve a bottle of red or white wine

or one of each on the table," Ivy piped in, sensing tension. "Speaking of receptions, have you chosen a venue?"

Alexis shook her head. Her mother was driving her batty, but Ivy's calm voice eased her nerves. "We desperately need your help," she asked, almost pleading.

Ivy pulled up a list of banquet facilities on her computer screen. "I'm afraid there won't be a lot of places available at this late date. Most are booked for the entire summer, but we might get lucky." Ivy held up two crossed fingers before scrolling through her list. "I have a couple of places in mind. The Renaissance is lovely and the staff is very accommodating. I'm going to call a couple other places too."

Ivy telephoned four different banquet halls as the four women waited patiently. Stress levels were high and no one spoke for fear of starting an argument.

Ivy looked slightly frustrated as she hung up after the last phone call. It seemed every place was taken for the last Saturday in August.

"Let's not give up hope, ladies," Ivy said, placing the phone back on the receiver and going through her list once again. "I'm going to call Meridian Banquets. I use them a lot in cases of emergency." Ivy lifted the receiver once more.

"This is an emergency," Gloria muttered loud enough for Ivy to hear.

Alexis prayed silently, watching Ivy as she spoke to the person on the telephone.

"I think we've hit the jackpot," she said, holding the palm of her hand over the bottom of the receiver. "Their grand ballroom is available for your date and it holds three hundred people!"

"It's too small," Josephine and Gloria cried at the same time.

Alexis didn't care though, she needed an elegant

place to have her reception and Meridian Banquets seemed like the last place that was available. She would have liked to consult Jaeden, but since he hadn't shown his face, she would have to make a decision without him.

"That will be fine, Ivy. Go ahead and book it," Alexis said, avoiding the displeased looks of her mother and soon-to-be mother-in-law. She looked in the opposite direction and glanced at Stephanie, who lifted her thumb and smiled.

Stephanie quickly lowered it when Josephine and Gloria turned, narrowing their eyes at her.

"Thanks, Benjamin, I'll get back to you later with more details," Ivy said before hanging up. "The Meridian is a beautiful facility over in Gary, which is not too far from here. It is a relatively new place," she told her clients. "They have luxurious banquet rooms with beautiful décors, which means we won't have to do a lot of decorating. I really believe you will be pleased with it," Ivy said to Josephine and Gloria when they looked at her blankly.

"One of the teachers at our school had her wedding reception there. I thought the place was gorgeous and the food was excellent," Alexis said, completely satisfied with her choice.

"We're going to have more than three hundred people at the reception," Josephine said, shaking her head. She couldn't understand why her daughter was being so stubborn.

"Then we'll have to talk about the guest list later," Alexis said curtly, ending the discussion before another argument started.

Josephine sucked her teeth and muttered under her breath. Alexis ignored her.

"You're penciled in," Ivy said cheerfully to the group, pretending not to notice the exchange. "So maybe Mon-

An Important Message From The ARABESQUE Publisher

Dear Arabesque Reader,

I invite you to join the club! The Arabesque book club delivers four novels each month right to your front door! It's easy, and you will never miss a romance by one of our award-winning authors!

With upcoming novels featuring strong, sexy women, and African-American heroes that are charming, loving and true… you won't want to miss a single release. Our authors fill each page with exceptional dialogue, exciting plot twists, and enough sizzling romance to keep you riveted until the satisfying end! To receive novels by bestselling authors such as Gwynne Forster, Janice Sims, Angela Winters and others, I encourage you to join now!

Read about the men we love… in the pages of Arabesque!

Linda Gill
PUBLISHER, ARABESQUE ROMANCE NOVELS

*P.S. Watch out for the next Summer Series **"Ports Of Call"** that will take you to the exotic locales of Venice, Fiji, the Caribbean and Ghana! You won't need a passport to travel, just collect all four novels to enjoy romance around the world! For more details, visit us at www.BET.com.*

A SPECIAL "THANK YOU" FROM ARABESQUE JUST FOR YOU!

Send this card back and you'll receive 4 FREE Arabesque Novels—a $25.96 value—absolutely FREE!

The introductory 4 Arabesque Romance books are yours FREE (plus $1.99 shipping & handling). If you wish to continue to receive 4 books every month, do nothing. Each month, we will send you 4 New Arabesque Romance Novels for your free examination. If you wish to keep them, pay just $18* (plus, $1.99 shipping & handling). If you decide not to continue, you owe nothing!

- Send no money now.
- Never an obligation.
- Books delivered to your door!

We hope that after receiving your FREE books you'll want to remain an Arabesque subscriber, but the choice is yours! So why not take advantage of this Arabesque offer, with no risk of any kind. You'll be glad you did!

In fact, we're so sure you will love your Arabesque novels, that we will send you an Arabesque Tote Bag FREE with your first paid shipment.

* PRICES SUBJECT TO CHANGE.

YOU'LL GET 4 SELECT ROMANCES PLUS THIS FABULOUS TOTE BAG!

ARABESQUE

Visit us at:
www.BET.com

THE "THANK YOU" GIFT INCLUDES:

- 4 books absolutely FREE (plus $1.99 for shipping and handling).
- A FREE newsletter, *Arabesque Romance News*, filled with author interviews, book previews, special offers, and more!
- No risks or obligations. You're free to cancel whenever you wish with no questions asked.

INTRODUCTORY OFFER CERTIFICATE

Yes! Please send me 4 FREE Arabesque novels (plus $1.99 for shipping & handling). I understand I am under no obligation to purchase any books, as explained on the back of this card. Send my free tote bag after my first regular paid shipment.

NAME _____

ADDRESS _____ APT. _____

CITY _____ STATE _____ ZIP _____

TELEPHONE (___) _____

E-MAIL _____

SIGNATURE _____

Offer limited to one per household and not valid to current subscribers. All orders subject to approval. Terms, offer, & price subject to change. Tote bags available while supplies last.

Thank You!

AN035A

ARABESQUE

Accepting the four introductory books for FREE (plus $1.99 to offset the cost of shipping & handling) places you under no obligation to buy anything. You may keep the books and return the shipping statement marked "cancelled". If you do not cancel, about a month later we will send 4 additional Arabesque novels, and you will be billed the preferred subscriber's price of just $4.50 per title. That's $18.00* for all 4 books for a savings of almost 30% off the cover price (Plus $1.99 for shipping and handling). You may cancel at any time, but if you choose to continue, every month we'll send you 4 more books, which you may either purchase at the preferred discount price. . . or return to us and cancel your subscription.

THE ARABESQUE ROMANCE CLUB: HERE'S HOW IT WORKS

THE ARABESQUE ROMANCE BOOK CLUB
P.O. BOX 5214
CLIFTON NJ 07015-5214

PLACE
STAMP
HERE

day we can go down, meet Ben, and taste the food before putting a deposit down."

"That's not necessary, we're going with Meridian," Alexis reassured her. She made a note of it in her Palm Pilot and then scribbled the name of the hall into her bridal book.

"Okay, so what are your colors and theme?"

Oh no, Alexis thought. Looking out the corner of her eye, she watched Josephine and Gloria flipping through their notepads. She hoped they wouldn't start blurting out suggestions. "Pink with silver as my accent color," Alexis blurted.

"There are several different shades of pink." Ivy rose from her seat and walked to the next room. She returned with a large thick book with fabric squares inside it and opened it on her desk. "Here are some of the popular pinks. Can you show us from one of these?" Ivy asked, turning the pages.

"I like this one," Josephine said, pointing to a striking deep pink.

Alexis shook her head. "That's not exactly what I had in mind. I'm thinking more along the lines of baby pink, not fuchsia," she said, pointing to another swatch in the book.

Ivy nodded and jotted down the model number. "Have you thought of a theme?"

"Yes, I'd like to use Make It Last Forever." Alexis heard her mother's sigh.

"What about the one I suggested?" Josephine asked impatiently.

"I don't think it fits," Alexis responded frankly.

Gloria leaned forward in her chair. "We should use the one I gave you. After all it is my son's wedding, too," she added, giving Alexis a knowing look.

Alexis adjusted her position in her chair and looked Gloria in the eye. "Your son's not here to give his opinion, now, is he, Mrs. Jefferson?" She turned her attention back to Ivy.

"Well," Gloria huffed in distaste. "I never—"

Josephine stared at the back of Alexis's head wondering, just what had gotten into her daughter today. She pouted her lips with disgust for Alexis's behavior.

Ivy rose from her desk. She needed to try to diffuse the situation before it escalated any further. "Why don't I take you to the bridal salon so you can at least choose your wedding gown and the bridesmaids' dresses? Maybe he'll show up by the time you're done with that."

"It won't matter then," Alexis mumbled, checking her watch. They'd been there over an hour and Jaeden hadn't even called.

"Did you say something, sweetie?" Josephine asked, looking in her direction.

"I'm going to try to call him again. You guys can go on ahead," Alexis said, rising from her seat.

"We'll wait for you," Gloria offered.

Alexis walked into the hall and dialed Jaeden's office number first, hoping he'd be there, but got the answering service again. Ending the call, she pressed another button to auto-dial his cell phone and immediately heard his deep voice on the prerecorded message. She left another message, telling him to contact her as soon as possible. "Where *are* you, Jaeden?" she said barely above a whisper.

Alexis tried to compose herself before going back into the room. She didn't want to look like she felt— disappointed and alone. Jaeden being with her every step of the way was what she wanted. After all, it was his wedding as well as hers.

"Lexie, you okay?" Stephanie asked, stepping into the hall.

"I don't know where he could be, Stef. Jaeden knew

what time we were supposed to be here." Alexis's eyes were glazed with unshed tears.

Stephanie hugged her. "Don't worry, he doesn't need to be here now since we're getting ready to choose our dresses. The important things like your invitations, cake, flowers, and other stuff, he'll be here to help you, I'm sure of it," she said, trying to reassure Alexis.

Readjusting the strap of her ivory silk tank dress, Alexis nodded in agreement and slipped her phone in the side pocket of her handbag.

"Did you reach him?" Gloria asked when the two women stepped back inside the room.

"No, he still didn't answer," she said softly. She tried to hide her despair, but it was obvious to everyone in the room.

Gloria rose from her chair and went to Alexis. "I'm sorry, sugah, but I know he has a good explanation for not being here."

"I can't wait to hear it," Alexis muttered before she gave Gloria a forced smile.

Ivy escorted the women into an elegantly decorated room with bridal displays for each season of the year. Alexis and Stephanie immediately headed to the summer gowns to get a closer look while Ivy searched for her sister. Soon, she walked from the back room with Violet, who was the same height and coloring as Ivy.

"Alexis, Violet will discuss your selections with me later and I'll contact you on Monday," Ivy promised.

"That will be fine. Thanks so much for everything," Alexis responded, giving Ivy a warm hug before she left.

"Have you thought about what kind of gown you'd like to wear, Alexis?" Violet asked, running her fingers through her short brown hair with blond streaks.

"I thought we'd choose the bridesmaids' dresses first," Alexis replied, hoping to get it out of the way so her mother could relay the information to her relatives.

"We could if you'd like," Violet said hesitantly. "But it's always easier to choose your bridesmaids' dress after you've chosen your gown first. Their dresses should complement yours. If you want something extravagant for them and understated for yourself, it won't be a good match."

"Well, I've always imagined my daughter in a beautiful Cinderella ball gown with the long train like Princess Diana wore," Josephine interrupted.

Alexis turned up her nose and shook her head. "No, Mom, I don't want to carry that much dress around all evening. Someone would have to go with me to the bathroom. I'd be uncomfortable and . . ."

Violet heard the frustration in Alexis's voice, so she moved closer and placed her hands on her shoulder. "Why don't we try on different styles of wedding gowns and then you can decide for yourself which you'd like better?" she recommended, hoping to ease the quickly rising tension. She'd felt it as soon as the foursome had walked into her room, but it was getting worse by the second. "Some gowns look better on the body instead of the hanger."

"That will be fine," Alexis said calmly.

"Good, follow me," Violet said to Alexis. "Once we slip the dress on, she'll come out and model it for you all," she explained to the others.

Josephine and Gloria took a seat in the Victorian-styled oak chairs in front of the mirror. Stephanie waited not far from the dressing room door where Alexis had disappeared to.

Alexis removed her clothes and stepped into a poofy slip with lots of scratchy material. Then Violet helped her into a white ball gown with long sleeves and lots of lace. When Alexis tried to take a step forward, it felt as if she were walking up a hill with a bowling ball chained to her leg.

As she stepped out of the dressing room, Stephanie assisted Violet by grabbing the other side of the long train.

"Lexie, this looks like my mother's good tablecloth." Alexis leaned forward and whispered, "And this stuff is making me itch." She rubbed her arms.

They lifted the gown so Alexis could see where to step up on the round podium in front of the three-way mirrors.

Josephine stood and went to Alexis. "You look like a princess, sweetie," she said, touching the scattered seed pearls on the sleeve of the gown. "I love it on you." She beamed with pride as she walked slowly around to the other side of her daughter. "What do you think?" she asked hopefully, clasping her hands together.

Alexis continued to scratch. "I hate it, Mom. I look like a stuffed turkey. It's too much dress and it makes me itch."

"How much is this gown, Violet?" Josephine asked.

"Twelve hundred dollars," she responded.

Gloria wiped her brow. "Wedding gowns are too expensive!" She sighed dramatically.

"I'm telling you the truth," Josephine said as she walked back to her seat without saying another word.

Alexis could sense her mother's disappointment.

Violet assisted Alexis down off the step. "Let's try on another one," she suggested. "I didn't think this one was quite right either."

Alexis tried on three more variations of the ball gown style and still didn't like any of them. The fourth gown Violet handed her was a white strapless fitted dress that flared at the bottom.

She didn't need any help stepping onto the navy blue carpeted circle with it on. This was a good sign.

"This is beautiful," Alexis said, fingering the alençon-beaded lace that went around the top of the gown. How much is this one, Violet?"

"Thirteen fifty," Violet replied, arranging the train on the dress so Alexis could get a better view.

Josephine turned up her nose. "I don't like this one, Alexis. It's too revealing."

"And expensive," Gloria added. "We could feed more people at the reception for that kind of money," she blurted out before she could catch herself. She put her hand to her lips. "I forgot, it's not *my* wedding," she added sarcastically.

You've got that right, Alexis said to herself.

"The dress shows every curve you have," Josephine added, getting up from her seat to get a closer look.

"You are right, Mrs. Shire, a mermaid-style gown does show all your curves, but your daughter has the body to pull it off quite nicely," Violet commented as she admired the dress on Alexis in the mirror.

"I don't believe she should wear something like that in the house of the Lord," Josephine said and looked over at Gloria for approval. "It's just not appropriate."

Alexis exhaled her frustration loudly before returning to the dressing room yet again to try on another dress.

After trying on several more gowns, Alexis was tired and annoyed. Every time she liked a gown, her mother didn't and vice versa.

"Let's try on this one," Violet recommended, handing Alexis a dress she'd pulled from the stockroom.

Alexis slipped the gown on and prayed both she and her mother would like it. As soon as she stepped out of the dressing room into full view, her mother and Gloria slowly rose from their seats with their eyes fixed on her.

"You don't like this one either," Alexis said, making her way to the mirror so she could see the gown for herself.

Once Violet arranged the cathedral-length train correctly, Alexis looked into the mirror. "This is so beautiful," she said, looking at her mother in the reflection.

"It's not a pure white or ivory color, they call it candlelight," Violet explained.

"Mom, what do you think?" Alexis asked her mother with pleading eyes.

"I really wanted you to have white white, but I agree, sweetie, it looks lovely on you," Josephine said, moving closer.

"We can order the gown in white, Mrs. Shire," Violet told her.

Alexis shook her head. "This color is gorgeous. I don't want to wear white," she said, rubbing the satin fabric.

"It's a lovely gown, Alexis," Gloria commented. "How much is it, Violet?"

"Nine hundred and fifty dollars."

"Now, that's more like it," Josephine told Alexis, who smiled in return.

"Stef, what do you think?" Alexis asked.

Stephanie smiled. "I think you look marvelous, darling."

"This is it," Alexis said, patting the strapless, duchess satin, A-line gown. In the mirror, she looked at the covered button detail in the back and train. "It's plain, but I think it's elegant. It's not too poofy or too straight."

"The train is just long enough," Josephine commented with a tear in her eye. "Alexis, you look beautiful."

"I feel beautiful," she replied, continuing to admire herself.

"An A-line gown is in between the straight and a ball gown. More and more bridal manufacturers are designing dresses with this style in mind," Violet offered. "I think this dress says classy, elegant. And with your bone structure and slender frame, strapless looks good on you."

"Now let's find a headpiece and veil." Violet walked

over to a glass display case filled with sparkling lace and crystals. She pulled out a beautiful silver rhinestone tiara and brought it over.

"I don't want a traditional headpiece or to wear a veil at all," Alexis said as Violet placed the round sparkling piece on her head.

Josephine and Gloria both gasped at the same time.

"O-kay," Violet said, preparing to lift the tiara from Alexis's dark brown locks.

"Wait just a minute, Violet," Josephine said, moving to where Alexis could see her. Violet froze at the sound of Mrs. Shire's tone. "You've chosen a gorgeous gown, why won't you wear a headpiece, Alexis? I think your face should be covered when you walk down the aisle."

Alexis looked at Stephanie, who hunched her shoulders.

"I didn't want to have the veil hanging from my head all night, mother," Alexis sighed.

"Then you don't want to look like a bride," Josephine said sternly.

"By whose standards?" Alexis raised her voice.

Josephine squinted and tapped her foot against the carpet. It was a sure sign she was about to explode with anger. Young lady—" Josephine began.

Alexis put her hands on her hips, ready for whatever Josephine was bringing.

"Why don't I create something for you?" Ivy suggested hurriedly, as she lifted the silver tiara from Alexis's head. "Maybe some flowers would look pretty in your hair or something."

"I guess that will be okay." Alexis agreed, not completely confident about Violet's suggestion, but hoping it would satisfy her mother. Alexis looked at Josephine. "If it pleases my mother, I'll consider a veil," she added unenthusiastically. She knew if she didn't at least try one on, her mother would never stop fussing.

Josephine waved her hand at Alexis. "Don't do me any favors, it's *your* wedding, remember?" she spat in return.

"Whatever," Alexis mumbled.

"I think a cathedral-length veil with scattered Austrian crystals will enhance your look," Violet suggested.

"If I may ask, what is cathedral length?" Stephanie said.

"It's the length of the veil. Cathedral length extends onto the floor at least six inches past the train of the wedding gown. They are used for formal weddings and look best when worn with a cathedral- or semicathedral-length gown. Alexis's gown has a cathedral train."

"I think that will be gorgeous, Lexie," Stephanie said.

"Do you have one I can try on?" Alexis asked. If she didn't like it, she'd go without one.

"Yes." Violet went to pick one out. She came back with two layers of flowing tulle held together on a clear comb.

After she made sure the comb was secure in the top of Alexis's hair, she stepped back so everyone could see how it looked with the gown.

"The front would cover my whole face?" Alexis asked, distorting her face.

"Yes."

"Do I want my face covered?" Alexis asked, looking at Stephanie in the mirror.

"Most brides are bawling when they come down the aisle, so I think it would be a good idea for you to hide your face," Stephanie said mischievously.

Alexis grinned. "You are so funny and are of no help to me," she said dryly.

"Don't be getting smart with me, get the veil, girl," Stephanie told her.

"Okay, okay," Alexis said, watching her mother and

Gloria sit tight-lipped and quiet. She was glad for the reprieve, but knew it wouldn't last long.

"Violet, I'll take the dress *and* the veil. We'll see about the flowers for my hair."

"Both are excellent choices. I'll need to measure you so we can order the right size dress," Violet said as she helped Alexis off the step.

"This size fits pretty well," Alexis replied, glancing in the mirror one more time.

"I know, but we can never be too careful."

They walked to the back of the dressing room so Alexis could remove the dress and get her measurements taken. After she changed back into her own clothes, she and Violet returned to the showroom.

"I have a small selection of bridal shoes. If there's anything here you like, let me know," Violet told her, motioning to a row of shoes.

"These right here." Alexis pointed to a pair of white sandals. They had five rows of rhinestones that wrapped around her ankle and tied in a little bow in the back.

"What size are you?"

"An eight and a half," Alexis said, picking up one of the shoes off the stand.

Violet brought a box of shoes out and Alexis moved over to one of the chairs in front of the display so she could try them on.

"Girl, those shoes are off the hook," Stephanie commented as she watched Alexis stand in front of the mirror on the floor.

"I love these shoes," Alexis said, watching the rhinestones glisten as she turned her foot in different directions. She glanced at her mother to get her opinion.

"How much are they?" Josephine wanted to know.

"I don't care, I want these shoes," Alexis stated before Violet could answer.

"They look rather expensive, Alexis," Josephine warned.

"It's okay, Mom."

"Then you'll pay for them," Josephine said. She and Gloria gave each other a meaningful glance.

"We're doing great, Alexis," Violet said. "We need to choose some jewelry for you and we're done. Let's look at the display over here."

A variety of jewelry was displayed in a case on the other side of the room. Alexis admired the sparkling necklaces, earring sets, and bracelets. She chose a small pair of vintage chandelier-style earrings and carried them closer to the mirror to get a better look.

"Beautiful," she said, tucking her long hair behind her ears.

"They will look lovely with your gown, Alexis," Violet said as she pulled out a matching necklace.

Violet helped put it on and watched as Alexis held her hair up and turned her head from side to side in order to get a feel for the jewelry. "I'll take it."

Violet recorded Alexis's choices in her file. "Are we having fun yet?" she asked, hugging Alexis to her side. "Now we can choose the bridesmaids' dresses. Ivy mentioned you wanted to use pink as your primary color and silver as an accent."

Alexis nodded. "I want something that's tea length so my bridesmaids can wear their dresses again and I want my maid of honor to try on some of them."

Josephine groaned loudly. "Alexis, that type of dress would be inappropriate. Remember what you've just picked out for yourself," she warned.

"I agree, Josie," Gloria said.

"Mom, she's just going to try on a couple," Alexis said, trying to keep her voice even. She attempted not to check the time since Jaeden still hadn't shown up.

After Stephanie modeled three different short dresses, Alexis wasn't satisfied. She had Violet pull out several long gowns, but she didn't like any of those either.

Finally, Stephanie stepped into the fitting area in a strapless satin A-line gown similar to Alexis's wedding dress. It had a back bustle and a slight train with a rhinestone clasp.

"That's the one," Alexis exclaimed with joy, admiring the red dress. "Stef, you look so beautiful."

Alexis turned to Violet. "Does this dress come in pink?"

"Yes, I believe it does." She flipped her swatch book open. "It comes in a rose pink," she added, pointing to the third swatch on the page.

"The color is nice and I like the way the fabric feels," Alexis said, rubbing the pink square between her fingers. "Would Stephanie wear the same color and dress as the bridesmaids?"

"That decision is entirely up to you. Keep in mind, even though the dress looks gorgeous on Stephanie, it may not look as flattering on the others depending on their body type," Violet reminded her.

Alexis had to stop and think about the sizes of some of her bridesmaids. Most she hadn't seen in a long time.

"LaTanya is full-figured, Alexis," her mother interjected.

Alexis didn't think now would be a good time to tell her mother she didn't want LaTanya in her wedding. "No, I think everyone will look nice in this gown," she said. "Everyone will wear the same thing."

"Good decision, Lexie, 'cause I'm loving this dress," Stephanie said, holding the sides of the dress out as she stared at herself in the mirror.

"Violet, by any chance do the shoes I picked for myself come in this color or can they be dyed?" Alexis asked Violet, who was adjusting the hem of Stephanie's gown.

"As a matter of fact, they do come in rose pink," Violet said happily.

"We need to be in a bridal magazine or on television so every person in America can see us," Stephanie said, still looking in the mirror.

Alexis noticed Stephanie staring. "You really like the dress, huh, Stef?"

Stephanie moved closer to the three-way mirror, raking her short curls with her fingers. "Girl, please, like, do you see how good it looks on me?" She laughed.

Alexis walked to stand beside Stephanie. "I'm so glad you're so sure of yourself," she said sarcastically.

"Don't hate me 'cause I'm beautiful. I didn't say anything to you when you had on that gorgeous dress a minute ago."

"Alexis, don't forget about your flower girls' dresses," Gloria reminded her. "I'll need to contact my niece Rhoda so she can order Arianna and Kaleece's dresses."

"I almost forgot," Alexis said before walking over to the display of tiny, frilly dresses. She pulled out a white tank dress with a tulle skirt. It had a white satin sash around the waist. Alexis held the dress up so the others could see it. "I love this little dress, but can I have a rose pink sash around the middle instead of the white one?"

"Yes, we can order it that way," Violet said, glancing at the tag to get the style number.

Alexis then ordered the flower girls' shoes as well as the bridesmaids' jewelry.

"Now, that's what I'm talking about. You made those decisions quickly and everybody agreed," Stephanie said. She'd been patient, but they'd been there more than two hours and she was ready to go. "I think we're getting somewhere."

"Stef, you are such a nutcase," Alexis said, relieved

that nobody had argued with her. "You can change clothes now."

Stephanie walked back to the dressing room.

Alexis walked over to Josephine and Gloria. "Are you going to look for a dress today as well?"

"We'll come back another day," Gloria said. "Everything you've chosen is gorgeous. Expensive," she noted. "But gorgeous nonetheless."

"I still think you should wear a tiara, it would complete the look," Josephine said, watching Alexis's facial expression change to frustration.

"Mom . . ." Alexis started.

Josephine held her hand up. "I'm going to leave it alone, though. I promise."

"Thank you." Alexis turned to Violet. "How long will it take for the dresses to come back?"

"We're going to have to do what they call a rush order, which increases the cost of each of the girls' dresses by forty dollars."

"Forty dollars?" Gloria exclaimed. "That makes that dress three hundred dollars per person!"

"I'm afraid so, Mrs. Jefferson. It usually takes fourteen to sixteen weeks for bridesmaids' dresses to come in and we don't have that kind of time. A rush cut comes back in six to eight weeks," Violet explained. "How many bridesmaids do you have?" she asked Alexis.

Alexis didn't want to say because she still hadn't decided. "Eight," she said at last.

"What do you mean eight, Alexis? There were ten names on the list we made," Josephine stressed.

"Mom, I'm sorry, I dropped LaTanya and Jessica," Alexis admitted. "I haven't seen or talked them since Cousin Gus's funeral four years ago. I just can't have all those people in my wedding. I wanted four, so I think I'm being generous."

Josephine frowned.

Alexis ignored her again. She found the more she did it, the easer it became. "Violet, I'll give you a list of names and telephone numbers." Alexis pulled out her Palm Pilot, a piece of paper, and a pen. She wrote down the contact information, then handed it to Violet.

"It's important everyone comes in as soon as possible. The dresses need to be ordered at the same time," Violet explained, scanning the list. She handed Alexis a legal-size piece of paper with a list of all her selections and their prices. "Keep this for your records."

"I will. Thanks so much for helping us," Alexis said, placing the paper in the planner Ivy had given her.

As they followed Violet to the exit, Stephanie threw her arms around Alexis and whispered in her ear, "My dress is da bomb," before catching up with Josephine and Gloria.

Alexis trailed behind them. Thinking about how Jaeden never showed up and didn't even call. Was this a sign of things to come? The thought made her stomach flip-flop.

CHAPTER ELEVEN

"Stef, will you drive us back to my mother's?" Alexis asked, throwing the keys to her.

"What's wrong? Are you sick?" Stephanie watched her friend's miserable expression as she opened the passenger-side door.

"I'm sorry Jaeden didn't show up. I'm sure it had to be important and he couldn't get away," Gloria insisted a second time.

"We need to talk about the girls you've asked to be in the wedding," Josephine said irritably as she opened the rear car door. "I want to make sure the list you gave Violet Hart matches the one we made at the house," she continued from behind Alexis.

Alexis sat quietly, hoping the Harts didn't think they were wasting their time with her because she kept assuring them her fiancé would show up and he didn't. Did they think he'd be too tied up to show up at the alter as well?

What could have been more important than planning their wedding? Her next thought was about whether she'd be able to pull off an extravagant wedding in the short amount of time. Would it become a total disaster?

Alexis had tuned out the comments her mother and Gloria were making from the backseat. She retrieved her Palm Pilot and began to make notes about her visit to the bridal estate. Even though Jaeden disappointed her by not showing up, she was pleased with the decisions she'd made.

As Stephanie drove down Josephine's block, they spotted Jaeden's SUV parked on the street.

Stephanie quickly glanced over at her. "Lexie, listen to what he has to say before you fly off the handle." She maneuvered the gearshift into park. "We'll be there in a minute," she said over her shoulder to Gloria and Josephine as they exited the car.

"Don't take too long, we still have things to discuss," Josephine said anxiously as she opened the door and stepped out.

Alexis watched as they disappeared up the walk.

"I think you're going to have a beautiful wedding. Everything you chose today was off the hook. I just don't want you to be upset about Jaeden not being there," Stephanie said to her best friend.

"He said he would though, Stef," Alexis whined. She turned away from her, blinking back tears.

"I know, Lexie, but things happen, you know that."

"He could have called me," Alexis said with the tears in her eyes threatening to fall.

"Remember what I said, Lexie. If you really think about it, we didn't need him there today, anyway." Stephanie squeezed Alexis's shoulder. "He's not supposed to see your gown and he wouldn't be interested in ours, so give him a break this time."

Alexis sat staring.

"Lexie, say something," Stephanie pleaded.

"Okay," Alexis said, resigned. "I'll give him a break, *this* time."

"Good. Now I have something I need to take care of, but if you need me, call." Stephanie pulled the handle to open the door.

She waited for Alexis to step out of the car before

throwing her keys to her. "Go talk to your man, girl." Stephanie laughed as she got into her own car and drove off.

Alexis stood in front of the house well after Stephanie had driven away. She wanted to pull her emotions together and wondered if every bride felt the way she did. She slowly made her way up the walkway, but detoured to the back of the house.

Opening the patio door, she stepped inside and took a seat on the chaise longue, further delaying seeing Jaeden. She'd had had enough arguments and disagreements for one day.

Alexis leaned back in the long green chair and closed her eyes. She began to relax as she thought about all the things she'd accomplished. The beautiful wedding gown she'd selected made her feel like a princess.

"There you are, baby," Jaeden said, closing the kitchen door behind him.

Alexis opened one eye, but didn't speak to him.

"What are you doing out here alone?" he asked, taking a seat at the bottom of the chair.

Alexis still didn't respond.

"Baby, don't be angry with me," he pleaded.

She opened both eyes, but still gave no response.

"Arnold called and asked if I could make a couple of changes to the sketches I presented in New York. I got so excited about the call that I met him at IHOP to go over them in person," Jaeden explained.

Alexis pulled herself up in one swift motion. "On Saturday morning, Jaeden," she spat. "You knew about this appointment a week ago and if I recall correctly, *you* were the one who didn't want a long engagement."

"Baby, you know how important this deal is to me."

"Oh, so our wedding isn't as important to you," Alexis snapped as she got up from the other side of the chair.

"Baby." Jaeden caught her arm so she wouldn't get away. "You know that's not true," he said, gently pulling her onto his lap. Snuggling against her neck, he continued. "Our wedding is very important to me," he said, placing kisses on her neck.

"Prove it," Alexis challenged, trying to ignore the feel of his lips on her skin. She was determined not to change the way she felt.

"What do you want me to do?" he asked, stroking her hair.

"Would you please talk to your mother about her guest list, and I'll talk to mine?"

"Sure I will, but what happened?" He pulled her closer.

"Every place the coordinator called was booked except for Meridian Banquets. The only room they had available holds three hundred people and both of our mothers think the place is *too small*," Alexis said sadly.

"How many guests do they think we're going to have?"

"I didn't want to ask, I was too stressed to even deal with it at the time. Your mother wants the wedding at your church and my mother wants the wedding at our church. It was too much and you not showing up didn't help matters." She looked down at him.

"I'm here now," Jaeden said before cupping the back of her head, and bringing her forward. He brushed his lips against hers.

At first, Alexis tried to resist, but as soon as she felt their lips connect, she melted against him.

Jaeden retreated and looked into her brown eyes. "Why don't we go to the movies and forget about all this wedding planning for the rest of the day?"

Alexis reached down beside the chair and went through

her purse to find her Palm Pilot. She turned it on and pulled up her wedding information.

"See this?" She held the small device in front of his face. "We have no time for recreation. I have a project for school due soon, plus we still haven't talked to our mothers about the engagement party." Alexis shook her head. "I'm almost scared to ask them about it. We don't even know if they've sent the invitations out and who they went to."

Jaeden rocked her from side to side. "About two months ago, I remember a beautiful woman once told me she didn't have time to go out with me, but she's wearing my ring today," he said, lifting her left hand. "Soon, she'll become my wife. You don't remember?" he asked.

He lifted her left hand even higher, so they could see the brilliant sparkle reflecting from her ring. "Does this jog your memory?"

Alexis giggled, playfully snatching her hand away. "Of course I remember."

"Come on, we'll talk to them now and then we're going to the movies."

"But we don't—"

Jaeden placed his forefinger over her lips. "That's final." He lifted her off his lap and pushed himself to his feet.

Alexis grabbed her purse and followed him inside the house. She couldn't help but forgive him, but she hoped he wouldn't leave her to make any more important decisions by herself.

Josephine and Gloria were sitting at the dining room table going over their lists when Jaeden and Alexis walked in.

"We need to talk to you," Jaeden said as he took one

of the middle chairs and Alexis sat in another. "First, I want to apologize for not being there with you today. Something came up at work that I couldn't overlook, but I promise I'll make the next meeting."

"I knew you had a good reason, son," Gloria said, looking over the top of her reading glasses.

"It's quite all right, Jaeden. We really didn't need you there today, anyway," Josephine piped in.

Alexis rolled her eyes.

"From what Alexis has told me, I should have been and that's why we need to talk," Jaeden said, placing his hands on the table. "Mama, even though Mt. Zion's sanctuary *is* larger than Pilgrim Branch's, I still think we should have the wedding there."

"I told your mother that, Jaeden. The wedding should be at the bride's church," Josephine said triumphantly.

Gloria leaned forward. "I still say Mt. Zion is a better choice. It's a new building with state-of-the-art equipment," she said firmly.

Josephine huffed. "I don't care how new it is, my daughter will marry at the church she grew up in," she spat.

Jaeden hit the table and jumped to his feet. "Ladies, please."

Both Gloria and Josephine looked at him as if they were taken aback by his gesture.

Alexis looked up at the scowl on his face. "See what I mean?" she muttered, glancing at both their mothers, who were acting like they were ready to participate in the WWF Smackdown.

Jaeden turned to Gloria. "Mama, please, let this go. We're getting married at Pilgrim Branch and that's the end of it."

Gloria sat quietly for a couple of moments, then she exhaled loudly. "Okay, but I want Pastor Dixon to at

least pray. I just wanted a place big enough to hold all
our guests."

"Pilgrim Branch holds four hundred people," Josephine clarified. "The sanctuary is a beautiful place to get
married.

"Ladies," Jaeden warned.

"I don't have a problem with Pastor Dixon participating," Josephine stated, trying to make peace. She knew
she needed Gloria as an ally if they wanted to get anything accomplished.

"It's settled then, the ceremony will be held at Pilgrim
Branch and Pastor Dixon will assist," Jaeden said, looking at each of them to make sure there were no further
objections. Jaeden glanced down at Alexis. "Baby, you
cool with that?"

"Yes. I'm just glad it's finally settled." Alexis shook her
head in disbelief at the way the older women had conducted themselves.

"On to the next subject, the guest list," Jaeden said taking his seat once again. He turned to his mother.
"Mama, it's crucial that we only invite people that are important to the two of us." Jaeden moved his finger between himself and Alexis, measuring his mother's
expressions as he spoke. "If the reception hall only holds
three hundred people, we have to divide three hundred
by four, which means we will have four lists, you and Pop,
Mr. and Mrs. Shire, Alexis and myself," Jaeden said, sensing his mother hadn't heard a word he'd said.

Alexis sat staring at the frown on her mother's face,
which grew deeper as Jaeden spoke.

"There are going to be people you just can't invite.
I'm sorry," Jaeden said sincerely.

"If your father and I are going to help pay for this wedding, I don't see why we can't invite as many people as
we want," Gloria began.

Alexis hunched Jaeden with her elbow because of the scowl that had grown on his face. "Let's talk about the engagement party," she said, moving to another topic. "How are those plans coming and when are you going to give us the date?"

"Everything has been handled. We called Ivy Hart the Monday after you told us you were using their services and they're handling the planning," Josephine said.

"It will be on the eighth of July at An Affair to Remember Banquets," Gloria added.

Alexis snapped her fingers, then pointed to her mother. "That's why you didn't comment much about the bridal estate when we visited today. You'd already been there. Why didn't you tell me, Mom?"

"You said you trusted us enough to make our own decisions and we wanted to surprise you with what we planned," Josephine explained. "It's still a surprise because we're not giving anything away, you'll just have to wait until July eighth."

"We do trust you," Jaeden said. "Don't we, baby?" He gently poked Alexis with his elbow when she didn't respond right away.

"Er, ye-yes, we trust you," Alexis agreed, wondering what the two women had up their sleeves. They were being way too accommodating.

"See, baby? We can still go to the movies."

"Great idea, son," Gloria said. "You two go and enjoy yourselves. Josie and I still have some things left to do."

Alexis raised her head. "We need to go over the guest list for the engagement party. We can't invite people to the engagement party and not to the wedding." She was beginning to loathe planning her own wedding. "How many invitations did you send out?" she asked her mother.

"Ivy told us to invite people from this area since the wedding was next month. So I would say we sent out about one hundred and fifty invitations," Josephine answered. She glanced over at Gloria, who nodded in agreement.

"See, baby? We have nothing to worry about. Let's go." Jaeden stood, gently pulling Alexis up from her seat.

"We'll see you two later," Josephine said and then smiled at Gloria.

Jaeden caught Alexis's hand as they walked to the threshold of the dining area.

"Don't forget to cut your lists for the wedding, ladies." Jaeden held up his hand when Gloria opened her mouth to disagree. "We'll talk about it later. That was just a reminder."

Alexis waved before they walked away. Her heart and her head told her that Josephine and Gloria were definitely up to something.

CHAPTER TWELVE

"Should we take your car or my SUV?" Jaeden asked Alexis when they stepped outside.

"We always take your vehicle, let's take my car," Alexis replied.

She caught him by the hand before he turned away. "I'm worried about the engagement party, Jaeden."

"Why, baby? They told us the coordinator is handling it, so stop worrying." He kissed her on the forehead.

"Follow me to my apartment and I can leave my SUV there," Jaeden suggested.

Alexis trailed Jaeden back to his apartment and pulled her car next to his SUV.

"Let's go inside and get the newspaper," Jaeden said, standing at the driver's-side door of her car.

Alexis grinned. "You could have looked at the movie listings at my mom's house. It doesn't take both of us to get one paper. What are you up to?"

"I don't want to leave you out here alone in the dark, baby," Jaeden said with pleading eyes.

Alexis got out of the car. "Jaeden, we're coming right back out, no detours," Alexis warned him.

"Baby, would I do that to you?" He smiled, showing perfectly straight white teeth.

"Don't give me that smile." Alexis pinched his cheek, but couldn't help but laugh at him.

Jaeden opened the door to his apartment, allowing Alexis to enter first.

"I told you we are not staying, Jaeden," she said after he picked up the remote control to his entertainment system and the soulful sounds of the Temptations singing "Tempt Me" floated through the air. She gave him a knowing look.

"What?" Jaeden said innocently. "It was already in the changer. I was listening to it this morning."

"Get the paper so we can go, I'm sure something's playing in the next thirty minutes," Alexis said.

"I love this song," he said, moving to the beat of the music. "We should practice your dance moves every chance we can, so you'll be a pro by the time we take the floor at our reception," Jaeden advised as he came closer to her. "Dance with me, baby."

Alexis decided not to argue with him. One dance and maybe they could get out of there.

She had a feeling he had set her up by the way he held her when she walked into his arms. She rested her head against him and he guided her to the beat of the music. She was right where she loved to be . . . in his arms.

Lifting her head, she looked up at him. "You didn't have to do all this," she managed to say before Jaeden claimed her mouth.

Her body responded to his touch and now she was unable to focus on what she'd been trying to say. His light kisses on her throat were driving her mad.

Jaeden moved slightly away from her so he could look into her eyes. "I'm sorry for not being there for you today. I can see now that it overwhelmed you, but I promise to always be there for you."

He picked her up, carried her to the sofa, and sat with her on his lap.

"I've already forgiven you," Alexis managed to say as her calm was shattered with the intense hunger of his kisses. He caressed her breast through the thin material of her dress.

"I thought we were going to the movies," she whispered. Jaeden continued without responding. "Don't you hear me talking to you, Jaeden? Are you going to answer me?"

"I am talking, baby. Can't you hear me?" he replied as he lightly pinched her nipple.

"You never planned for us to go to the movies, did you?"

The pleasure became too intense. She reached over to turn out the lamp near the sofa and concentrated on making love to her man. She'd worry about everything else tomorrow.

The next Wednesday, Alexis waited for Jaeden at Hearts and Flowers. He had promised to be on time after she warned him of the consequences if he didn't.

She had been waiting fifteen minutes when he sped into the parking lot and jumped out of the SUV, smiling. "Sorry, baby, I woke up a little late, dreaming about you of course." Jaeden kissed her on the lips.

"Glad you made it. Now let's go inside, I want to get as much completed today as possible," Alexis said as they walked to the front of the bridal estate.

Announcing their arrival, she opened the door and stepped inside with Jaeden following her.

"Wow, can we afford this place?" Jaeden inquired as he looked around at the rich décor.

"I thought the same thing, but they are very reasonable," Alexis replied.

Ivy met them in the waiting room and Alexis introduced her to Jaeden before they headed to Ivy's office.

"I'm glad you both are here because we've got a lot of ground to cover today," Ivy said as she offered them a seat at a table in the corner. "We need to choose your dinner menu and table linen choices," she said, handing the brochure to Alexis.

Holding the paper with the selections between them, Alexis and Jaeden began to scan over their choices.

"My suggestion is to have hot and cold hors d'oeuvres served by a butler and a family-style sit-down dinner," Ivy said, glancing at the paper.

"Sounds good, what do you think, Jaeden?" Alexis asked.

"Fine by me, whatever you say, baby," he replied nonchalantly.

Alexis looked at him and prayed today wouldn't end up a disaster.

"The prices you see include a four-hour premium bar, which is all your more expensive liquors," Ivy informed them.

"How much would we save if we didn't have the bar at all?" Alexis asked.

Ivy turned the page of the little booklet. "You'd save twelve dollars per person."

Jaeden looked at Alexis. "Baby, I think we should keep the bar, I have people in my family who drink."

"Our moms would probably have a fit if we don't, so I guess you're right." Alexis agreed to keep the open bar.

"I'll fill in your selections on Meridian's banquet form and give you a copy for your records as well," Ivy replied.

"I was thinking for my table linen I'd like to have white table skirts, silver damask tablecloths, and white chair covers with matching silver sashes."

Ivy smiled. "You've been doing your homework. I love your choices."

"I'm finally getting excited," Alexis said, staring at Jaeden, who seemed to be gazing into space.

"Next, we need to choose invitations," Ivy said, rising from her seat. "I have a good variety in the other room. If you'll follow me."

She led them into the next room where there was a large mahogany table and bookshelf filled with huge sample invitation catalogs.

Jaeden and Alexis skimmed through three books before they found something they really liked.

"I think this is the one." Alexis pointed to an elegant light pink card with a ribbon attachment. "It matches my colors perfectly," Alexis said. "Honey, what do you think?" Alexis tapped Jaeden, who seemed to be someplace else.

"It's fine with me, baby."

"How many do you want to order?" Ivy asked, getting a blank from the tray on the table.

"I don't have a good grasp on that number. Our mothers are still working on their lists," Alexis replied.

"When ordering invites, you must count at least two people per invitation," Ivy informed them.

Jaeden and Alexis looked at each other. "We're in trouble," they said in unison.

Ivy chuckled. "Maybe I can help you. To get a better idea of the number of people you'll be feeding, also count yourselves and your wedding party, as well as your parents. There should be a separate count for all your service people like the photographer and videographer, disc jockey, et cetera. We can usually get a lower price for their food."

"This means we should only order a hundred and fifty invitations, right?" Alexis asked, trying to remember the last number on her mother's list.

"Correct."

"We're definitely going to have a problem, Jaeden."

Alexis tapped him. She was getting increasingly frustrated with his absentmindedness.

He jumped. "What?"

Alexis just sighed before turning her attention back to Ivy. She could see he had no intention of concentrating on what they were doing.

"My mother's list alone is double that," Alexis said to Ivy.

"There are several solutions to your problem," Ivy began. "You can invite more people to the wedding and less to the reception. And if that's not an option, you'll have to cut the guest list."

"My mother probably has a long list as well," Jaeden said.

Thank God, he's listening, finally, Alexis thought. "We need to think about this one, Ivy." she said.

"I understand it can cause a bit of confusion."

"Confusion is not the word that fits here, it's going to be more like World War Three with our mothers," Jaeden added.

"We've been clashing with them since we started planning the wedding; this could send them over the top. Neither has any intention of cutting her list." Alexis shook her head.

"Well, why don't I take you down to see Rose so you can order flowers?" Ivy pushed her chair back before standing. "Did you decide where the wedding will take place?"

"Pilgrim Branch," Jaeden said.

"I'm glad that worked out, and everything else will too, you'll see," Ivy said.

"I truly hope so," Alexis commented as they followed Ivy out of the room.

A soft chime sounded as they walked into the design studio and Rose came from the back to greet them.

"They're all yours, Rose." Ivy walked over to her sister. "Alexis has already been added to the online database, so you can pull up her information."

Rose smiled thanking her sister before she left the room. Then she walked over to the couple. "Good morning," she said. "Are we ready to create?" Rose's voice was filled with excitement.

Alexis appreciated her enthusiasm. "Yes."

"Let me show you some of the designs I have on display." Rose led them into the floral showroom.

"These are so beautiful," Alexis said as her eyes tried to soak in all the lovely designs.

Rose picked up a large bouquet. "Thank you so much, I'm fond of them too," she said, laughing.

Alexis touched several different samples. "I like them all. How do I choose just one?" She looked at Jaeden for an answer.

Jaeden held his hands up. "Don't look at me. I have no clue about this kind of stuff," he said in a hurry.

Alexis exhaled loudly.

Rose patted her on the back. "That's quite all right, we'll go through everything together," she assured her. "What are your colors?"

"I'm using rose pink and silver accents," Alexis replied. She liked Rose's pleasant and easygoing demeanor.

"Would you like to carry something small or extravagant?" Rose asked, handing Alexis a small bouquet.

Alexis still couldn't make up her mind. She had had no idea there were so many choices to make and Jaeden wasn't contributing an iota to the decision-making.

"It's okay." Rose gave Alexis's hand a gentle squeeze after she saw the confused look in her eyes. "Let me make a suggestion." She picked up a bouquet with a mixture of toscanini and emma roses wrapped tightly together with silky ribbons. "This would be lovely in different shades of pink. I could add some greenery, some pink spray roses, and wrap it in silver shimmer ribbon," she suggested.

"That sounds beautiful," Alexis said.

"Good, we could use the same flowers for your attendants in various hues to contrast their gowns, but I can make them into round balls we call pomanders using the same ribbon for the handle." She picked up a sample from the display and slipped her hand through the handle to demonstrate how the flowers should be carried.

"That's different," Alexis said, studying the two bouquets.

"Your throwaway bouquet would be a very small version of the one you'd carry down the aisle."

"What about the guys?" Alexis asked, handing the flowers back to Rose.

"We would use the same roses, adding different things to enhance the designs I'll create."

"I love your ideas," Alexis said, looking at Jaeden for his input.

Just as he was about to comment, his cell phone rang. He excused himself, got up from his chair, and moved quickly out the door so he could take the call.

Alexis had hoped they wouldn't be interrupted until they'd finished everything she had planned for the morning. It was a weekday, and she understood he had business to conduct. But if she could complete her tasks, she could go home and finish her report on the benefits of teaching using animated graphics.

While they waited for Jaeden's return, they talked about decorations for the church, then moved on to the reception décor.

Rose placed the flowers back on the display stand and lifted her finger. "I want to show you a new vase that just came in. I'd like to use it for your table centerpieces at the reception."

"Okay," Alexis said, watching the door and wondering why Jaeden hadn't returned.

Rose came toward her with a tall crystal trumpetlike vase.

Alexis's jaw dropped at the sight of the beautiful glass container. "This is so gorgeous," she said as she took the vase from Rose.

Rose grinned. "I would fill them with different shades of pink blossoms. They would kind of run over from the top." Rose demonstrated with her hands.

Alexis was filled with excitement. "If you have any other ideas for the wedding or reception, I trust your decision," Alexis said, handing the vase back.

"You'll need to give me a definite number of the boutonnières, corsages, and table centerpieces you'll need," Rose said, placing the container on the table in front of them.

Alexis pulled out her Palm Pilot to retrieve the information and scribbled the numbers on a sheet of paper. "This is a tentative number. I'll call you if anything changes," Alexis said as she gave Rose the information.

"I know the count for the centerpieces will change depending on the number of responses you receive, and that's fine."

Alexis glanced toward the door just as Jaeden returned.

"Baby, how much longer do you think we'll have to be here?" he asked when he retook his seat.

"I'm not sure. Why?" Alexis asked before she took a quick look at the wall clock.

"Marie from the office called and I really need to get back."

"But we're not done yet." Alexis hoped he sensed her disappointment.

"Let me get Ivy for you," Rose said, walking back over to her desk. She pressed a button on the phone and spoke to her sister. "She'll be here in a minute," she said after she hung up.

Ivy gracefully strolled into the room a few minutes later.

"What else needs to be done today?" Jaeden asked Ivy as he continued to glance at his watch.

"He needs to get to the office," Alexis explained.

"Your wedding cake selection."

Jaeden rose from his seat, and Alexis followed. He walked out of earshot of the two women and pulled Alexis into his arms. "Baby, whatever you choose would be fine with me. I really need to go," he said before he kissed her forehead.

Alexis pulled back from him. Her eyes tried to hide the regret she felt.

Jaeden gently captured her face and held it in his hands. He kissed her lightly on the lips. "I'll call you later tonight."

"Okay," Alexis said, her voice barely above a whisper. She watched as he retreated from the room.

Rose went to Alexis. "You're going to have a gorgeous wedding," she assured her.

There might not be a wedding at all if he keeps this up, Alexis thought.

"Lili's waiting for us, sweetheart," Ivy said as she gently grabbed Alexis's hand and gave it a reaffirming squeeze.

Alexis waved good-bye to Rose and walked with Ivy.

"Everything will work out in the end, I promise," Ivy said as she led Alexis from the room. "We're going to work hard to make this wedding the best Taylor's ever seen."

"I bet you tell all your clients the same thing," Alexis said, looking at the sophisticated-looking woman.

Ivy chuckled. "I do whatever it takes to make sure she has a smile on her face when she leaves this place," she said as they walked down the corridor to Alexis's next big decision.

Lili Hart sat at the marble-topped table in her showroom waiting for Alexis. She walked over to shake her hand.

"Nice to see you again, Alexis." Lili looked toward the door. "I thought your fiancé would be joining us this morning?"

"He had to go to the office," Alexis replied sadly.

Ivy gave her baby sister a look that had become their secret code when the bride was having problems. "She's ready to choose one of your fabulous cakes," Ivy said.

"I've been trying to come up with something unique. I thought about making the groom's cake in the shape of a baseball cap since that's your fiancé's business," Lili said, gesturing to Alexis to have a seat at the table.

"That is unique. What a great idea," Ivy said to her sister.

"Thanks, Vee." Lili smiled, then waited for Alexis's response. "Do you think Jaeden would like the idea?"

"Oh yes, I think it's lovely. I've never seen a groom's cake made that way," Alexis said, trying to concentrate on cakes and not on Jaeden's departure.

"I've made a preliminary sketch of how the cake will look." Lili opened the manila folder on the table. "If you approve, all you have to do is tell me what type of flavor, filling, and icing you would want."

"I really love the idea, so you can choose all that."

"Why don't you think about it first and let me know? In the meantime, let's pick out a wedding cake," Lili suggested.

"I'll be back later, Alexis," Ivy said before she disappeared through the door.

For the next hour, Lili presented Alexis with photos of cakes she'd created. Then they moved to an array of cakes on display and Lili explained the many different styles. It was so much information, Alexis could barely process it.

"You'll probably need a cake that would feed two hundred and seventy-five people," Lili said.

"But I'm going to have at least three hundred guests at the reception," Alexis corrected.

Lili watched Alexis's eyes shift in confusion. "Ivy told me, but there are a lot of people who don't eat cake, so this way you won't have so much left over. If you want to order a cake for three hundred, that's not a problem," she added.

Alexis touched Lili's arm. "I'm sorry, I know you're the expert, I don't know what to do anymore. I'm not comfortable making a decision like this without my fiancé's input," she said honestly.

"Is he a big cake eater?"

"I really don't know." Alexis wondered if she really knew Jaeden at all.

Lili waved her hand dismissively. "Well, that's no problem. We can make some choices and you can go over them with him. If he disagrees, you have a week before the wedding to make changes."

"That's a relief. At least I don't have to feel bad if he doesn't like what I choose," Alexis said.

Lili pointed to a display cake. "I suggest five round stacked cakes iced with a smooth layer of royal fondant and decorated with lots of beautiful roses cascading from the top to the bottom on one side."

"Ooo, how pretty." Alexis's eyes brightened. "What is royal fondant though?"

"It's a smooth icing made of sugar and other ingredients. Here is what it will look like," Lili said, pointing to several cakes on display. "The roses would be in different hues of pink with some greenery to give it that extra touch."

"I've heard horror stories about how the pesticide used on live flowers can make people sick," Alexis said with concern.

"Rose will probably decorate the cake table with live flowers, but all the flowers on your cake will be hand-made of sugar," Lili clarified.

"Oh, you really are talented, Lili," Alexis complimented.

"Besides the bride's gown, the wedding cake is the focal point of any wedding," she said reassuringly. "Now you've chosen the presentation of your cake, now pick a flavor and filling for each tier." Lili, pointed to a list for Alexis to choose from.

She chose golden yellow cake with raspberry cream filling for the bottom tier, lemon with lemon curd filling for the second, dark chocolate with chocolate mousse for the third, coconut with coconut crème for the fourth, and chocolate cake with raspberry filling for the top tier.

"Great variety," Lili said making sure she'd written down all Alexis's selections correctly.

"Do you have a photo of what you're proposing, so I can show it to my fiancé and my mother?" Alexis asked, knowing she would be bombarded with questions later.

Lili pulled out a white binder from in front of her. Flipping the pages, she tore one out and gave it to Alexis.

Alexis studied the photo. "Thanks, it'll be so much easier than trying to describe it to them."

"No problem. What about a wedding favor for your guests? Did you want to go with something edible or were you going to talk to Ivy about it later?" Lili asked.

"I don't think I'll have time later. You mentioned something they could eat . . . like what?"

"Here is a book with some photos and pricing of personalized cookies and chocolate CDs, et cetera, that I've done in the past."

"I love the chocolate CD idea," Alexis said, studying the book sample. "Let's go with that. My fiancé loves music and I love chocolate."

Lili wrote down the information. "They're four dollars each. How many would you like to order?"

"I don't know. What do you think?"

"You could do one per couple since you'd need so many," Lili suggested.

"That's probably best. Although I can already hear my mother complaining about spending four dollars on the CDs," Alexis replied.

Lili handed Alexis a sheet of paper with her order written on it. "We're done here. Why don't I walk with you back to Ivy's office?" she asked, rising from her seat.

Alexis stood and followed Lili out into the hallway. "Lili, can I ask you a question?"

"Shoot."

"Do all brides act like this?"

"What? Nervous? It's very normal. This is an exciting and stressful time."

They walked into Ivy's office and found her sitting at her desk.

"We're back," Lili announced.

Ivy smiled as Alexis walked toward her. "Are you satisfied with your selections?"

Alexis nodded. "My cake is going to be simply gorgeous."

"I know it's been a long morning, but we have accomplished a great deal," Ivy said, looking at her computer screen. "Once Lili adds your selections to the file in the computer, I will be able to evaluate our progress."

"Oh, I meant to remind you," Lily said. " Since your parents are hosting the wedding, be sure you have their names on your invitation. A lot of people may not be familiar with you and your fiancé's names, but will recognize your parents' immediately."

Alexis chuckled. "I'm sure we were going to have the names of both parents printed on the invitation. Both our mothers would probably have a fit if we didn't."

"You must remember, your invitations need to be sent out as soon as possible. I'll need your wording and the number you want ordered by Monday," Ivy insisted.

"Can I take a look at my choice one more time?"

"Sure, let me get the book. You can have a seat at the table." Ivy retrieved the large burgundy binder and placed it on the table in front of Alexis.

Alexis flipped to page 64. She rubbed the pink shimmer of pearlescent paper. "This is so gorgeous," she commented. "I just love the look."

Ivy flipped to the front pages. "Why don't you choose the lettering, ink color, and look over the wording samples?"

After glancing at all the selections, Alexis made a decision. "I like the invitation the way it's shown in the book. If Jaeden doesn't like it, then too bad, he should have been here," she said, pushing the book aside.

"I agree it's beautiful just the way it is," Ivy said, jotting down the information from the page and ignoring Alexis's comment about Jaeden.

Alexis wrote down the wording from the invitation.

"Okay, that should do it for today, Alexis," Ivy said when she finished writing. "At the next appointment we should talk about music for the ceremony."

"Thanks so much for everything, Ivy," Alexis said, rising from her chair. They hugged before Alexis left.

On her way to the parking lot, Alexis decided she'd better head home to finish her papers for school. Since the weight of the wedding planning was falling on her shoulders, she needed to get that out of the way.

She got in her car and pulled out of the gates with a new determination.

CHAPTER THIRTEEN

Alexis was determined to use Saturday to finish up the assignments she hadn't completed for her class. Jaeden had gone to the office and everyone else was busy with their own tasks.

Alexis sat at her breakfast bar with her Palm Pilot on one side and her laptop in front of her. She scanned her notes to find the place where she'd left off earlier in the week.

The telephone rang, interrupting her thoughts. Alexis looked at the caller ID and quickly answered when she saw Hearts and Flowers on the screen. "Hello."

"Alexis, this is Violet Hart calling."

"How are you, Violet?"

"I'm very well, thank you. I'm calling to inform you that two of your bridesmaids still haven't come in."

Just what I need, Alexis said to herself, rolling her eyes. "Violet, can you give me their names, please?"

"Brianna and Cherise Clark," Violet read from the list in Alexis's computer file.

"I knew it," Alexis said. "Go ahead and order the other dresses. Don't worry about them coming in."

"Are you sure about that?" Violet asked.

"One hundred percent. They won't be participating in the wedding and we don't have any more time to wait," Alexis said, her anger building. She knew her cousins weren't going to cooperate, and that was the main reason she hadn't wanted them in her wedding in the first place.

"Has everyone else come in and given you their deposits?" she asked.

"Yes, everyone has paid half of the amount due. I'll give you a call back once the manufacturer has given me an approximate ship date."

"Thanks for calling," Alexis said.

"I'm so sorry to have to be the bearer of bad news."

"There's no need to apologize. You've actually helped me. Thanks again."

Alexis ended the call and rapidly punched in her mother's phone number.

"Mother," Alexis yelled when Josephine answered on the second ring.

"What's the matter, sweetheart?"

"I wanted you to hear this from me first," Alexis said in a hurry.

"Okay," Josephine said, expecting the worst.

"I told you they didn't need to be in my wedding." Alexis continued to speak rapidly.

"Who? I can barely understand you. Slow down and tell me what happened."

"Brianna and Cherise."

"What about them?"

"They still haven't been measured for their dresses, so I told Violet to order the others."

"But I spoke to Florence the same night we went to the shop and she told me she would make sure they went the next day," Josephine said, confused.

"Aunt Florence shouldn't have to keep reminding grown women about their responsibilities unless she lied to you," she bellowed.

"Alexis, watch your tone with me," Josephine demanded. "You're flying off the handle for no reason."

"Mom, I didn't want them to be in my wedding in the first place," she said, lowering her voice.

"Fine, now they won't. Did Violet say if everyone else has been in?"

"Yes, so now I have six bridesmaids."

"You should be satisfied then."

"I hope nothing else happens."

"There are no promises in life, sweetie. Things happen and you're going to have to learn how to deal with them when they do and stop having a fit," Josephine admonished.

"I'm not having a fit. I just want my wedding to be perfect and not have people telling me lies."

"I thought you hired Ivy Hart to take the stress from you. It sounds to me like you're worrying more now than before," Josephine commented.

"I'm getting married soon, there's a lot to worry about," Alexis said sternly.

"I'm aware of that," Josephine countered, becoming exasperated. "But if you don't pull yourself together, you're going to be in a padded room soon," Josephine warned. "I don't think your cousins intentionally set out to destroy your wedding plans, Alexis. There has to be a good explanation for what happened. I'll call Florence and ask her."

"Don't worry about calling Aunt Florence, Mom. I've made my decision and I'm sticking to it."

"We'll chat later when you've calmed down."

"I'm still not changing my mind," Alexis said, fully riled up.

"Go finish your paper," Josephine said, disconnecting the line.

Alexis clicked off her phone and set it on the counter. She was too rattled to go back to where she'd left off with her paper, so she just stared at the computer screen.

Suddenly, she realized, she'd forgotten to remind her mother about the guest list. But she didn't feel like going back and forth with Josephine just yet.

Alexis sighed wearily. The chaos of the morning had worn her out. She decided to take a nap. Maybe once she got up, she'd feel better and could finally finish her assignment.

The ringing of the telephone startled Alexis out of her sleep. Rolling over, she looked at the clock on her bedside table; it read three o'clock. She couldn't believe she'd slept so long. Throwing the covers back, she swung her legs to the side of the bed, sat there, and waited for the telephone to ring again.

"Hello."

"Were you asleep, baby?"

Alexis pushed her tousled hair off her face. "Taking a nap."

"You've been so busy trying to plan our big day, you haven't taken any time for yourself," Jaeden said with concern.

"Speaking of wedding planning, I had to drop two of my bridesmaids today," Alexis told him.

"Why, what happened?"

"They didn't do what I'd asked them to do, but it was expected."

"It wasn't my cousin Nicole, was it?"

"No, they were my cousins," Alexis said, shaking her head.

"Have you ordered the tuxedos yet?"

"No."

"Aw, Jaeden," Alexis moaned.

"I will, I promise," Jaeden assured her, trying not to upset her further.

"Jaeden, please make sure you do it soon."

"I said I would, baby, stop worrying."

"Well, you don't need two of the guys now, unless you want to use them as ushers."

Jaeden heard the frustration in her voice. "I'll take care of it. Hey, let's go out tonight and forget about all the wedding-planning nonsense. Just have a good time together for a change. We haven't done that in a while." Jaeden hoped she'd agree.

Alexis thought about the work she still had to do. "I don't know. My assignment still isn't finished, so I planned on finishing it today and go over my guest list one more time."

"Why don't I pick up some DVDs and come over later, then?" Jaeden suggested.

"I'll try to have my work done so we can relax together," Alexis promised.

"We both need some downtime. I've never known you to take naps in the middle of the day," Jaeden observed. "There's been a lot of activity in such a short amount of time. I want us to enjoy each other and not have to think about the wedding."

Alexis let out a big breath. "You're right, I need to relax. I'll see you later."

"Any new DVD releases you'd like to see?"

"No, whatever you choose will be fine."

"I can't wait to see you, baby," Jaeden added before hanging up.

Alexis placed the phone back on the base and sat quietly for a moment. She got up and strolled to the kitchen to get a bottle of Arizona Iced Tea so she could get back to work.

As Alexis pulled on the refrigerator door handle, she stopped before opening the door. Her handwritten list stuck out like a sore thumb. She picked it up and a satisfying smile grew on her face as she went through each goal she'd already accomplished.

Suddenly, Alexis didn't have a taste for something cool to drink, but wanted to finish her work. She couldn't wait to draw a line through the last two goals on her list. In order to reach that goal, she'd have to buckle down and focus. No more breaks or interruptions.

Alexis was still trying to complete her paper on "The Principles of Teaching in the Digital Age" when Jaeden arrived. She opened the door for him and went back to her computer. She felt she needed to revise the last two pages.

"Baby, you aren't done yet?" Jaeden asked, looking over her shoulder.

"No, I've been planning the wedding, so I've put it on the back burner. I'm going to finish it tonight," she replied.

"I thought we were going to put everything aside and relax this evening." Jaeden set his packages on the counter. "I brought over some Chinese food so you wouldn't have to cook." He pulled the containers from the plastic bag.

Alexis barely heard a word he'd said she was so engrossed in her paper.

"Baby," Jaeden said, moving closer to her. He hugged her from behind, causing Alexis to lean back against his chest.

He kissed her on the side of her neck. "Why don't you take a break and eat with me?" he suggested, rocking her.

"You go on ahead, I really need to finish this," she said, patting his hand.

"I'm not taking no for an answer," he said, slowly turning down the lid of her laptop.

Alexis lightly pushed him away. "Jaeden, don't, I'm already two assignments behind. I'd like to hand them in on Tuesday," she said, watching Jaeden continue to close the lid.

"You can go back to it later, I promise," Jaeden said, still trying to coax her away from her computer.

Alexis picked up her Palm Pilot before moving over to the sofa.

"Stay there and I'll get everything we need." Jaeden went back to the kitchen to gather plates and glasses. He returned to the living room and set them on the table in front of the television.

He saw Alexis typing on her Palm Pilot and he gently removed the device from her hands.

"Why did you do that?" Alexis asked, watching him lay it on the table.

"Eat your dinner, baby," Jaeden said softly, handing her a plate before picking up his own.

"I know we're supposed to be relaxing, but I want you to hear what I want the wedding invitation to say." She put down her plate, picked up her Palm Pilot and brought up the notes she'd written.

Let this be our destiny
to begin each new day together
to share our lives forever . . .
Mr. and Mrs. Robert Shire
along with
Mr. and Mrs. Donald Jefferson
request the honour of your presence
at the marriage of their children
Alexis Renee
and
Jaeden Leon
on Saturday, the twenty-seventh of August
two thousand and five

                    at four-thirty in the afternoon
                    Pilgrim Branch Church
                    1548 West Tenth Avenue
                    Taylor, Indiana

Alexis smiled after she read the words to him. "Do you like it?" She watched him for a reaction.

"Baby, you know I don't care. Whatever makes you happy," Jaeden said as he bit into his egg roll.

Alexis sighed, then picked up her chopsticks. As she ate, she glanced at Jaeden from the corner of her eye. She was becoming more than annoyed by his "whatever" attitude when it came to the wedding.

After church Sunday, the family met at Jaeden's parents' house for dinner to finally get the guest list in order. Alexis needed to get the list to Ivy the following day.

"I'm going to excuse myself so you all can get to work," Robert said, rising from the dinner table. He patted Josephine on the shoulder before leaving the room.

Donald got up from his seat as well. He turned to Jaeden. "I've already given your mother the few names I wanted to add to the guest list," he said before he followed Robert out of the room.

"I hope you two have taken some of the people off your guest lists because the invitations are going to be ordered tomorrow," Alexis said to Josephine and Gloria.

"Make sure you have both parents' names on the invitation," Josephine reminded Alexis.

"Let me show you what I have written for the wording," Alexis said, handing her mother the sheet of paper she'd printed that morning.

Josephine read the paper and passed it to Gloria. "This is beautiful."

After both women read the document, Alexis prayed they wouldn't want to change the wording. She wanted to move on to the guest list anyway. She gently grabbed the paper from her mother's hand, so she could make sure she was listening. "We're concerned about the number of people we're inviting."

"Are you two still worried about that?" Gloria asked, shaking her head.

"Yes, Mrs. Jefferson, it's a big concern," Alexis said as she retrieved her Palm Pilot to read her notes. "I was thinking maybe we should order more invitations to the ceremony and only enough for the reception to have three hundred guests."

"Alexis, we can't do that!" Josephine shouted. "That's disrespectful." She looked at Gloria. "Don't you agree?"

Gloria's unpleasant expression answered her question. She removed her reading glasses. "Yes, I do. How can we tell people they can come to one and not the other?"

"People do it all the time, Mrs. Jefferson," Alexis said.

"It's disgraceful," Josephine said in disgust.

"I agree with my mother on that," Jaeden said.

Gloria hit the table with her hand. "Well, I'm glad one of you is thinking straight this evening."

Alexis thought she'd stare a hole into Jaeden. "You agree with what?" Alexis all but shouted. She couldn't believe the words were coming from his lips.

"We should cut the list period," Jaeden said.

Everyone looked at him as if he'd grown two heads.

"What?" Jaeden said, hunching his shoulders.

"I don't care what you do," Alexis snapped, her eyes only on Jaeden as she scraped the floor with her chair. In a hurry, she got up. "You guys can figure it out. Here's my list." She tossed the paper on the table. "I'll need a combined one before I leave tonight." She went to the family room.

Robert and Donald were watching television when she appeared in the doorway.

"What's the matter, baby girl?" Robert asked, concerned with the anguish he saw on his daughter's face.

"Nothing," Alexis said quietly as she moved over to the other end of the sofa with her head bowed.

Robert scooted down next to her.

"Something's wrong." He pulled her into his arms. "Since you were a little girl you only act this way if something's wrong," he said, placing his chin on the top of her head.

"I'll give you two some privacy," Donald said, rising from his recliner. "I'm going to find out what this is all about." He walked out of the room.

Robert moved away from Alexis so he could see her face. "It's just the two of us now, so tell me what happened."

Alexis explained to her father the situation with the guest list and the hall.

"If it will help, I'll talk to your mother. I'm sure she'll understand."

"Daddy, I've told Mom over and over again and I'm still not getting through to her. I need to give my guest list to my coordinator so the invitations can be ordered and mailed. I'm going to have to pay extra just to get the invitations overnight."

"Everything will work out, baby girl, you'll see." Robert kissed her forehead. "I think you've got a case of wedding jitters. It's normal for a young woman to get nervous about getting married."

"Maybe you're right." Alexis looked up at her father for confirmation.

"Aren't I always?" Robert said, smiling.

He rose from his seat and held out his hand for her to join him. "Let's go see if we can't resolve this matter."

Alexis was relieved her father understood. She prayed he could get her mother and Gloria to understand why she asked them to cut the list.

The closer Alexis and her father came to the dining room, the louder the voices became.

"This is getting on my last nerves," they heard Gloria say.

"What exactly is bothering you, Gloria?" Robert asked.

"How do we choose who can or can't come to the wedding? It's just too hard," she explained as Robert and Alexis took a seat at the table.

"I have an idea," Robert said, looking at all the papers on the table. "Why don't we eliminate people who have small children?"

"Daddy, it's an adults-only reception. That's not the problem," Alexis said.

"Josie, let me look at our list for a minute," Robert asked, reaching for the yellow-lined paper. He studied several sheets before speaking. "You can cross off Aunt Imogene. We know she's not coming because she's too frail to travel. Uncle Freeman too, he's staying with his daughter Ruby now," he said, scanning the list again. "Cousin Pearlie is in a nursing home. Where did you get these names, Josie?"

"I went through all our address books we had in the kitchen drawer so I wouldn't forget anyone."

"Well, that's three you can take off, so I'm sure we can find more," he said, giving the list back to his wife.

"Donald, look over your list, see if you and Gloria can find people you can remove."

Gloria scanned the pages, then handed them to Donald. Jaeden looked over his father's shoulder as he studied the list carefully. "Mama, I know you weren't inviting Cousin Harry." Jaeden pointed to a line on the paper. "He's a drunk and always wants to fight. I don't want him to ruin our day."

"You shouldn't say such negative things about your kinfolk, and nobody's ruining anything," Gloria replied.

"He's right, Glo," Donald said. "Harry always tries to start an argument when he's tipsy. Remember last month at Jesse's place how he wanted to fight Toot?" He scanned the list again and pointed out several other people they could eliminate too.

"Donald, Harry is still kin," Gloria said in her own defense.

"Alexis, you and Jaeden look over your lists again, too," Robert suggested. "You might be surprised who you can eliminate."

"Instead of sending invitations to all those grown folks at Florence's house, send one," Robert said to Josephine.

"Thank you so much, Daddy, for your help." Alexis kissed her father on the cheek.

Robert glanced at his wife. "How much are we paying that coordinator, Josie? I need a refund for this part of her commission," he said, laughing.

After working another twenty minutes, they had shortened the list tremendously, but Josephine insisted on keeping a few of the names.

"Are you feeling better, baby?" Jaeden asked as he sat down beside Alexis.

She wanted to be angry with him, but found she couldn't. Each time he came close to her, the heat from his body caused her to seek refuge in his arms.

"Yes, I'm fine. I will feel even better when the invitations are in the mail, though." She leaned closer to him. "I still don't think our mothers are too happy about cutting their lists," Alexis whispered so only Jaeden could hear her.

"They'll get over it," Jaeden said, watching their parents going over the names again.

"Why don't we get out of here and go somewhere?"

"Not yet," Gloria said overhearing her son. "Josephine and I wanted to make sure you two don't forget the engagement party."

"I haven't forgotten," Mrs. Jefferson," Alexis said and then took a fleeting look at Jaeden. "He had better not have, either."

"Wouldn't miss it for the world," Jaeden piped in.

CHAPTER FOURTEEN

Alexis's heart overflowed with joy as she and Jaeden stepped inside An Affair to Remember on Friday evening. She held on to his arm as he escorted her to the Signature Ballroom.

At the door, an enlarged version of their engagement invitation had been encased in an antique silver frame that sat on an easel. The richly tailored card had been decorated with flowers and it epitomized elegance. Alexis immediately stopped to read it.

Where love reigns
the impossible
may be attained

Please join us to honor
the engagement of
Alexis Shire
and
Jaeden Jefferson
Friday, July eighth
eight o'clock to eleven o'clock
An Affair to Remember
2565 Castle Drive

Given with love by
their parents

Jaeden embraced her. "Baby, don't cry," he said when he saw her eyes water.

"This is so beautiful," Alexis said as she carefully wiped her tears so that she wouldn't smear her makeup.

"You look gorgeous," Jaeden said, staring at the strapless pink dress she wore. She had pinned her hair up and left an array of curls spilling from the top.

"You don't look so bad yourself," Alexis said.

Jaeden had worn black slacks and dinner jacket with a white shirt and black bow tie.

The crowd immediately applauded when they stepped inside the banquet room. Alexis looked around at the elegant shades of ivory and bone that adorned the round intimate room, and the beautiful chandeliers hanging from the ceiling. There were many windows and from the balcony she could see the twinkle of lights in the faux trees and ivy.

The tables had been decorated with pink organza over white tablecloths. Five-prong candelabras were encircled by unique centerpieces in various colorful spring flowers.

Josephine and Gloria greeted the couple. "You look so beautiful, sweetie," Josephine commented, opening her arms wide.

"Mom, everything is so lovely." She hugged her mother in a warm embrace.

"Nothing's too good for my girl," Josephine said as unshed tears filled her eyes.

"Mrs. Jefferson, you all have done an awesome job," Alexis said as tears slipped down her cheecks. She looked around the room at all the familiar faces.

"How can we thank you, Mama?" Jaeden said as he kissed his mother on the cheek.

"You just did, son, now let's have a good time," Gloria said as she led them farther into the room.

Alexis spotted her father and went to him. "Daddy," she said as she ran into his embrace. "This is so wonderful."

"I told your mother everything would be fine. You women worry too much," Robert said as he held his daughter tightly.

Alexis withdrew and found Jaeden standing next to her.

"Mr. Shire." He held out his hand for his future father-in-law to shake, but Robert hugged him.

Alexis's tears came even faster.

Ivy Hart approached them. "Here's the happy couple. Why don't we take our seats now so we can get started?" she suggested.

Robert and Donald escorted their wives to their table in the front of the room. Ivy led Jaeden and Alexis to the head table.

After they had been seated, Alexis leaned over to Jaeden. "This is so beautiful," she said, looking out at the crowd. "Look." She pointed to the cake nestled in the corner. She pushed her chair back and stood up.

Jaeden caught her hand and waited until she bent to hear him. "I thought they were about to get started," he said.

"Come on, we need to see this now," Alexis said.

Jaeden followed her to a wonderfully decorated table. Striking candles and crystal Eiffel Tower–like vases filled with flowers decked out the table with a large sheet cake that reminded them of a Bible. Alexis's baby photo and name decorated one side and Jaeden's was on the other.

"Oh my God! No, she didn't," Alexis said in disbelief. "I knew they were up to something."

"I guess you didn't hide that photo album so well after all." Jaeden laughed, but turned silent when Alexis stared at him. "Baby, I think you look pretty," Jaeden said, snuggling behind her.

"I can't believe she did that. My mother knows how much I hate those pictures," she insisted.

"You were such a pretty girl and now look how you've grown into an even more stunning woman," Jaeden complimented her as she turned to face him.

"You really think so?" Alexis asked him naively.

"I know so," Jaeden said before capturing her lips in a sensual kiss.

They were so caught up in each other, they hadn't noticed that the photographer and some of their guests had surrounded them, until they released each other.

Alexis turned quickly toward the cake so no one could see her blushing.

"Sweetie, I couldn't resist," Josephine said from behind Alexis. She nodded toward the cake.

"It's lovely, Mom," Alexis said honestly.

"I'm glad you're pleased, Alexis, it was my idea," Gloria said. "Josie told me you didn't like your baby pictures."

"I didn't, but this is unique." Alexis squeezed her mother's hand affectionately.

"Come on, baby," Jaeden said, leading Alexis back to their table. After they were seated, Alexis looked down at her plate and saw a sugar cookie made in the shape of a miniature wedding cake and iced in their wedding colors. It had their initials and wedding date on it as well. The treat had been placed inside a clear cellophane bag and tied with a silver bow.

She brought it to Jaeden's attention, pointing to the one in his plate. "Wow, this is more than I ever could have asked for," she said to him.

Jaeden leaned closer to her and said, "All I've ever wanted was you," before he kissed her softly on the lips.

Alexis began to tear up again. "If I keep this up, I won't have a lick of makeup on," she said, brushing the tears from her face.

When the room quieted, Robert and Donald started the evening with a toast to the couple. After they finished, Jaeden suddenly stood and Alexis didn't know what would happen next. His father handed him the microphone.

"I'd like to make a presentation to my beautiful fiancée," Jaeden said, watching Alexis's surprised expression.

She nervously stood to join him.

Gloria handed Jaeden a small package. "This is just a small token of my love for you. I can't tell you in words how happy I am that you agreed to spend the rest of your life with me," Jaeden said before giving the box to Alexis.

Her hands shook as she slipped the white bow from the package. Finally opening it, she found another charm for her bracelet. This time it was her initial.

She pulled Jaeden to her and whispered in his ear, "You don't have to keep giving me gifts, baby," she said, lightly touching his face with her palm.

"You deserve it." Jaeden placed a kiss on her lips after everyone started lightly tapping their glasses with their silverware.

Jaeden gave Alexis the microphone, but she was so emotional she couldn't speak at first. "We would like to thank all of you for being here this evening to share in this special moment in our lives." She felt herself wanting to cry, but willed herself to keep going. "To our parents, for always being the wind beneath our wings," she managed to say and then she took a deep breath. "I'd better stop now before I get too weepy."

Everyone laughed.

"Enjoy your evening. Thanks again." She handed the microphone to Ivy and took her seat as she became overwhelmed with emotion.

Food stations were situated in different locations

throughout the room. They were decorated with floral displays and unique serving pieces for an eye-catching effect.

One chef carved a roast, and one made chicken crepes. Ice-carved boats filled with jumbo shrimp and crab legs had their own space. There was even a beverage station where guests could design their own drinks. Beautiful displays of cheeses with bread and fresh fruits were featured in baskets.

After Alexis got herself together, she and Jaeden left their table to walk around the room and greet their guests.

"Lexie," Stephanie called out.

Alexis was standing by the cake table talking to one of Jaeden's cousins. She turned to find her best friend standing beside a very tall man whose coloring reminded Alexis of Hershey's chocolate.

She hugged Stephanie and their eyes began to fill with tears. "I've never cried this much in my life," Alexis said, blinking back her tears.

"At least they're happy tears," Stephanie said, wiping the lone tear that spilled down Alexis's cheek.

"I'd like you to meet Charles Ervin," Stephanie said, giving Alexis a deliberate stare.

"Chucky?" Alexis raised an eyebrow in disbelief.

"Yes," Stephanie confirmed, ignoring the smirk on Alexis's face.

Alexis extended her hand. "Nice to finally meet you." She had thought Chucky was a figment of Stephanie's imagination and never predicted he'd look like the tall dapper gentleman standing before her.

"Congratulations on your engagement," Charles's voice boomed.

"Thank you very much." Alexis turned to Stephanie. "I didn't see you when we came in."

Stephanie could barely meet Alexis's gaze. "I—I know, w-we just got here," she stammered out.

"I'll find us a table and you two can talk," Charles said, planting a kiss on Stephanie's lips. "It was great meeting you, Alexis," he said before walking off.

Alexis leaned closer to Stephanie. "Where have you been hiding him?" she whispered.

"A girl can't give away all of her secrets," Stephanie said. "I've got to keep some things to myself." Stephanie followed Charles's retreating back with her eyes.

"When I turned and saw him standing next to you, all I could think about was chocolate," Alexis said with a laugh.

Stephanie shook her finger at Alexis. "You're getting married in less than eight weeks, you better keep your eyes off my man, girl," she teased.

"Your *man*, huh?" Alexis began. "I thought you were only friends."

"Shut up, Lexie," Stephanie said, turning her attention to the cake that sat on a table near Alexis.

"Maybe Jaeden and I will host an engagement party for you and Chucky in the near future," Alexis whispered in Stephanie's ear.

"Not." Stephanie held up her hand. "Chucky's a great guy, but marrying him? I don't think so."

"We'll just have to see about that," Alexis said, strolling away.

"Oh, no, you don't, missy," Stephanie said, catching Alexis by the hand before she got too far. "No matchmaking, Lexie."

"I'm not like you, dear." Alexis winked as she walked off, leaving Stephanie standing alone.

Alexis saw Jaeden coming toward her.

"Come with me, baby," he said, redirecting her path to the middle of the parquet-tiled dance floor.

"Please, no more surprises, I don't think my heart

can take any more," Alexis said, laying her head against his shoulder.

"I requested the deejay to play a song for us."

Alexis gave him a puzzled look.

Jaeden pulled her close. "I just need to feel you in my arms," he whispered in her ear.

Alexis nestled against him when the music began and the words of "We Both Deserve Each Other's Love," an old-school classic by LTD, resonated in the air.

"Listen to the words of this song, Alexis. I believe this with every fiber of my being." Jaeden kissed the tip of her earlobe before snuggling against her neck.

The feel of his breath against the side of her face made the hairs on the back of her neck stand up. She lay her head against Jaeden's shoulder and sighed dreamily.

By the second verse, there were more couples on the floor, including the parents of the bride and groom-to-be. Alexis glanced to her left and saw Stephanie in Charles's arms on the dance floor as well.

"What are you thinking about?" Jaeden asked, bringing Alexis's attention back to him.

"I don't want this night to end," she said before readjusting her arms around his neck.

"We will have many more great evenings like this, I promise," he said before giving her a long kiss.

CHAPTER FIFTEEN

"Why didn't your mother and Aunt Glo come with us?" Stephanie asked as Alexis drove down Seventy-first Avenue toward Hearts and Flowers. "They've been like your shadows this whole time."

"I didn't want to hear their comments if there was something they didn't like, so I didn't tell them about the fitting. I need peace," Alexis said with her eyes on the road.

"I've heard some horror stories, Lexie, so let's pray you'll have it," Stephanie said as Alexis drove through the gates of the mansion.

"Oh no," Alexis exclaimed, pulling into the nearest parking space.

"What is it?"

"We haven't applied for our marriage license," Alexis said in horror. She immediately pulled everything out of her purse until she found her Palm Pilot.

"I'm losing it. It totally slipped my mind," she said, retrieving her calendar. "I don't even have a note on the calendar."

"Don't panic," Stephanie warned.

"I don't know, maybe Ivy can tell me how long it takes," Alexis said, stuffing her belongings back into her purse. "I'm ready now." She got out of the car.

As they climbed the stairs, Alexis kept thinking how

disappointed she was in herself for not keeping her priorities straight.

She was relieved to find Ivy in the bridal salon talking to Violet.

"Ladies, how are you today?" Ivy asked when the two women entered.

"Can you tell me how long before the wedding we have to apply for a marriage license?" Alexis asked in a hurry.

"Typically a month before the ceremony," Ivy said, looking curiously at Alexis. "Don't panic, you have time."

"What do we need to do?"

"Both of you have to go to the county courthouse to apply. Take your birth certificate and any other form of identification showing your current address and date of birth."

"How long does it take to get it after we apply?" Alexis asked, making notes in her Palm Pilot.

"There is a fee of eighteen dollars to be paid in cash and you usually get the license the same day. It's good for up to sixty days after it's issued," Ivy informed her.

"Excuse me for a minute, I'm going to call Jaeden so we can get down there as soon as possible." Alexis strolled out of the room.

She dialed his number, but got his voice mail. Frustrated, she turned the phone off and dropped it in her drawstring bag.

"What did he say when you told him?" Stephanie asked when Alexis returned to the room.

"Voice mail, a-gain," Alexis replied. "I always get his voice mail," she mumbled.

"Are you ready to try on that gorgeous dress of yours?" Stephanie asked in an attempt to get Alexis's mind focused on a happier subject.

"The bridesmaids' dresses came in on Tuesday and

the flower girls' dresses came in on Thursday," Violet said, walking toward the dressing room.

"Excellent," Alexis said thankfully. "At least something's going right."

She followed Violet to the dressing room where her dress and shoes were waiting. Quickly, she put them on.

Alexis heard a loud gasp when she stepped out into the room.

"What's the matter?" Alexis asked Stephanie in a panic, looking down at her gown.

Stephanie covered her mouth with her hands. "You are so gorgeous," she said, following Alexis to the mirror.

"Stef, don't start. You know I'll cry if you look at me hard," Alexis said as she moved closer to the triple mirrors. She studied the woman she saw looking back at her and for a few moments she couldn't say anything.

"Alexis, you look stunning," Ivy and Violet said together.

Violet wrapped a magnetic straight pin holder on her arm. "I'm so glad we ordered the size six instead of the eight. There are only minor alterations needed on this one," she said as she began to adjust the hem of the garment.

The receptionist buzzed and told Ivy another client had arrived. "I've got to run, but I'm so happy everything is working out for you," she said to Alexis before she left.

Alexis turned her attention back to the mirror. "Awesome," she said to the mirrors. "This *is* beautiful." She continued to study herself in the mirror. "I wish my mom had come."

"Bring her with you for the next fitting," Violet said, sticking a straight pin in the material she'd just folded under Alexis's arm.

"Stef, look at my shoes," Alexis said, kicking one foot out from under the hem of the gown.

"Don't move, Alexis." You wouldn't want an uneven hem," Violet said as she measured it and placed several pins in the fabric.

"Lexie, I'm lovin' the shoes, girl," Stephanie said, getting a closer look.

"There." Violet pulled the hem down in the front to make sure it was even. "How does it feel, Alexis?" she asked as she raised herself up off her knees.

"It feels snug under the arms," Alexis replied.

"Strapless gowns are supposed to be snug so everything can stay in place," Violet said knowingly. "It's not too uncomfortable?"

"No, it feels okay."

"Good, I want to show you the headpiece I've created for you." Violet walked slowly around to the front of the dress, brushing the gown as she went to retrieve the veil.

She returned to Alexis with one open rose and an orchid intertwined on a comb. The hairpiece complemented the dress perfectly.

"How had you planned to wear your hair for the wedding?" she asked Alexis.

"I think Jaeden likes my hair down, so I guess I'm going to wear it like I have it now," she replied.

"I think you should wear it with lots of curls," Stephanie advised.

Violet held the custom-made piece in front of Alexis so she could get a good look at it. "Before you say no, I want you to see it in your hair," she said, reaching to put it in place.

She slipped the comb in on the left side of Alexis's hair. "Wait, let me go and get the veil so we can see the ensemble together." Violet swiftly walked to the display case and returned with the veil.

Putting it in place on Alexis's head, Violet stepped back to give her client a full view of the mirror.

Stephanie stood next to Alexis, admiring the ensemble. "It's different, Lexie," she said. "But I like it."

"Do you really?" Alexis studied the overall look. "Or do you think I should wear a tiara like my mother wanted?"

"You should only wear what you are comfortable with," Violet interjected.

"I like it, too," Alexis said, staring in the mirror. She smiled. "Can I have a smaller version made for my flower girls?"

"I wouldn't make it exactly like yours, but we can make a little something for them."

"Great. Stef, try on your dress on so I can see how it looks next to mine," Alexis said anxiously.

Stephanie followed Violet to the dressing room, leaving Alexis alone with her thoughts.

As she stood in front of the mirror it dawned on her that she was really getting married. Butterflies began to rumble in her stomach. In a month she'd become somebody's wife. Could she handle it? Would she be a good wife? Would things change between her and Jaeden? Alexis had a lot of questions and no real answers.

The swooshing sound of the dressing room door opening caused her to turn.

Alexis's eyes immediately filled with tears as Stephanie stepped out in her flowing rose-pink gown. She wondered if the tears came because she was overwhelmed by the beauty of the gowns or was it because she was scared to death to get married?

"Girl, this dress is major," Stephanie said, making her way to the mirror. "I can't wait to see myself." She settled on the stand next to Alexis.

"Alexis, you are going to have a beautiful wedding, dear," Violet commented as she began to adjust Stephanie's gown.

"Thanks to you and your sisters," Alexis retorted.

"Oh yeah, look at *my* shoes with this dress, girl," Stephanie said, sticking her foot out as she mimicked Alexis.

"You can't move, dear, I don't want to stick you," Violet told Stephanie as she tried to put the last straight pin the material.

"Sorry, Vi," Stephanie said, snickering.

"Violet, are you going to help me get out of this dress without me getting stuck by the pins?" Alexis asked.

"I'll help you both when you're ready."

"We're ready," Alexis said, dragging her best friend from in front of the mirror.

After they changed their clothes they were ready to leave the bridal mansion.

"Thanks so much for everything, Violet, I love my dress." Alexis hugged her.

"I'm going to look better than the bride," Stephanie teased, embracing Violet as well.

"I don't think so, girlfriend," Alexis snapped playfully.

"Both gowns should be ready for a final fitting a week or two before the wedding," Violet informed them.

Alexis pulled out her checkbook, remembering that Violet needed to be paid for the dresses.

Violet motioned for her to put it away. "Your mother came in last week and paid the balance. By the way, I didn't charge you for the headpiece."

Alexis hugged her again. "Thanks so much," she told her before she and Stephanie left the building. In the parking lot, Alexis pulled her cell phone out and turned it on so she could call her mother and thank her for paying. As she was about to dial, the phone rang. Alexis looked at the caller ID and rolled her eyes.

"Yes?" she said casually into the phone after pushing the Accept button.

"Hey, baby, where are you?" Jaeden asked.

"I'm leaving the bridal salon. Why haven't you been answering your phone?" Alexis snapped.

"You've been trying to reach me?" Jaeden's voice was filled with innocence.

"Uh, yeah."

"I was tied up."

"Obviously," she spat.

Jaeden heard the aggravation in her voice. "What happened this time?" he sighed.

"We haven't applied for a marriage license."

"When does it have to be done?" he inquired evenly. He knew if he panicked Alexis would too.

"As soon as possible." Alexis thought if she didn't tell him it was urgent, it would never get done.

"I can't go this afternoon, I've got a meeting with my staff," Jaeden said, checking his watch. "I don't think the county office is open on Saturday. That is where we have to go, right?"

"Then let's go first thing Monday morning."

"I'm meeting Arnold Monday at nine o'clock."

Alexis counted to ten, willing herself not to go off on her future husband.

"Alexis, baby, are you still there?" Jaeden said after a long pause.

"I'm here. Why don't you look at your calendar and tell me when you can pencil me in then, Jaeden?" Alexis said, her voice rising.

"Tuesday morning is good. I'll pick you up and we can have breakfast afterward."

"You sure it won't interfere with your meetings?" she asked sarcastically.

"Alexis, what I'm working on is going to pay off for us both, I know it will." After another long pause, Jaeden said, "Look, baby, I've got to run to a meeting. I love you." He disconnected the call.

Alexis turned and looked at Stephanie with one hand on her hip, and holding the phone away from her body.

"I know what you're going to say already," Stephanie began. "But in Jaeden's defense, most men aren't as involved in planning a wedding as the woman is," Stephanie tried to explain to her.

"Whatever, I need to call my mother." Alexis hit a button on her cell phone. She didn't want to talk about Jaeden anymore.

CHAPTER SIXTEEN

For the next couple of weeks, Alexis's life went into fast-forward. She and Jaeden had picked up their marriage license and the responses from the guests had started pouring in.

Alexis, Josephine, and Gloria sat at the dining room table, which had become a conference room of sorts since they began planning the wedding, to compile a list of the responses.

Alexis pulled out all the reply cards they'd received from a shoe box her mother had been keeping them in. "Looks like everyone said yes," she joked as she turned on her laptop.

"I've been getting lots of compliments on the invitations," Josephine said.

"Me too," Gloria added. "My brother asked if he should wear a tuxedo to the wedding after receiving his."

"I hope you told him he had to dress up," Alexis said, distributing the cards between the other two women. "Mom, why don't you take this pile and Mrs. Jefferson can take one, while I type? I think we can get this done much faster." Alexis ignored the scowl her mother gave because of her comment to Gloria.

While she set up her document on the computer, Gloria and Josephine started opening the envelopes. As they took the cards out and stacked them up, they started to see problems.

"Uh-oh," Gloria said, staring at one of the guests' response.

Alexis looked up from her computer screen. "What's wrong?"

"Helen Murphy responded with six people as her guests."

"Who is she?" Josephine asked calmly.

"She used to live next door to us over twenty years ago. She's known Jaeden since he was a boy."

"I don't care who she is, we can't allow all six of those people to come to the reception," Alexis said harshly before she'd realized it slipped out.

Both Gloria and Josephine glared at her, but neither said a word. They knew Alexis was under tremendous pressure because usually she was very polite.

"Please, put that one aside until we can figure out what to do with it," Alexis then said calmly.

The women nodded and continued with their tasks.

"Here's another one," Josephine said, lifting the small card in the air. "Brenda Hill replied seven."

"Mom, this is ridiculous. Mrs. Hill only has one daughter. She must have included Gwen and her five kids. Didn't she read where it said *adult reception*?" Alexis's voice rose an octave.

Josephine reached over and patted her hand.

"Don't get excited, Alexis. I'll call Brenda and remind her that the only children allowed are those in the wedding party."

"Looks like I have a new headache," Alexis muttered as she went back to her spreadsheet.

As they continued to compile the list, they came across several other reply cards that had an excessive number of guests wanting to attend the reception.

"Alexis, I don't have the heart to tell these people they can't come. Some of these people we've known since before you were born," Josephine said when Alexis insisted they couldn't come.

"Give me their numbers, *I'll* tell them," Alexis replied.

"Umph, umph, umph," Josephine said, shaking her head.

"Mom, you and Mrs. Jefferson may not have a choice, because seating at the hall is limited. Where are we going to put these people? They can come to the ceremony, but after that I don't know what to tell you," Alexis said, quickly running out of patience.

Gloria dropped the paper in her hand on the table. "We're not starting that again," she snapped.

Alexis looked at her watch, ignoring Gloria. "It's time to go to my fitting. We need to be there by one o'clock, so I'd like to get going. We can finish this when we return."

Alexis drove to Hearts and Flowers, anxious for the mothers to see her in her wedding gown.

Once they were inside the mansion, Violet took Alexis to change while Josephine and Gloria waited. Tears came to both of their eyes when Alexis came out of the dressing room wearing her wedding ensemble and custom headpiece.

"Violet, it's lovely," Josephine said, moving toward her daughter so she could get a closer look.

"Mom, you really like it?"

"I love it, sweetie. It's not what I envisioned for you at first, but it's a close second, don't you agree, Gloria?"

Alexis looked up to the ceiling. She just couldn't win.

"My son is a lucky man," Gloria said. "You are a beautiful bride, Alexis."

"Look at my shoes, they are so gorgeous with the

dress." She stuck a foot out so they could see the way her shoes sparkled.

"Thanks again, Mom, for paying for them." Alexis bent to kiss her mother.

"You should be thanking your father," Josephine said. "Those shoes were expensive." She waved her hand and shook her head.

"Alexis, I think everything is in order. There's no need for further alterations," Violet said, brushing the skirt of the wedding gown.

"I'm satisfied," Alexis replied, looking at her reflection in the mirror.

"Mrs. Shire, are you pleased with everything?" Violet asked.

"Perfect."

"I'll have the dress steamed and delivered on the day of the wedding then."

"Thank you so much," Alexis said to Violet.

"You're quite welcome. Now, I want to get you out of this and update you on the rest of your party," Violet said, assisting Alexis off the step.

After Alexis was dressed, Violet went to put the dress away. The three women waited for her to return.

"I almost forgot. You still have two bridesmaids who haven't come for their initial fitting," Violet said entering the room.

"Who?" Alexis's voice was so loud, it carried.

"Kendra Mitchell and Tiffany Ross. I've left several detailed messages for them and I haven't received a return phone call."

"I'll contact them," Alexis said, disgusted.

"And today, I received a phone call from Nicole Johnson saying she can't participate."

"What!" Alexis screamed. "Why?" She began to walk

back and forth. "I'm getting married next Saturday. Why would she bail out on me now?"

"Did something happen to the young woman?" Josephine asked.

"Why would Nicole do such a thing?" Gloria said with disappointment. "She didn't mention a word to me when I spoke to her last weekend. Did she give you a reason?"

"She's pregnant," Violet said, surprised the young woman hadn't told Gloria.

"Pregnant?" Gloria exclaimed.

Violet raised her shoulders. "That's what she told me earlier today. I'm sorry, but you'll need to pay the remaining balance on her dress or find a replacement."

Alexis dropped into the nearest chair. "This is a nightmare. I can't believe this is happening to me," she mumbled, holding her head in her hands.

"Well, I'll be," Gloria said. "No wonder every time I saw her she had on one of those big tops. I just assumed it was the way young folks wore their clothes nowadays."

Alexis jumped up from the chair. "I'll get a replacement, Violet."

"This type of thing happens all the time, Alexis, so don't let it get you down." Violet patted Alexis's back to console her. "I'm confident you'll find someone to take Nicole's place," Violet assured her. "Please, don't forget to have Kendra and Tiffany call me as soon as they can."

"I won't," Alexis said, moving swiftly toward the door. She waited for her mother and Gloria to join her.

Alexis was shocked, angry, and disappointed that so many people had let her down.

When they got into the car, Alexis pulled out her cell phone and called Nicole.

"Why didn't you tell me you were pregnant?" Alexis shouted when Nicole answered.

After she gave no response, Alexis's anger increased.

"How far along are you and why didn't you say something before we ordered the dresses?" she demanded.

Alexis paused for a few seconds to try to get a hold of herself. She knew she was acting out of character and could feel a major headache coming on.

All of a sudden she didn't hear anything, no static, no interference, nothing. She looked at her screen and saw the call had dropped.

"No, that heifer didn't hang up on me," Alexis yelled.

"Alexis!" Josephine called her name sternly as she snatched the cell phone from her hand. "Pull yourself together. If I've told you once, I've told you a million times, things happen. Okay, the girl didn't tell you she was pregnant. Find a replacement and move on. You're going to give yourself a nervous breakdown or worse."

Alexis rolled her eyes.

"How will you be able to enjoy your wedding day if you're on medication, crazy as a loon?" she added.

Gloria rubbed Alexis's shoulders from the backseat. "Honey, your mother's right. I'm sorry Nicole did this to you, but you're getting married next weekend, so we've got to concentrate on finding a replacement. If it makes you feel any better, I'll pay for the dress."

Josephine patted her shoulder. "Not to worry, we'll help you find someone, sweetie."

"I think you two have helped me enough," Alexis replied, snatching her cell phone back from her mother.

Josephine pointed her forefinger at her daughter. "We're going to let that one slide because you're upset."

They sat in the car silent for a while before Josephine spoke again. "Why don't we get a bite to eat?" she suggested.

"I could use a little something myself," Gloria said.

Alexis exhaled loudly and started the engine. "Okay,

there's an Applebee's on the way back to your place, Mom."

By the time Alexis pulled into the restaurant parking lot, she felt drained.

When the hostess seated them, Alexis pulled out her Palm Pilot, searching for Kendra's and Tiffany's phone numbers.

"I guess nobody's where they're supposed to be today," she said after getting voice mails for both of them.

She dialed again and left a message for Kendra and now she was about to leave one for Tiffany. "This is Alexis. Please contact Violet Hart *today* about your dress for my wedding. If you don't want to be in the wedding, I need to know *today!*" she said before ending the call.

"Alexis, that wasn't nice to leave that kind of message on someone's phone," Josephine admonished after her daughter hung up.

Alexis studied her mother's unpleasant expression. "What they're doing to me a week before my wedding isn't nice either," she snapped. "At least I didn't lie. One person has already dropped out. If I need to replace more I would like to know now."

"Do me a favor, sweetie, put the wedding planning aside for about an hour to give yourself some time to get your emotions in order," Josephine suggested sweetly. She was seeing the worst in her usually pleasant daughter and knew Alexis was close to her breaking point.

Gloria put her menu down on the table. "I've heard wedding planning is chaotic, but I never thought this one would end up this way."

Alexis stared silently at the two women. It was as if they had no idea of the role they'd played in bringing her to this level of anger. She had always had her life in order and had always been slow to get upset. She laid her electronic device down, pushing it aside and out of the way as she picked up her menu.

"That's my girl. I think you'll feel better after you've eaten something," Josephine said, glancing over the entrées.

They placed their orders and tried to talk about something other than the wedding.

The three women ate in silence. Before they could settle the bill, Jaeden called Alexis's cell phone.

"It's about time you called," Alexis said, reaching for her wallet to pay the tab.

Gloria stayed her hand. "Go ahead, we'll take care of it," she said, pulling several bills from her handbag.

"I called you earlier," Alexis shouted into the phone as she swiftly moved through the restaurant and out the door.

Josephine and Gloria rushed out to the car after paying the bill. As they approached, they found Alexis sitting in the driver's seat staring out the window.

Josephine sat in the front passenger seat and Gloria sat in the back behind Alexis.

"What did he say, sweetie?" Josephine asked as she placed her pocketbook on the floor.

Alexis turned to her mother and broke down in tears. "He doesn't care, Mom," she cried. "Every problem we've faced, I've had to fix by myself."

"Aw, sweetheart, he cares," her mother said, trying to pull Alexis as close to her as she possibly could with the console between them.

"Alexis, honey, Jaeden loves you. He's just trying to get his business straight so he can take care of you after you're married."

"I don't need him to take care of me," Alexis wailed. "I can do that myself." She spoke in anguish. "I need him to take some of the responsibility for this wedding. He hasn't done anything. Yeah, he physically attended a couple meetings, but his mind was always someplace else."

Alexis cried harder.

Josephine got out and went to Alexis's side of the car and opened the door. "You're in no shape to drive, so let me."

Alexis stared at her mother for a few moments, then slid from under the steering wheel and walked around to the passenger side. Josephine took her place, secured her seat belt, and started the engine.

Alexis continued to cry the entire way back to her mother's house.

"I hope you feel better, honey," Gloria said to Alexis as she stepped out of the car when they reached their destination. "Josie, I'll call you later once I talk to my sister about Nicole," she said, hugging her.

Alexis embraced Gloria and watched as she got into her car and drove away.

"Mom, I'm going to lie down in my old room for a while, if that's okay."

"Of course it is, sweetie," Josephine said with concern as she followed her daughter into the house.

Alexis headed up the stairs and down the hall to the last room.

Leaning on the door for strength, she placed her hand on the knob and took a deep breath before gradually opening it. Her eyes scanned the room she'd spent every night in growing up.

Walking over to her grandmother's antique rocking chair, Alexis pulled an old quilt from it and carried it to the bed. As she lay across the bed covering herself, so many thoughts swarmed in Alexis's head, it started to throb.

She covered her eyes with her arms, hoping doing so would help keep all her mixed-up thoughts away, but it didn't. Pressure and problems had been building for quite some time now. Alexis didn't want to think about Jaeden, but she couldn't concentrate on anyone or anything else.

She lay quietly for a while before finally falling asleep.

Twenty minutes later, Alexis's eyes fluttered open and she found Jaeden sitting in the old rocking chair next to the bed.

"I didn't want to wake you," he said softly seeing she was awake.

Alexis closed her eyes and turned her back to him.

Jaeden slid to the edge of the chair. "Baby, I'm sorry if I upset you earlier. There's a lot going on at work," he said.

Alexis turned to face him quickly. "Have you found someone to replace your cousin?"

"I haven't had a cha—"

"Then why are you still here?" Alexis asked harshly, cutting him off.

Jaeden sighed. "I came straight here after you disconnected us earlier," he tried to explain.

Alexis pulled herself up to a sitting position. "Why can't you help me with this one thing? You haven't done anything else for this wedding," she yelled.

"You don't have to raise your voice," Jaeden said calmly.

Alexis's face contorted. "I bet if I were Arnold Herswick, you would've jumped through hoops when I asked you to do something," she spat.

"That's not fair."

Alexis flew off the bed. "*Fair?* Let's talk about what's not fair. I've taken all the smart remarks and listened to both our mothers bicker, complain, and worry me to death. It wasn't fair I had to do it alone. You didn't think about fairness then, so I think it's time you share in the anxiety."

Jaeden leaped up so fast, the chair was still rocking. He pushed his hands into his pockets and walked toward her.

Alexis moved away. "All I asked you to do is find someone to replace Nicole. She's *your* cousin and should easily be replaced, since you have so many people in your family." She went back over to the bed and dropped down.

Jaeden paced back and forth without looking at Alexis. Finally, he turned toward her. "Alexis, has it ever crossed your mind that I'm working hard to make a good life for us?" He stopped and exhaled before moving over to her. He tried to put his hand on her thigh, but Alexis moved swiftly over to the rocker.

Jaeden gave her an intense stare before he spoke again. "Alexis, do you want to know what the real problem is?"

Alexis tilted her head to the side and glared at him. "I'm waiting," she said when he didn't continue.

Jaeden shoved his hands in his pockets. "You're always trying to run everything," he said, his voice grew louder. He began pacing again. "If things aren't done the way you think they should, it's wrong. You can't control every little thing that happens!"

"I do not try to control everything! Don't get mad at me because I don't like disorder and chaos," Alexis hollered back. Suddenly, she got up from the chair and walked over to the window. "Maybe things happened too fast between us and we really don't know each other well enough to get married."

Jaeden moved his head from side to side and exhaled loudly. "See what I'm talking about, Alexis? Just because we're having a disagreement doesn't mean we weren't meant to be together." Jaeden went to her.

"Think about what you're saying, baby. We both said things we didn't mean."

"I meant every word I just said." Alexis's voice increased in volume.

"The stress of the wedding has taken a toll on you. I think you need to go to the spa or something to try to relax, relieve some of this stress," Jaeden advised as calmly as he could.

Alexis threw back her head and laughed, then turned to him. "I've asked you to help me a million times so I wouldn't be stressed, but you didn't, and now *you* want to tell *me* how to relieve stress?" She moved back over to the bed. Jaeden followed her and sat down with her.

Alexis moved back to the rocker. They sat staring at each other for a while. "I think I've found a solution," she said finally.

Jaeden had relaxed, so he scooted to the edge of the bed. "Good, let's hear it."

Alexis tugged at her finger. "I know just how I can get rid of all the problems and stress I've been experiencing for the past four months."

Jaeden looked horrified. "What are you doing?" he asked, fearing the absolute worst.

"I'm relieving stress." Alexis continued to pull at the ring until she got it free. She tossed it in his lap and then sighed contently. "Now, that was a real stress reliever," she said, getting up from the chair once again.

Jaeden picked up the ring and held it in his hands. "The wedding's next Saturday, Alexis!" he pleaded.

Alexis crossed her arms under her bosom. "Can't have a wedding without a bride."

Jaeden couldn't believe what she was saying. "W-what? Alexis wait."

"The wedding's off," she yelled. "Get out of here." She

pointed to the door, wanting him to leave before her tears began to fall.

Jaeden didn't move. He just stared at her with his mouth hanging open.

When Alexis saw he wasn't going to leave, she decided she would. She slipped her feet into her sandals and ran down the stairs to the kitchen where her parents were sitting at the table.

"The wedding's off," Alexis cried from the bottom of the stairwell.

Robert rose from his seat and went to her. "Why?" he asked, pulling her into his arms as his eyes collided with Jaeden, who was standing at the top of the stairs.

Alexis turned around and glanced at Jaeden before breaking free from her father. She ran out of the house and jumped into her car.

Jaeden followed her, but it was too late. She sped away from the curb with Jaeden chasing after her car.

CHAPTER SEVENTEEN

Jaeden's heart plummeted as he stood in the middle of the street watching Alexis's car move farther and farther away until it was completely out of sight.

Robert and Josephine stood nearby encouraging him to come back into the house.

"I'm going to go after her," he said, pulling his keys from his pocket.

"It's not a good idea right now. Let her settle down and think things through," Robert said, patting him on the back.

"She'll come around, Jaeden, I just know it," Josephine said with tears in her eyes.

Jaeden rubbed his hand over his closely cropped hair and looked one last time up the empty street. "I'll be at my parents' house. If she calls, please tell her that I love her," he said before he climbed into his SUV.

"Mama," Jaeden yelled as he marched through the house. "Mama!"

"What is all the commotion about?" Gloria asked as she got up from her spot on the sofa.

Jaeden stormed into the family room sooner than she could get to her feet.

"What is your problem?" Gloria looked up at her distraught son.

"She called the wedding off!" Jaeden yelled, walking back and forth with his hands in his pockets.

"What do you mean she called the wedding off?"

"Do you need me to spell it out for you?" Jaeden's voice roared.

Gloria held her hand up to stop him. "Now, wait just one minute, young man, I know you're upset and you have a right to be, but remember who you're talking to," she said in a stern voice.

Jaeden pulled the engagement ring from his pocket and handed it to his mother. "She gave it back to me," he said as he dropped down on the sofa.

Gloria moved closer to him and sighed deeply. This was a delicate situation that had to be handled with care. "Why don't we talk about the reason Alexis gave for calling the wedding off?" she said softly.

"There is no valid reason why she had to call off the wedding, *if* she loves me like she claims," he said, his voice cracking for the first time.

Gloria turned her body toward him and picked up her son's hand. "Yes, there are several reasons why she had the right to call off the wedding. You two just met in April. You fell in love and you asked her to marry you a month or so later." Gloria pointed to his chest.

"What difference does it make when we met? I love her and I thought she loved me too."

"You told her you didn't want a long engagement, which meant she had to pull together the wedding of her dreams in less than three months. The girl is overwhelmed and every time she thinks she can count on you to help her, you're not there."

"But—" Jaeden started.

"I know you can't help it because this business deal is something you've always dreamed about," she said.

"But—" Jaeden began again.

"Wait, now, let me finish." Gloria held her hand up. "I'm not saying you're wrong for doing that. All I'm saying is you both have the best intentions, but you have to put every aspect of your life in perspective. The Bible says 'he that finds a wife, finds a good thing and obtains favor from the Lord.'

"You've found a good thing in Alexis, now don't you think the Lord would grant you favor to get the business deal done? Think about it." Gloria patted his knee.

Jaeden stared at his mother. "I never looked at the situation like that before."

"I know," Gloria said, smiling.

He sat silently for a couple more minutes. "I guess you're right. I've been so busy that I've neglected the most precious person in my life."

"That's right," Gloria said, squeezing his knee again. "You need to straighten this out with Alexis because your father and I would like to rock a grandbaby or two in our arms before we're too old." Gloria laughed, getting up from her seat.

"Mama," Jaeden called.

Gloria turned. "Yeah, son?"

Jaeden stood and hugged her. "Thanks for everything."

"You two belong together," Gloria said with a tear in her eye. She pulled back from him. "Now, you're going to have to wait until tomorrow when she's had some time to be alone. I just hope she's not like I used to be, because I made your father wait a whole week before I'd talk to him after we had an argument."

"I don't have that long and I'm sure there are still things that have to be done for the wedding."

"Well, I guess you've got your work cut out for you, then."

"I'll talk to you later, Mama," Jaeden said before he left.

Gloria picked up her purse and keys; she'd decided to pay Josephine a little visit.

Gloria barged through the open door of Josephine's house. "We need to talk."

Josephine closed the door behind her and led her into the living room. They settled on the beige sofa. "How's Jaeden?"

"Confused. I had to really talk to him so he could see where Alexis was coming from. The funny thing was as I shared with him the things he'd been doing wrong, I thought about how miserably we failed them both."

Josephine's eyes bugged. "I've supported my child from the very beginning. We paid for the coordinator, her gown, and half the wedding reception, so I don't understand what you mean," she said defensively.

"Yes, I agree we've both been there monetarily, but every decision Alexis made, you disagreed with it."

Josephine pointed to herself. "Me? You were the one giving those kids hell about the church and the guest list," she said.

"That was both of us, Josie, and you know it."

Josephine exhaled. "Gloria, why are we arguing about this?" she asked. "Both of our children are hurting."

"A combination of things led to Alexis's outburst and we contributed to them. Now we have to make sure they get married. I know in my heart my son loves her," Gloria said.

"I believe they should be together too," Josephine replied. "But what are we going to do about it?"

Gloria raised her finely arched brow. "What we do best."

"Let's get to it, then," Josephine countered. "I'll call Ivy to make sure nothing is canceled."

Gloria nodded in agreement. "Good, I intend to hear wedding bells next Saturday."

Alexis tossed and turned all night. Even if the telephone hadn't been constantly ringing, she wouldn't have been able to sleep. She swung her legs to the side of the bed and sat up. She heard the repeated chime of the doorbell, but didn't go to the door right away, just in case it was Jaeden.

Alexis rose from the bed and finally made her way to the door. "I'm coming," she called. She looked through the peephole and saw it was Stephanie. Alexis opened the door. "Why are you leaning on my doorbell?"

Stephanie walked quickly inside. "I was about to call the fire department if you hadn't answered when you did. She sat down on the sofa. "Why haven't you been answering your phone?"

Alexis closed the door behind her best friend. "I didn't feel like it. What are you doing here so early on a Sunday morning?"

Stephanie turned around in her seat. "Why aren't you getting ready for church?"

"I'm not feeling very well today," Alexis responded, standing in the middle of the floor in her pajamas.

"I know, I've heard." Stephanie patted the empty place beside her. "Come over here and sit with me, Lexie. I think we need to talk."

"If you want to talk about your cousin, I said all I had to say to him yesterday." Alexis moved closer to the sofa. "I guess the word is out that the wedding is off."

Stephanie stood and walked over to Alexis. "It better not be. I've spent all my money on that dress. Shoot, I wanted Chucky to see how fine I am in it," she said, laughing. She tried to bring a smile to her best friend's face, but her attempt wasn't working.

Alexis took a step back. "I'll refund everybody's money, but I'm not marrying Jaeden."

"Don't get smart. It's me, your homegirl, you're talking to. I know you, Alexis Renee Shire." Stephanie pulled Alexis over to the sofa. "Look at me, Lexie." She waited until Alexis turned to face her. "I know you love Jaeden. I feel that the two of you were meant to be together."

Alexis's eyes filled with tears. "That's what I thought, but I was wrong, so could we please drop the subject? I've made my decision and I'm not going to change my mind."

Stephanie had tears in her own eyes. "Lexie, have you ever tried to look at this situation from his point of view?"

Alexis opened her mouth to speak, but Stephanie stopped her.

"Before you say anything, I want you to understand that I'm not taking anyone's side in this. I love both of you dearly. I've seen you both grow individually and flourish as a couple."

"Dang, Stef, I've asked you nicely to please drop it." Alexis left the couch and went to the breakfast bar. Leaning on the back of the bar stool, she let the tears flow.

Stephanie followed her. She hesitated before placing her hand on Alexis's shoulder. "It's okay to be upset with him, but do you really want to throw away the love of your life?" She rubbed Alexis's hair affectionately.

Alexis turned and laid her head on Stephanie's shoulder and sobbed. Stephanie patted her back to try to calm the tears.

After several moments, Alexis lifted her head and looked at Stephanie. "He said I was controlling," she cried.

"Well, you are, Lexie," she said as nicely as she could.

Alexis jerked back. "How can you say that to me?"

"Haven't I always told you the truth?"

Alexis nodded.

Stephanie led her back to the sofa and sat beside her, waiting until Alexis's tears subsided. "Lexie, everything in life is not black and white. You've always lived your life by rules and lists." Stephanie put her hand on top of Alexis's. "You've never gone outside the box before. For the first time in your life you took a chance and fell madly in love with a great guy. But things aren't like you thought they should be. So you want to throw all of that away." She shook her head. "Love has no rules, it's not a fairy tale. Remember, this is real life and it can be a trip to deal with, but it's even worse when you're alone."

"I only wanted him to help me plan our wedding. I hadn't asked anything else of him. Was it too much to ask?" Alexis cried.

"I know and I agree with you that he should have been more considerate. What I'm trying to get you to see is his side of things, what he thinks and how he feels." Stephanie rose from the sofa. "Now, the decision is yours. I wouldn't want you to marry someone you really didn't love."

"I do love Jaeden," Alexis said before she could catch herself.

Stephanie pointed to her. "I knew that, I just wanted to hear you say it. I've got to go now, but if you want to talk, you know how to reach me."

Alexis pulled herself up from the sofa. Tears flowed once again as she hugged her friend.

Stephanie rubbed her back. "It's going to be all right."

Alexis pulled away after several moments. "Thanks for coming by, I really appreciate it."

"Talk to you soon," Stephanie said as they walked to the door.

Alexis opened the door so Stephanie could leave. After closing it behind her, Alexis could see the light on her answering machine blinking rapidly. She'd turned the volume down last night so she couldn't hear Jaeden's voice when he called.

Alexis didn't have to play the messages to find out who they were from. Still she couldn't help herself, she wanted to hear his voice now. She walked over and pressed the button.

In message after message, Jaeden told her how sorry he was for what happened between them. He didn't hang up before telling her he loved her each time.

After listening to the first four messages, she deleted them all, not wanting to listen to any more. She was more confused than ever about what to do.

To get her mind off the wedding, she decided to play solitaire on her PDA. She picked up her purse off the chair to get her Palm Pilot out. After she pulled everything out, she found it wasn't there.

Alexis tried to think and not panic. She rummaged through her entire apartment and still couldn't find it.

Slipping on her pink jogging pants and a white T-shirt, she ran to the car hoping she'd left it there, but there was no sign of it anywhere.

She ran back into the apartment to call her mother.

"Mom," Alexis said in a panicked voice.

"What is it, sweetie?" Hearing her daughter's voice, Josephine was immediately alarmed.

"I can't find my Palm Pilot. Did I leave it there by any chance?"

"No, sweetie, the only thing you left here was your laptop."

"Oh no," Alexis cried.

"Have you looked in your car?"

"Yes, it's not there."

"You were moving pretty fast yesterday."

"I've looked everywhere," Alexis cried.

"Did you go straight home when you left here?"

"Of course." Alexis didn't feel like explaining her whereabouts to her mother. "Call me if you find it."

"You know I will," Josephine replied.

Alexis clicked the Off button before Josephine could ask anything else and laid the phone down on the counter, then put her head in her hands and cried.

She cried because she failed herself. She'd always been focused on what she wanted and for the first time she was unsuccessful. In a matter of days, she'd lost her Palm Pilot and, more importantly, the love of her life.

CHAPTER EIGHTEEN

On Tuesday morning, Gloria called Josephine on the phone. She desperately wanted to do something to erase her son's sadness.

"Josie, this has gone on long enough. My son comes over every day, walking around here like a zombie. I have to make him eat and that's odd for Jaeden. I look at him and can tell he's not sleeping well either," Gloria said with concern.

"I know. Alexis was already beside herself, now she's worse since she lost that darn Palm Pilot. You would think she's mourning a child or something. I'm thankful she had completed her classes before all this mess happened."

"She still didn't find it, huh?" Gloria asked.

"Nope."

"Josie, what are we going to do? The wedding is Saturday."

"I know, I know. I've tried everything I know to talk to her, but she's so despondent."

"Did you call Applebee's to see if it turned up there?"

Josephine grinned. "Yes. Did you tell Jaeden about her losing it?" she asked.

"No. Whenever I talk about her, he doesn't want to hear it, so I stopped trying. But I know one thing, I'm sick of him moping around here," Gloria huffed.

Josephine laughed. "Is he there or at work?"

"He's at his apartment. He said something about having a meeting later in the evening. Why?" Gloria whispered into the phone, sensing Josephine was up to something.

Josephine hoped her simple plan would work. "Alexis is supposed to come over here later, so if I can get Jaeden to come over too, maybe we can get them to talk to each other."

"What are you going to say to him to get him over there?"

"I'm going to ask him to go over to Applebee's and talk to the manager in person."

"Huh? Why? I thought they didn't have the Palm Pilot," Gloria said, confused.

"I said I called. I didn't say they didn't find it," Josephine clarified, hoping Gloria had caught on to her plan. "We've got to do something, so what could it hurt? Nothing beats a failure but a try."

"I understand," Gloria said with a giggle. "Call me back after you talk to him."

"I'll do that." Josephine hung up the phone. She looked up Jaeden's number from her phone book and dialed. He picked up after the first ring and Josephine knew he probably hoped it was Alexis calling from her house. She hated disappointing him, but hopefully if her plan worked they'd be together soon. She told him about Alexis losing her Palm Pilot.

"Jaeden, do you think you could help me?" Josephine asked when she'd completed the story.

"Mrs. Shire, I'm sorry, your daughter has made it very clear she doesn't want anything to do with me. She won't even return any of my phone calls."

Josephine's heart hurt for them both. "I know and I understand that, but I'm asking you to help *me*."

Jaeden released a deep sigh. "Sure. How can I help?"

Josephine smiled. "I need you to go to Applebee's and ask the manager if anyone found her Palm Pilot."

"Why didn't you tell Alexis to go there herself if you're so sure she left it there?"

"She's too distraught after everything that has happened," Gloria lied. She hoped the Lord would forgive her. She was only trying to find a way to make Jaeden and Alexis happy. "She hasn't been thinking straight."

Jaeden ran his hand over his close-cropped hair. "Okay, but I wouldn't get my hopes up. Several days have passed already and people don't usually turn in something like that."

"Thank you so much, Jaeden," Josephine said with a hint of hope in her voice.

"No problem, I'll call you when I find out something," he said before he disconnected the call.

Jaeden walked into his bedroom, opened the bottom drawer of his armoire, and retrieved the ring box. He'd put it back in the box the night Alexis threw it at him.

Taking the box over to his bed, he flipped open the lid. There sat the sparkling diamond that once belonged to his soul mate. He studied the platinum piece carefully before removing it from its holder.

Slipping the ring into the front pocket of his slacks, he got up and went to the living room to grab his keys from the cocktail table on his way out the door.

Jaeden drove to the restaurant and asked the hostess if he could speak to the manager. A short woman with curly blond hair came from the back of the establishment.

"Yes, sir, how can I help you?" she asked, adjusting her name tag.

"My fiancée had lunch here a couple days ago and I think she left her Palm Pilot."

The woman grinned at the handsome customer. "I had hoped the owner would return for it. An elderly couple gave it to one of my servers. Someone called to ask about it over the weekend, but no one picked it up. After that I called the numbers I found in it, but kept getting voice mails. I left several messages, but haven't received a return phone call. Excuse me for one sec and I'll get it."

"No problem," Jaeden said, understanding he'd been set up. Pulling his cell phone from the clip on his waist, he telephoned Josephine. "Mrs. Shire, I can't believe it myself, but it's here, the manager went to the back to get it for me." Jaeden played along with the trap Josephine had obviously set for him. He knew it was a ploy to get him to her house and he wondered if Alexis would be waiting when he got there. Now he was glad he'd brought the ring. "Mrs. Shire, are you there?" he asked after he didn't hear a response right away. He was afraid his phone had lost its signal.

"Yes, Jaeden, I'm still here. Would you mind bringing it to the house? I'll make sure Alexis gets it."

"Sure, I'll see you in a few minutes, the manager's coming back with it now."

Jaeden disconnected the call.

"Your fiancée's very lucky," the manager said, handing the small device to him.

"No, I think I'm the lucky one," he said.

It only took ten minutes to get to the Shires'. Jaeden noticed Alexis's car as well as his mother's parked on the street nearby when he pulled up to the house.

He stepped out of the car telling himself he wouldn't pressure Alexis into talking to him if she didn't want to. He'd have to live with her decision not to marry him.

Once he closed the door to his vehicle, he knew he couldn't convince himself the latter was true. He knew in his heart Alexis loved him. There was no doubt in his mind about that. He patted his pants pocket to make sure the ring was still there as he made his way up the walkway.

Swinging the white door to the patio open, he stepped inside. "Hello?" he called as he opened the door that led to the kitchen.

There was no answer.

"Hello," he repeated, walking farther into the house.

"In here," he heard Josephine say.

Jaeden walked into the dining room area not knowing if he would run into Alexis there or not.

"You found it," Gloria said as Jaeden kissed her on the cheek.

"What are you two up to?" he asked, looking at the cards on the table.

"Just going through more responses we got today," Gloria said.

"Thanks so much, Jaeden, for getting it for us," Josephine said, casting Jaeden off before he could speak. She hugged him tightly and kissed him on the cheek.

"She was lucky," he said with a smirk as he handed Josephine the device.

"Where did you find it?" Alexis asked from behind him.

Jaeden hadn't realized she had walked into the room. He slowly turned to face her. A rush of emotions overwhelmed him and all he wanted to do was sweep her into his arms and carry her to the nearest bed, *but that's not how she wants it*, he reminded himself.

His gaze was fixed on her as she nervously bit her bottom lip. It only made him want to feel those same lips against his own.

"Applebee's. An elderly couple gave it to your server."

"Um, h-how did you know I'd lost it?"

Jaeden glanced at Josephine, who gave him a sheepish grin. He turned his attention back to Alexis.

"We've counted two hundred and fifty-five people from the responses," Gloria announced.

Neither Jaeden nor Alexis commented. They both stood in place gazing into each other's eyes.

"Jaeden," Josephine called.

He dragged his dark eyes slowly from Alexis to her mother.

She handed him the Palm Pilot. "You give it to her," she said cheerfully, knowing her plan had worked like a charm.

Jaeden accepted the device and moved closer to Alexis. Their eyes collided as Alexis reached for the small PDA.

Jaeden held it out to her, but didn't release it once she possessed it. "Can we talk alone for a minute?" he asked, his voice barely above a whisper.

Alexis's eyes fluttered as she tried to keep them on him. She finally nodded in agreement.

Jaeden turned and said to the two older women, "We'll be back."

"Take all the time you need," Josephine said, giving Gloria an eager pat on the knee under the table.

Jaeden held out his hand for Alexis to take. He hadn't realized he'd been holding his breath until her soft hand latched on to his.

Jaeden sat on the bed next to Alexis when they entered the upstairs bedroom, but she quickly moved to the rocker next to it.

They both sat quietly, then Alexis turned on her Palm Pilot. She took occasional glances at Jaeden, who sat silently, never taking his eyes off her.

"You wanted to talk," Alexis said softly.

"Only if you're up to it," Jaeden replied.

"I'm listening."

"Did you get my messages?" he asked.

Alexis looked at him under her lowered lashes. "Yes," she whispered.

Jaeden leaned forward so he could feel closer to her, but not cause her to move away at the same time. "I didn't realize how important planning this wedding was to you. Spending the rest of my life with you was all I wanted. I didn't care about the fanfare that went along with it. Evidently you did. All I wanted was you," Jaeden repeated, dropping to his knees in front of the rocker. "Baby, I don't think I can sleep another night with this wedge between us." Jaeden laid his head in her lap and gently grabbed her hips, rubbing his face against her. "My heart is hurting and I feel empty inside." His voice was ragged. "I can't breathe without you."

Alexis couldn't move. Looking down at Jaeden, knowing in her heart he was telling the truth, she finally traced his hairline with her fingertips as the tears began to seep from her eyes. She loved him so much.

Lifting his face in her hands, she bent so their lips were mere inches apart.

"I'm so sorry," she whispered before brushing her lips lightly against his.

"Baby, you have nothing to be sorry for." Jaeden lightly rubbed his face against the side of hers as he took her hands in his.

"Oh, yes, I do." Alexis allowed the tears to continue to fall. "I'm sorry for always blowing up every time something happened. There was little in my life that was spontaneous, then you came along and it seemed my world was turned upside down. I didn't think things through anymore, I just did what felt good."

"Spontaneity is good, but I still should have been there for you," Jaeden said. "I was busy trying to get my professional life in order when I was neglecting the most important person in my life . . . you."

Alexis reached out and touched his face. "All I want is to be your wife, a good wife to you, and the mother of your children. I want to find you beside me when I'm old and gray. I know you are my soul mate."

Jaeden pulled himself to his feet and reached into his front pocket. "I have something that belongs to you," he said, pulling out the sparkling diamond.

Alexis quickly covered her eyes to get the tears to stop, but they kept coming.

Jaeden got back down on his knees, picking up her left hand. "This is where it belongs," he said, sliding the ring inch by inch onto her finger. "I don't want you to ever take it off." He kissed her hand.

Alexis stood, shaking her head. "Never." She hugged him to her tightly.

Jaeden lifted Alexis into his arms and moved backward over to the bed and laid her on one side while he lay on his side next to her.

"I can't wait to watch the sunrise on your face every morning for the rest of my life," he said, truthfully.

Josephine glanced up from the cards she'd been sorting and bumped Gloria with her knee when she saw the couple walking into the room.

Gloria peeked over her glasses and saw Alexis and Jaeden holding hands as they stood in the doorway of the room. She held up her ring finger and gave them a dazzling smile.

"You're getting married?" Josephine asked excitedly.

Alexis nodded, squeezing Jaeden's hand tighter.

"Thank God." Josephine and Gloria both looked toward the heavens.

"I'm sorry if I caused either of you any stress," Alexis said as she went to hug her mother and Gloria.

"You have nothing to apologize for. We were a little overbearing at times ourselves," Josephine admitted.

"A little?" Alexis said, raising her brow playfully before she took a seat at the table.

Jaeden sat in the empty chair beside her.

"We're just relieved you two are going on with the wedding," Gloria added.

"My heart felt like it had been ripped out," Jaeden said. "Now I'm better and after Saturday, I'll be made whole."

"Aw, isn't he cute?" Alexis said, pinching his cheek. "I know there are a lot of things that still need to be done."

Both mothers beamed with happiness. "We've found a replacement for Nicole. My niece Vonda has already been fitted for her gown and the shoes fit perfectly," Gloria said proudly. "And all the men have been measured for their tuxes."

"I haven't ordered programs," Alexis said. "I'll have to call Ivy to see what my options are," she added, moving out of her seat in a hurry.

Josephine stopped her. "No, you don't, sweetie. Gloria and I have already spoken with Ivy."

Alexis couldn't believe her ears. "You did?"

"We told her you were a little under the weather and asked if she would go over with us everything that was left to be done."

"We took care of the programs and menu cards for the reception. We approved all the floral arrangements, the cake, and even designed the cover for your wedding favors," Gloria said, smiling while Josephine nodded in agreement.

"And we asked Ivy to select your toasting glasses, cake server, and accessories," Josephine concluded.

Jaeden squeezed Alexis's hand, then looked at his mother. "Mama, you and Mrs. Shire did all this for us?"

"We sure did. Josie and I realized you were upset, but we also felt in our hearts you were going to get married, so we didn't hesitate to keep all the plans you made intact."

"Thank you so much for everything!" She took Jaeden's hand in hers.

At that moment, his cell phone rang. Jaeden pulled away and Alexis rolled her eyes. *Here we go again,* she thought, thinking the worst. Jaeden looked at the caller ID.

"Jaeden," Alexis pleaded disappointedly.

"I need to take this," he said, softly walking from the room into the kitchen.

Alexis watched him leave, then turned to face their mothers.

"Sweetie, don't be upset," Josephine said.

"I'm okay," Alexis tried to reassure them although she was certain they could tell she was lying.

Jaeden walked back into the room. "Baby, don't be angry with me, but I've got a dinner meeting with Arnold this evening."

Alexis nodded, wondering if Jaeden had changed at all.

Jaeden pulled her to him. "I promise to come back right after the meeting is over and do whatever you need me to do. I've been waiting for him to show me the marketing plan for my product, so this could be big. I can't cancel." He gave Alexis a soulful kiss.

Alexis stepped out of his embrace and took a deep breath. She remembered that Jaeden was working hard to secure their financial future and she couldn't fault him for that. "I understand. I'll probably still be here when you come back. I want to go over everything."

"My baby's back," Josephine said, laughing.

"I'll see you all later." Jaeden pulled Alexis along with him from the room. "Are you going to be okay with this?" he asked, resting his forehead against hers.

"Yes," she whispered. "I know how much this means to you."

"You know that I love you, don't you?" Jaeden asked, looking deep into her eyes.

"I love you, too," Alexis replied softly.

"I'll call you on my way back," he promised.

Alexis watched him leave, hoping she'd made the right decision by taking him back.

CHAPTER NINETEEN

"Where are we going? Alexis asked Stephanie. "We have reservations at Shaw's for dinner at seven." She looked over at her friend. "You know they're always crowded."

Stephanie shook her head. "That's only on the weekends. It's Thursday and you've already called twice anyway. I need to stop by my aunt Sherly's for a sec. She can't find a red afghan and she swears I threw it away when I helped her clean out the attic a while back."

Alexis twisted up her nose. "Stef, you did say she had a lot of junk up there. Are you sure you didn't just get tired of going through boxes and put her afghan in the trash?"

Stephanie laughed, hoping Alexis was buying her story. "I will admit there were a lot of things I wanted to throw out, but she was watching me like a hawk. It's probably up there with the rest of that junk she kept." She pulled into the driveway of her aunt's house and cut off the engine.

"I'll stay here. That way you can tell her someone's waiting in the car so we can get going," Alexis said, hoping Stephanie would move faster.

"If Aunt Sherly finds out you're in the car and didn't come in to speak to her, she going to have a fit. So come with me now, I don't feel like hearing her mouth asking me why you didn't come in," Stephanie pleaded.

Alexis sighed, got out of the car and walked to the door.

Stephanie rang the doorbell and they waited. "Hey, Auntie," Stephanie said, kissing Sherly on the cheek when she answered the door.

"Stef, I looked in all the boxes in the attic, so it must be downstairs in the basement or you trashed it and don't want to admit it," Sherly said, closing the door behind them.

"Aw, Auntie. I'm getting ready to go to dinner. I don't want to look through all those dusty boxes in the basement," Stephanie moaned.

"Girl, stop whining," Sherly said, walking from the foyer down the hall. "Alexis, would you mind going down with her?"

Alexis glanced at her watch, then at Stephanie. "Not at all," she said. "Your auntie is something else," she whispered to Stephanie as they followed Sherly to the basement door. "She didn't even speak to me when we walked in."

Sherly turned and waved her finger at them. "I bet you my life you put my afghan in that bag we threw in that Salvation Army Dumpster, Stef."

"I don't remember seeing it, Auntie, honestly. Maybe it is down here," Stephanie said, stepping back so Sherly could open the basement door.

Stephanie led the way down the stairs, but once they hit the bottom step, the lights went out.

"What's wrong with your aunt, Stef? She just turned the lights out on us," Alexis complained.

"Wait, there's a switch down here," Stephanie said, patting the wall nearby. "Here we go." She flicked the switch.

"Sur-prise," everyone yelled.

Alexis's hands flew to her mouth. "Oh my God." She looked over at Stephanie, who was doubled over with laughter.

"I gotcha," Stephanie said in between laughs.

Alexis walked around to the other side of the staircase and looked at all the women in the room. Her eyes went right to her mother's tearful ones. Gloria stood right next to Josephine. All of Alexis's aunts and cousins were there, as well as Jaeden's relatives.

"Mom," Alexis screamed as her mother came toward her.

"Sweetie, you look so pretty in your pink pantsuit." Josephine hugged her daughter, patting her own face with tissue so she wouldn't ruin her makeup.

"Stephanie suggested I wear it because we were supposed to be going to a fancy restaurant for dinner. Were you in on this?" Alexis put her hands on her hips and glared at her mother playfully.

"Of course, your mother and I both knew about Stephanie's surprise," Gloria piped in, giving Alexis a peck on the cheek.

Stephanie came back over and hugged her.

"Congratulations, Lexie," Stephanie said before putting a white sash across Alexis's body with the word BRIDE written on it with silver glitter.

"You planned the shower even though I had called off the wedding?" Alexis exclaimed.

Stephanie nodded. "Girl, everybody knew you were going to marry Jaeden." She grabbed Alexis's hand and led her over to an antique-styled chair. "This will be your throne for the evening. Enjoy yourself," she said before hugging her best friend.

"Everything is so beautiful," Alexis commented as she looked at all the balloon decorations. She saw the food table was filled with salads, barbecue ribs, chicken drumettes, ham, bologna, turkey, salami finger sandwiches.

As she sat, Alexis was greeted by so many people, she stopped trying to count once she got to fifty. She couldn't believe the number of relatives and friends who came out to shower her with love and gifts, especially Brianna, Cherise, LaTanya, and Jessica, whom she'd been so mean to.

The guests played lots of games to entertain themselves and instead of a piece of cake, each guest was given a mini-gift box cake for dessert. Each one was iced with Belgian chocolate ganache mixed into a pink color.

When Alexis opened her gifts, Stephanie would take the bows and ribbons and put them on a paper plate to make Alexis's bridal hat. Alexis had a wonderful time and all her friends and current and future relatives laughed as they took pictures with her in her new headwear. But, after she thought she'd opened all the gifts, Stephanie came back with one more.

"I almost forgot about this one," she said, handing Alexis a box perfectly wrapped in pink foil.

Alexis held it up to her ear and shook it. "Well, it's not ticking, so that's a good sign," she joked.

Everyone laughed.

"I hope not, it's from your husband-to-be," Stephanie said.

Alexis's eyebrows raised in confusion. When did he have time to pick up something? Jaeden was truly extraordinary.

"Open it," the ladies cried in unison, eager to see what special gift Jaeden had purchased.

"I hate to tear the paper, it's so pretty," Alexis whined as she slid the bow off the package.

"Do you need some help?" Stephanie asked over Alexis's shoulder. She wanted to know what was in the box almost as bad as Alexis did.

"No, thank you, I can handle this myself," Alexis quipped as she ripped the rest of the paper off, revealing the gift.

"I can't believe him," Alexis squealed. "He bought me a new Palm." Grinning wildly, she held the box up over her head so everyone could see it.

"Jaeden doesn't know it yet, but he's created a monster," Stephanie told the crowd. "If he thought the girl was bad with her old trusty Palm, he'd better watch out because not only is this thing a Palm, it's a digital camera, a telephone, and she can send and receive text messages. Alexis will never put this thing away." Stephanie laughed at the mystified look on her best friend's face.

Alexis stood and hugged Stephanie. "Thanks so much for everything. This was a wonderful party."

Upon their departure, all the guests were presented with a pink mini wedding cake candle. It was hand painted with frosted-wax pearl roses and bows and placed in a clear box with a pink organza ribbon and a tag that said "Alexis and Jaeden."

"Stef, this was one of the best days of my life," Alexis said, grateful her best friend had done so much to celebrate her wedding.

"*One* of the best days," Stephanie said in return. "Your wedding day will top this."

"It will be on the list, but the best day of my life was the day I met Jaeden," Alexis said, her eyes watering.

"Aw," Stephanie squealed, pulling Alexis in for another hug.

They quickly withdrew, wiping the tears from their eyes, and Alexis hoped her friend would soon find the happiness she felt at that very moment.

Alexis looked impatiently through the square glass panel at the main entrance of Pilgrim Branch Church Friday evening. The rehearsal couldn't start until all the participants had arrived and she was waiting for the rest of her bridal party.

Jaeden walked behind her massaging her shoulders. "Baby, why don't you come into the sanctuary and sit? They'll be here."

"Tiffany begged to be in the wedding and has given me nothing but problems since," Alexis said, trying to look farther up the street. Things had gone so well with the wedding since she and Jaeden had reunited. Alexis worried they were in for another round of drama.

Jaeden gently pulled her away from the door, leading her up the stairs. "Stop worrying."

Alexis knew he was right and focused her attention elsewhere. She turned and, from the back of the sanctuary, envisioned the transformation that was taking place. Tomorrow it would be filled with lots of relatives and friends who would bear witness to her union with Jaeden.

"It's going to be breathtakingly beautiful by the time Rose gets done," Ivy said, interrupting Alexis's daydream.

"That's exactly how I want it, Ivy," Alexis responded, seeing Ivy approaching from the church's middle aisle.

Ivy looked at her watch when she reached Alexis. "We're going to have to begin in the next fifteen minutes. I almost forgot," Ivy added, moving toward a pew in the back of the church. She stooped and pulled out a large box from beneath the bench. "I picked up your programs."

She retrieved a rose-colored booklet from the box and handed it to Alexis.

Never in her life had she been made to cry so much.

She stared at the photograph on the front of the program. It was the picture she and Jaeden had taken at their engagement party. She ran her fingers across the white vellum cover. "This is beautiful," she said.

Jaeden looked at it over Alexis's shoulder. "Our mothers did a good job," he said proudly.

"Yes, honey, they really did." Alexis read each line of the order of service. Every song she and Jaeden had chosen to incorporate in the ceremony was being used.

She turned to the next page, which explained the symbols of a covenant marriage. Alexis looked up, darting her eyes between Jaeden and Ivy. "Whose idea was this?"

"I suggested it would be appropriate for this ceremony," Ivy said. "Your mothers thought it would be a nice idea."

"What a nice touch," she said softly, awed by the detail her family had exhibited to make sure she had a perfect day. She would have to be sure to apologize to her mother again for her behavior throughout the initial wedding planning.

Ivy nodded and smiled. "I'm so glad you approve," Ivy said, checking her watch again.

Alexis flipped to the next page, which listed the names of the wedding party. The last page expressed Alexis and Jaeden's appreciation to their guests.

Alexis stood and walked into Jaeden's arms. "I couldn't have done a better job with the program myself. They are so beautiful," she said before handing her copy to him.

Jaeden kissed her. "They only wanted us to be happy, baby." He looked down at their photo. "Baby, we look like we're stars," he said, pointing to the paper.

"You're my star," she said, giving him another kiss.

By six-thirty, everyone had arrived and the rehearsal was ready to begin. Ivy had hired an organist and the church's audio technician would assist them with the recorded music. She demonstrated for the ushers how they should walk down the aisle, light the candles, and, when it was time, pull the aisle runner.

After the bridal party went over how they should walk, Ivy asked if they could put everything together with the music. Kendra and Tiffany sashayed down the aisle with their escorts. And when all of the couples had gone down the aisle, Pastor McCree, who would be conducting the ceremony, explained the sanctity of marriage to all those in attendance.

Alexis was disappointed because she wasn't allowed to participate. Her mother said a bride should only walk down the aisle once. Alexis's uncle Darren's girlfriend had been asked to stand in for the rehearsal while Alexis observed the proceedings from the back of the sanctuary. She was pleased that after the wedding party had gone through the whole processional twice, everyone seemed to have perfected it.

The wedding party went to the Jeffersons' house for the rehearsal dinner.

Alexis and Jaeden stood to thank everyone for participating in their wedding before the meal was served. Then they gave the bridesmaids pearl heart-shaped boxes. Each of the girls' names and a short message was engraved inside the heart. The groomsmen received a clock made of a lead crystal basketball. The brass backboard and hoop had a wood base where their names were engraved.

"I have one last announcement to make," Jaeden said, glancing at Alexis as she took her seat. "I'd like to thank all of you for encouraging me to pursue my dream. This morning I received the final decision from Arnold Herswick," he said with everyone's eyes on him. "They've offered me a position heading their new urban division!"

Squeals of excitement were heard throughout the room. Alexis jumped up and grabbed him. "I'm so proud of you, honey," she bellowed, pulling him toward her again.

Jaeden pulled back from her after a few moments and looked into her eyes. "Now, baby, if you want to go to school full-time, so you can meet your goals sooner, you can," he said before capturing her lips.

After they broke the kiss, he waved his hands to quiet everyone down. "Wait," Jaeden yelled over the loud voices. "That's not all. They've offered a million dollars for my designs," he said, smiling.

Now they had much more to celebrate.

CHAPTER TWENTY

The following morning, Alexis sat in a brown folding chair in one of the Sunday school classrooms at her church that had been designated as her dressing room. She and Stephanie shared a room while the bridesmaids and mothers dressed in rooms down the hall. Ivy had provided them with a makeup artist and Violet came to help them get dressed.

The morning had been hectic. Alexis and her bridesmaids had gone to breakfast and to the beauty salon. She loved the way Sharon styled her long locks off her face. Wisps of her beautiful dark brown hair flowed down her back in big curls.

Alexis sat quietly trying not to concern herself with the events of the day. She kept reminding herself the wedding was in capable hands.

She had just finished putting on her undergarments, stockings, and shoes when the makeup artist had arrived to do her face. Now she waited for Violet to help her into her gown.

Just as Violet removed the hanger from the hook, Stephanie ventured from the other dressing room.

"Were the girls all right?" Alexis asked, making sure the tops of her stockings were securely fastened.

"Yes, Desiree is making up Kim's face as we speak.

Everyone else has their clothes on and makeup done," Stephanie said proudly.

"How do they look, Stef?" Alexis asked nervously.

"Everybody looks gorgeous. Tiffany is complaining about her shoes, but other than that all is well." Stephanie took her dress from Violet.

"What's wrong with her shoes?" Alexis asked in a panic.

"Not a thing from what I could see." Stephanie slipped out of her blue jean dress and wiggled into her gown.

Alexis twisted her mouth downward. "See? I told you she gets on my nerves."

"Girl, I wouldn't worry about it." Stephanie waved her hand. "I think Tiffany likes to hear herself talk," she said, moving over to Violet so she could zip the side of the dress.

Alexis's hands flew to her face when Stephanie was dressed. "You look lovely, Stef," she squealed.

"I think they turned out rather well," Violet said proudly. "You have beautiful bridesmaids who enhance the dresses even more." She removed the wedding gown from the hanger.

"I told you we should be on television, Lexie," Stephanie said, trying to pull down her strapless bra through her dress. "I'm glad I walked around in my shoes when we got here. I'm use to wearing fatter heels than these." She raised her foot up to show the two-and-a-half-inch heel. "I'm in love with these shoes, though." She pranced over to Alexis. "It's your turn now, girlfriend. Let's get your dress on," she said, putting her street clothes in her bag and dropping it on the floor.

"What time is it now?" Alexis asked.

"Three-thirty." Stephanie pointed to the digital wall clock. "There's a clock up there, Lexie."

"I don't know why I didn't notice it," Alexis said, untying her robe and slipping it off.

"You're nervous, that's why," Stephanie said as she helped Violet open the dress wide enough to put over Alexis's head without ruining her hairstyle.

After zipping it and making sure Alexis was comfortable, Violet placed the headpiece in her hair and Stephanie pulled her hair in place.

"Jaeden is going to go crazy when he sees you," Stephanie said, looking at her friend through the mirror. "This is no dress rehearsal, girlfriend. This is the real deal."

"Gee, thanks, Stef, for reminding me," Alexis replied. She couldn't believe the time had finally come. Her palms began to sweat.

"We can put the veil on now or wait until it's almost time for the wedding to start," Violet offered.

"We can wait," Alexis said, trying to figure a way to sit without wrinkling her dress.

Violet moved the train out of the way. "Just sit," she said, watching Alexis bop down in the chair. "You're ready now, so I'm going to see if Ivy needs me for anything. I'll be back to check on you."

"Thanks again for everything," Alexis said as Violet left, closing the door behind her.

Alexis noticed Stephanie staring at her. "What? Stef, don't start crying, your makeup is going to have to be done over," Alexis said, tears welling in her eyes also. "Mine too, if we keep this up." She flicked the tears away, but it was too late, the tears had already started streaming down Stephanie's face.

"Oh." Alexis got up from her seat and went to her friend. They hugged each other. "My pictures are going to look horrible."

Alexis stepped back. "I never thanked you for everything you did for me. Wait a minute. This reminds me," she said, reaching for her bag.

"Please don't tell me you're looking for your Palm

Pilot. Not today, Lexie," Stephanie said with her hands on her hips.

"No, I have something for you."

"For me? What?" Stephanie asked curiously.

"You'll see in a minute, if I can get it out of this bag." Alexis continued to feel around inside.

She pulled out a square package. "I know how much you like opening packages, so I wrapped it," she said as she handed it to Stephanie.

Stephanie held the package as the tears continued to roll down her brown cheeks.

"Aren't you going to open it?"

Stephanie tore the silver wrapper off the white box. A hand-carved pewter frame with the word "sisters" printed at the top slid out. The border around the photograph had both their names around it. The photo in the middle was of the two of them at the first school picnic Alexis had attended after she began teaching at Nobel.

"You still have this picture? I had forgotten all about it," Stephanie said, looking at Alexis with tears in her eyes again.

"I didn't forget," Alexis said, her eyes tearing as well. "If I had a sister, I would want her to be just like you . . . sometimes."

They both laughed.

"This is so special, I will treasure it," Stephanie said, embracing Alexis. After they'd consoled one another, Stephanie said, "Let me go and make sure the girls are all right."

"Why don't you bring them in here? We're all dressed now, so it should be okay," Alexis said as Stephanie headed out the door.

When she was alone, Alexis caught a glimpse of herself in the mirror and couldn't help but go over and look. She kept thinking to herself that her courtship and engagement were all a dream, but by tonight she would be Mrs. Jaeden Jefferson.

Before she could finish her thought, there was a knock at the door.

Alexis turned toward the sound. "Yes?" she said, waiting for the person to speak.

Josephine glided into the room. "Look at my baby." She and Alexis walked to each other and embraced. "You are a beautiful bride." She placed her hand against her daughter's face. "You're glowing, sweetie," she said with a tear in her eye. "I can see you are truly happy."

"I'm happy, nervous, and jittery," Alexis started. "How about all of the above?" she joked. She admired her mother's dress. "You look so pretty," she said of her mother's silk chiffon gown. She fingered the lace beading at the top. "You didn't show this dress to me."

"There are some things you just don't need to know," Josephine said, smiling.

"I love it on you." Alexis looked down at her mother's feet. "You went all out, didn't you, Mom?"

"Of course, my only baby is getting married today."

They both laughed.

"Do you have your old, new, borrowed, and blue?" Josephine asked, assessing her daughter's gown.

"I hadn't thought about it." Alexis started wringing her hands together.

Josephine held her daughter's hands still. "It's okay."

"My dress would be my new and I have on a beautiful blue garter with white lace, but the old and borrowed I'm missing," Alexis said, looking into her mother's eyes.

"I brought your something old." Josephine pulled out a gold-embroidered ivory handkerchief from her purse and gave it to Alexis. "This belonged to your great-grandmother Georgia. She carried it on her wedding day, my mother carried it, and I even had it with me when your father and I married."

She placed her hands on top of Alexis's. "I always dreamed of this day, giving this to you. Since you don't have old and borrowed, use it for both," Josephine said before pulling Alexis into her arms.

"Mom, words can't express how thankful I am for everything you've done for me." Alexis took a deep breath. "Even when I said mean things to you, your love never wavered. I hope I'm as good a mom to my children as you've been to me." Alexis hugged her mother for several moments.

Finally, Josephine stepped back so she could get a good look at her daughter. "I love you very much, sweetie. I'm not going to worry about you because I know Jaeden is a strong, hardworking young man who will take care of his family," she said, unsnapping her box purse once again.

She pulled out a small box beautifully wrapped with rose-colored foil paper and a thin silver bow. She looked at Alexis before passing it to her.

"What's this?" Alexis asked. "You and Daddy have done more than enough already."

"Jaeden gave it to me a minute ago to give to you," she said.

Alexis's hands were shaking as she accepted the little gift. "You saw him?"

"Yes, he looks so handsome. All the men do. They were on their way to take pictures in the Fellowship Hall."

Josephine had to take the package from Alexis, her hands were shaking so badly. She tore the pretty foil paper off and held it so Alexis could remove the lid herself.

Alexis gasped at the contents inside. "Huh?"

"You're going to need a new bracelet in a minute," Josephine said.

"It's beautiful. Mom, look at this," she said, lifting the fourteen-karat heart from its cushion. It was filled with pave diamonds just like the first charm Jaeden had given her.

As Alexis admired the gift, Stephanie and the rest of the bridesmaids came into the room.

"Lexie, the photographer wants to know if you're ready for him," Stephanie said, heading toward Alexis to see her new gift.

The rest of the girls followed behind her.

"This is gorgeous." Stephanie stared at the sparkling piece of jewelry. She noticed Alexis's tearstained face. "You need a makeup fix before the photographer comes in." They all laughed as Stephanie hurried from the room.

Alexis admired the gift Jaeden had sent and hoped she'd be as good to him as he was to her.

Ivy stuck her head in the door. "It's time to line up."

Alexis looked at her mother with a panicked look in her eyes. "Mom, Stef's—"

Before Alexis could get the words out, Stephanie walked around Ivy into the room with the makeup artist following her.

"We're ready to start and it's just four thirty-five," Stephanie said, almost out of breath. "Most people don't start on time and Ivy's not playing either." She pretended to wipe her brow.

"Mom, I forgot to put my veil on," Alexis said as her makeup was being repaired. Butterflies began to swarm in her stomach.

"I thought you didn't want to wear one." Josephine mimicked the way Alexis had said it the first time she'd suggested she wear one at Hearts and Flowers.

"I bought one, remember?" Alexis pointed to the see-through material on the table. After her makeup had been reapplied, she stood to check it in the mirror.

Josephine picked up the veil. "I'll put it on for you," she said, walking behind the chair and placing the comb in her daughter's hair.

Once she secured it, Alexis was ready.

Just before Josephine pulled the blusher over Alexis's face, she said, "The next time I see you, you'll be a married woman." Her eyes misted as she lowered the netting over her daughter's head.

All the groomsmen had gone to the Fellowship Hall and Jaeden sat in the room alone.

"There's my baby," Gloria said, walking into the choir room where the men had dressed.

"You look so great, Mama," Jaeden said, rising to give her a kiss on the cheek.

"Thank you, sir," Gloria drawled as she modeled her silver-beaded gown for him. "Nervous?" she asked as she brushed his lapel and readjusted his flower.

"A little." Jaeden looked down into his mother's eyes. "I just want to thank you for always being there, for helping me see things the way they really were when it came to Alexis." He grabbed her hand and they moved over to the empty chairs in the corner. "I knew she was the one I've been waiting for all my life."

"I figured it out before you did. That day back in April when Stephanie brought her to Tommie's house and you walked in, your body language changed after you laid eyes on that beautiful young woman. I knew you were a goner." She squeezed his hands.

"You didn't say a word to me," Jaeden said in surprise.

"I wanted you to figure it out on your own, but I was praying all the time. Gloria checked her watch and rose from her seat. "It's time for us to go."

She walked to the door, but suddenly stopped. She

turned to face her son. "Son, never forget to let God lead, you 'cause he's a mighty good leader."

"I won't, Mama, I promise," he said, wrapping his arms around her. He led her out of the room and down the hall.

CHAPTER TWENTY-ONE

The balcony and the main floor of the sanctuary were filled to capacity with family and friends.

The ushers held the brass candle lighters with their right hands and placed their left hands behind their backs as they marched down the aisle in unison to ignite the spiral candelabras that sat alongside the arch at the altar.

Lighted pew candles were placed along the inside of the aisles, which were adorned with various shades of pink rose bouquets draped with tulle.

The organist softly played Regina Belle's "If I Could" as Donald Jefferson was escorted to his seat by a hostess. He grinned as friends and relatives snapped pictures of him in his black tailored four-button tuxedo.

All of Alexis's and Jaeden's aunts and uncles formed two single lines and were escorted to their seats down front.

Jaeden and Gloria appeared in the entrance of the sanctuary. He was dashing in his black long coat with a three-button single-breasted front, his triple-pleated satin notch-lapel shirt with a self-top collar, white full-back vest, and Windsor tie.

They walked hand in hand slowly down the aisle, until they stood underneath the arch covered with tulle, white lights, and flowers at the altar.

Gloria and Jaeden turned to face each other. She

looked deeply into the depths of the dark brown eyes of her son, who after today would be starting his own family.

"Son, as we walked down the aisle, I reflected back to several stages in your life, the day you were born, your first day of school, and your high school graduation. You have made me so proud." Gloria's voice began to tremble. "I feel so blessed to have been chosen by God to bring you into the world," she said with tears spilling from her eyes. "Alexis is an amazing young woman and I know she will make a wonderful wife. I love you."

After a long embrace, Jaeden escorted his mother to her seat in the second pew. She sat next to his father, who was wiping his eyes with his white handkerchief. He leaned over and kissed his wife's cheek. Dabbing the tears of joy from her eyes, Gloria was grateful everything had turned out for the best.

Josephine Shire beamed as she appeared in the doorway in a beautifully beaded silver silk chiffon cap-sleeved gown. She seemed to glide down the aisle. As Josephine took her seat, she pulled out a lace handkerchief and dabbed the corners of her eyes too.

The guests couldn't seem to stop passing Kleenex. Tears of joy continued to flow from just about everyone.

The charming tempo of Luther Vandross's "So Amazing" filled the air and the guests watched in admiration as the bridal party marched two by two along with the beat of the music.

Jaeden's cousin strode midway down the aisle of the sanctuary in his black long coat with a three-button single-breasted front and white shirt with a rose-pink Windsor tie and vest. He turned to a bridesmaid, who stood at the door waiting for him. He held out his hand, inviting her to join him.

The lovely young woman held her head high as she

stepped gracefully toward her escort. A beautiful rose pomander hung from her dainty wrist by a satin ribbon.

Her escort bowed in front of her before taking her arm in his as they walked together to their positions at the top of the stairs of the choir stand.

Kendra and Ronald, Tiffany and Tony, Vonda and Dwayne, and Rhoda and Darren all executed their steps in sequence with the same precise manner. Each bridesmaid stood on the step below the groomsmen, three couples on the groom's side and two on the bride's.

Stephanie was the last to make her entrance as maid of honor. She walked slowly down the aisle on Gregory's arm. She gave Jaeden a big smile before taking her place at the left side of the altar.

The ring bearer looked handsome in his tux. Hesitating before taking a step toward the front, he dangled his pillow from his finger and stopped several times before he made it to the front next to Gregory.

Two male cousins moved swiftly with one hand behind their backs, each picking up one side of the corded white handle that held the white bridal runner. Pulling it as they moved slowly backward, they laid the foundation on which the bride would make her journey.

The flower girls entered and they were lovely in their dresses as they sprinkled rose petals on the white carpet. Ivy had promised both the cute five-year-olds that she'd give them a dollar if they successfully threw the petals on the white runner.

Glenn Jones's soulful voice resonated in the room and the guests looked toward the church door, which had been closed. They were waiting for the bride to be revealed. Little by little, the entrance to the sanctuary opened, revealing Alexis and her father.

The bride looked gorgeous in her strapless matte satin gown with a cathedral train. She clung to her father's arm, knowing every step she took would bring her closer to Jaeden.

While the room resonated with words of finding that perfect love, that one-of-a-kind love most people only dreamed about, a teary-eyed Jaeden watched as Alexis make her way to him.

It seemed as if she was moving in slow motion. As he thought about the words of the song and allowed them to sink in, his heart raced and his palms were sweating in eagerness.

He was so thankful for the beautiful woman that would soon become his wife.

Finally, she stood before him.

Robert lifted the veil that revealed his only daughter's tearstained face. He wiped a tear with his thumb, kissing her on the forehead. "I love you, baby girl," he whispered before replacing the transparent material.

"Who gives this woman to be wedded to this man?" Pastor McCree asked with authority.

"Her mother and I do," Robert responded, glancing at a weepy-eyed Josephine. She'd stood when her husband and Alexis stopped next to her pew. Robert turned to Jaeden and several emotions ran through him before he spoke. "Take care of my baby girl," he said with a tear in his eye before placing Alexis's right hand into Jaeden's.

Taking two steps backward as Alexis moved toward her soon-to-be husband, Robert took his seat next to his wife. Josephine patted him on the leg and he lifted her hand, brushing his lips against her knuckles.

Alexis and Jaeden stood staring as if they were looking into each other's souls. Their eyes were fixed only on each other.

"You look stunning, baby," Jaeden whispered huskily.

"Thank you for my gift, I love it," Alexis whispered in

return. She'd given the delicate piece to her mother to keep so she wouldn't lose it.

She clutched her hand-tied rose bouquet and heirloom handkerchief in her left hand.

"Dearly beloved . . ." Pastor McCree began with power, making the couple realize they weren't alone.

Their heads jerked slightly in his direction and they could hear the snickers from the congregation.

Alexis handed her bouquet to Stephanie, but held on to the handkerchief.

When it was time to recite their wedding vows, Jaeden recited the vows he'd written first. "Alexis," he began, looking attentively into her eyes. "You are a precious gift from God and bring so much joy into my life." He could barely finish his statement. "I affirm the special bond between us and promise to keep it alive always. I promise to be your confidant, your best friend, sharing your hopes and dreams."

His right eye began to twitch as he tried to hold back his tears. "Now, I know I Corinthians Chapter thirteen is true. Love is patient and it is kind, it always protects, always trusts, always hopes, and always perseveres. Love never fails," Jaeden said, believing those words in his heart.

As he allowed a tear to slip down his cheek, he slipped the platinum wedding band on the third finger of Alexis's left hand next to the platinum engagement ring he had given her.

When it was Alexis's turn she could barely speak. Looking down at the two rings that now graced her finger, she was immediately filled with so much love, joy, appreciation, and admiration for the man she was about to pledge the rest of her life to.

Alexis had to clear her throat several times in order to speak her vows. "Jaeden, I've heard people say love is the light that lights the world and kindness paves the road to happiness." Her voice began to falter.

She cleared her throat once again, so she could continue. "I promise to love, honor, and cherish you all the days of my life. You've shown me what real love is and I'm so grateful for your gentleness and friendship," she said, gradually slipping his platinum wedding band on his finger.

They looked at each other and spoke as one. "Love bears, believes, hopes, and endures all things. Love never fails."

Pastor Dixon recited a powerful prayer before Alexis's cousin repeated it in song. Josephine and Gloria rose from their seats as the piano intro to BeBe Winans's "For the Rest of My Life" echoed in the room.

The two women crossed the room and flicked the buttons on their long lighters to illuminate each side of the carved candles that were nestled in a decorative stand to represent the two families. They embraced each other before taking their seats.

Alexis led Jaeden over to the lighted candles. They each picked up the one their mothers had lit. Holding them in the air, they brought them together until it was no longer two flames, but one.

Lowering the single flame, bringing light to the middle candle, they extinguished the candles they held, unifying the two families into one. They placed the candles back into their holders before strolling hand in hand to stand in front of the pastor once more. Alexis and Jaeden turned to face each other again and continued to hold hands.

"I love you," he whispered to Alexis, taking a step closer.

"Son, I haven't said you can kiss the bride yet," Pastor McCree interrupted with a chuckle.

The congregation laughed too.

Jaeden didn't care. He wanted to get to the good part.

At last, Pastor McCree held up his hand. "By the power vested in me by Almighty God and the state of Indiana, I now pronounce you newly married husband and wife." Pastor McCree then nodded to Jaeden. "*Now* you may kiss your bride."

The audience applauded as Jaeden kissed Alexis so fiercely she bent backward.

Natalie Cole's "This Will Be" rang out in the sanctuary and the bridal party marched happily out into the vestibule to the cheers of the audience.

After the guests filed out of the church, Ivy asked the bridal party to return to the sanctuary for the photo session. It moved along rather quickly and soon they were headed to the reception.

The driver opened the door to the limo and congratulated the couple before they climbed inside.

Alexis rested against Jaeden's shoulders and held on to him tightly when they were finally alone.

Jaeden looked down at her. "Baby?"

"Yes," she whispered.

"What's the matter? Why are you so quiet?"

"I'm just so happy," Alexis said. Jaeden pulled back from her slightly and lifted her chin. There were tears of joy brimming in her eyes.

"And it's going to be this way for the rest of our lives," Jaeden promised. He kissed her with such passion, she could hardly catch her breath.

EPILOGUE

Two years later . . .

"Baby, it's time to go," Jaeden said as he walked into the nursery. He found Alexis sitting in the rocking chair with their eight-month-old son, Jaelen Alexander.

"I don't want to leave him," Alexis said tearfully as she looked down into his angelic face. She touched his hairline lightly as he smiled back at her. Lifting him to her chest, she held him closely.

When Alexis had found out she was pregnant, she and Jaeden decided she would go to school full-time. She received her master's of science degree in educational administration several months before Jaelen was born.

"You don't want to miss your first day at your new job. You've worked too hard to get it." Jaeden came over and reached for the baby.

Alexis continued to hold him. "I know, but I've never been away from him all day before." Her face was filled with worry as she handed the baby to his father.

Jaeden took Jaelen back to his crib and laid him down. He turned to Alexis and stretched his arms out. "Come here, baby."

Alexis walked into the strong arms of the man that had been her rock for the past two years while she dealt with graduate school and pregnancy.

Jaeden hugged her, drawing tiny circles on her back to comfort her. "Jay's going to be fine. Your mother should be here any minute and my mother will be here this afternoon."

"I know, but—"

"No buts." Jaeden placed his finger over her lips, then replaced it with his mouth. After they broke the kiss, he stepped back and looked into her eyes once again. "You'll be back home with him in no time."

"I guess you're right." Alexis walked over and looked at her son lying in his crib, playing with his feet.

"You go ahead. Let me change him and I'll bring Jay down so we can see you off," Jaeden said.

"Okay." As Alexis started down the stairs, the doorbell rang. She jogged the rest of the way to the door. "Mom, I'm so glad you're here," she said, opening the door.

"What's the matter?" Josephine asked as she hurried inside. "Is there something wrong with my grandbaby?"

"No, mom. He's wonderful. I just don't think I can leave him."

Josephine smiled and walked over to her daughter. "Sweetie, it's natural to have these feelings, but you've always wanted to be an elementary school principal."

"I told her he would be fine, Mrs. Shire," Jaeden said as he came down the stairs with Jaelen in his arms.

Josephine's eyes lit up when she saw her precious grandson. She took him out of Jaeden's arms when he reached the bottom step.

"She'll get used to leaving him with me," Josephine said, placing little kisses on the baby's temple.

"Come on, baby, it's getting late," Jaeden said to Alexis.

"I just need to grab my briefcase," Alexis said, but didn't move. She kissed her son's forehead again.

"He'll be fine, sweetie. If something happens, I'll call."

Alexis's eyes widened. "Something like what?" Her voice was filled with panic.

"Have a good day, Alexis," Josephine said, smiling as she remembered the way she'd overreacted the first time she'd left Alexis alone.

Jaeden brought Alexis her briefcase and began to gently pull her toward the door.

"I'll call you later, Mom, to check on him," Alexis said before walking out the door.

Alexis greeted the office staff at Benjamin A. Banneker Elementary School. She was elated when she was offered the position as principal of the newly built school.

She walked to her office and rubbed her hand over her engraved initials before opening the door.

Placing her briefcase on the desk, she opened it and pulled out the picture frame Stephanie had given to her at her baby shower.

Alexis stared at the three photos encased in the pewter frame. The first was of her pregnant in her cap and gown standing next to her husband. The second was their first family portrait with Jaelen. The third was of Jaelen sporting the new line of urban clothing his father had designed.

Alexis sat down in the large brown leather chair and pulled out her goal list. She'd taken it off the refrigerator the night before. She picked up a pen and smiled as she read through the list she had made over ten years ago.

Alexis had done everything she'd ever set her mind to and now she could add marriage and motherhood to that glorious list.

Dear Friends:

I pray you enjoyed the ups and downs of Alexis and Jaeden's journey to the altar. I loved sharing their experience with you.

Planning a wedding can be a stressful time. In most cases it is the largest event you'll ever plan. It can also be a beautiful and exciting experience to be enjoyed by all, creating memories that will last a lifetime.

I would like to thank everyone who supported me in this endeavor. I hope to give you more wonderful wedding stories in the near future.

I would love to hear from you. You can write me at P. O. Box 11203, Merrillville, IN 46410 or e-mail me at seandyoung@comcast.net.

Don't forget to visit my Web site, www.seandyoung.com, for contests, my favorite wedding links, and upcoming events.

All Good Things,

Sean D. Young

Wedding Tip: Be sure to get specifics in contracts from your vendors. Bridal Shops, bands, DJs, florists, caterers, and bakeries—have everything in writing. Ask for additional costs that could be charged to you such as traveling, overtime, sales tax, etc. Insist on all the details in the contract. Be suspicious if your vendor doesn't like this.

We hope you enjoyed Sean D. Young's first novel, *Total Bliss*. We have included an excerpt of her next novel, *With This Ring*, which will be in stores in Spring 2006.

Happy Reading!

CHAPTER ONE

"You may kiss the bride," the preacher announced joyfully.

Rose Hart's eyes fluttered as she watched the groom, Nicholas Damon, slowly lift the veil that covered her cousin's round face. She studied the couple as they gazed deep into each other's eyes before sharing a kiss that left them both breathless. Rose could feel the love permeating between them, and that brought a smile to her face.

She was extremely happy for Destiny, who stood at the altar in a breathtaking satin gown with a Queen Anne neckline and long illusion trumpet sleeves. Destiny had waited a long time for this day, and Rose was thrilled to stand next to her as the maid of honor.

The women had been close ever since they were chubby little girls fantasizing about all their hopes and dreams for the future. Each of them had a detailed wedding-day fantasy, but unfortunately, Rose's vision of a happily ever after had been shattered years ago. Destiny's wedding would have to serve as a victory for both of them.

Rose looked up at the gold bridal arch which she'd decorated earlier that day. She and her sisters Violet, Lili, and Ivy operated Hearts and Flowers, a one-stop bridal mansion that took care of all of a couple's wedding needs. Rose was responsible for the floral arrangements, Lili designed cakes, Violet ran the bridal salon, and Ivy took care of the general coordination of events.

Keeping with the theme of the October wedding, Rose had skillfully adorned the arch with ivory tulle that had fall flowers, leaves, and berries intertwined in it. The mixture of mango, gold, and brown colors were magnificent against the yellow flicker from the lights of the candelabrum.

The thunderous applause from the audience, followed by the upbeat tempo of "The Best Is Yet to Come," brought Rose out of her daydream. Dabbing her eyes with an embroidered white handkerchief, she glanced at the women standing behind her and noticed that the other bridesmaids also had to catch the tears threatening to slip down their brown cheeks. She turned around to find Jonathan Damon, the best man, standing with his arm extended and waiting for her to take it.

Jonathan was a devastatingly handsome man who had to be at least six feet tall. Rose had observed his good looks when she met him at the wedding rehearsal. He reminded her of a dark chocolate cover model with his clean shaven look. *Hmm,* she grunted in appreciation, noticing that in his black one-button notch lapel tuxedo he looked like he could strike a runway pose any minute.

"I'm sorry, Jonathan," she whispered, stepping forward.

Jonathan took in the lush beauty standing before him. He admired the way her strapless mango-colored gown clung to every curve of her body. Her shiny shoulder-length black hair had been pinned into a neat French roll that gave her an elegant appearance. He wrapped her arm over his and patted her hand.

"It's okay," he responded in a rich baritone voice as they made their way up the aisle. They walked through the church's vestibule, with the rest of the bridal party following behind them.

When they separated, Rose noticed sweat clinging to Jonathan's brow and leaned closer to him. "Are you okay?" she asked, her voice filled with concern as they entered the holding room.

"I felt fine this morning. I don't know what happened," he said hoarsely.

Rose studied him for a moment and then frowned. "You don't look so good." She guided him over to the nearest chair. "Why don't I try to get you something cool to drink?"

Jonathan pulled a handkerchief from the inside pocket of his jacket and wiped his forehead. "I think I'll be fine, but thanks."

Rose decided to get him some water anyway. When she returned, she found him scrunched down in the chair with his head resting against the wall. She handed him the Styrofoam cup filled with water from the fountain in the hallway. "Here you go, sweetheart."

Jonathan pulled his long frame into an erect sitting position before accepting the cup from her. "Thanks," he said, taking a small sip.

Rose took the empty seat next to him and watched as he drank. Even though Jonathan looked sick, she noticed it did little to diminish his strikingly good looks. "Did that help any?" she asked softly.

"Yes, thank you, but I think I'm going to leave right after we take pictures. I hate to do that to Nick, but I just need to lie down for a while."

"That's probably a good idea."

Rose was watching him use his hankie to dab at the perspiration when her sister Ivy walked into the room.

"The church has been cleared, so we're ready for our photo session," Ivy announced to the crowd. She looked down at Jonathan and her brows creased with concern.

When the bridal party began to file out of the room,

Ivy pulled Rose aside as she passed by. "Is he okay?" she asked, pointing to the best man.

"He's not feeling very well," Rose whispered, watching him sweep the now-damp handkerchief across his brow again as he walked through the doorway.

She followed Ivy out of the room and into the sanctuary where their father, Andrew Hart, had already started the photo session. As they took pictures, Rose tried to keep her eye on Jonathan, who seemed a little off balance at times. When Andrew paused to reload his camera, Jonathan took a seat on the front pew. Rose walked over to where he sat and touched his forehead once more. He was burning up.

"Jonathan, maybe you should leave now. You're starting to look kind of funny and you have a temperature."

He looked up, piercing her with his coal-black eyes. "I feel even worse, but I wanted to talk to Nick before I left." Jonathan reached into his pocket and pulled out a slip of paper. "I wrote my speech for the toast so I wouldn't forget anything. Can you have my brother read it for me?" he asked meekly.

Rose had no idea who his brother was. "Who is—Oh, never mind," she amended, seeing a fresh layer of perspiration form on Jonathan's face. "I'll talk to Nicholas. I'm sure he'll take care of everything."

Jonathan rose from his seat on shaky feet. "Thanks. Please tell him I'll catch up with him later."

Rose reached out and grabbed his hand. "Do you want someone to walk with you to your car?" she asked, watching him skeptically.

"No, it's not so serious that I can't drive." He squeezed her hand before releasing it. "I would kiss you for being so sweet to me, but I'm not sure if I'm contagious," he joked.

Rose smiled at the thought of his full lips descending upon hers and then realized that that probably wasn't what he meant. "That's quite all right," she said, rubbing his back gently. "Just take care of yourself."

"I will." Jonathan offered her a sad smile, attempting to assure her that he was okay before he walked away.

With a shake of her head, Rose watched one of the finest men she had ever seen exit the sanctuary and then sent her attention back to the photographer. Her father was now taking a photo of both sets of parents posed with the bride and groom.

"Mr. Hart, can we get one more with the entire wedding party?" Ivy called out. She always called her father Mr. Hart when they were on a job, to make things seem more professional. Quickly, Ivy looked around the church, counting the bridal party. There were nine people present when there should have been ten. "Where is Jonathan?" she asked loudly when she realized who was missing.

"He started feeling worse, so he left," Rose explained, looking down at the slip of paper Jonathan had given her. She walked to where her sister stood and handed her the speech. "He gave me this for the reception and asked if his brother could read it."

"Who is his brother?" Ivy asked, glancing at the note and then at her sister.

Rose hunched her shoulders. "I have no idea. I told him I'd give the paper to Nicholas."

Ivy sighed heavily, trying to keep her composure. She hated when things didn't go according to plan. "I'll give it to him now and explain what happened. I hope Jonathan feels better," she added before walking away.

"Me, too," Rose mumbled, thinking of the handsome best man who'd exited her life just as quickly as he'd entered it.

After the photo session, the wedding party headed to the reception. Rose beamed when she walked into the main ballroom at the Crystal Palace, an elegant banquet facility in Taylor, Indiana. With its winding staircases, multiple fireplaces, and antique décor, it made guests feel like they were celebrating in a real palace.

The ballroom, with its countless crystal chandeliers, a marble dance floor, and high ceilings, was gracefully decorated in ivory and gold. Since Rose was part of the wedding, she'd made arrangements to go to the facility earlier to decorate. Her goal had been to bring Destiny's childhood vision of the perfect wedding to life.

Destiny had chosen raw silk tangerine tablecloths, so Rose designed a tabletop centerpiece of deep burgundy hydrangeas, black magic roses, orange leonidas roses, and calla lilies. She also placed beautiful gold lamps on each side of the centerpiece to complete the look. Since she'd left to get ready for the wedding, the waitstaff had placed gold-trimmed china and flatware on the tables, along with beautiful antique gold frames with the table numbers printed in calligraphy. Rose was proud of the outcome of her hard work, and she knew she'd accomplished her goal when she saw the tears brimming in Destiny's eyes as she looked around the room.

Soon, the wedding party was announced, and after the bride and groom received their guests, everyone was prepared to eat dinner. Pastor Bobby Grayson gave the invocation, thanking God for the couple as well as the food.

Rose picked up a dainty cellophane bag next to her place setting. Chocolate-shaped leaves wrapped in gold, orange, and copper foil had been placed in the small pouch. It was tied with a sheer rust-colored ribbon. The favors had taken Lili forever to complete, but the hard work had been well worth the result, Rose thought.

"Rose!"

She looked up to see Ivy, who was headed in her direction with a panicked look on her face.

"What's wrong?" she asked her sister, rising from seat. It looked serious.

"Nicholas just told me Jonathan's brother, Marc, is going to take his place," Ivy spat out, waving her hands.

Rose frowned in confusion and grabbed her sister's hands, holding them to keep them still. "What's wrong with that?" she asked calmly.

Ivy pulled a hand out of her sister's grip and took several deep breaths to calm herself. "He's going to take Jonathan's place!"

Rose crinkled her nose, puzzled. Her sister tended to be a little dramatic sometimes. It was an odd trait for a wedding planner. "Vee, you're confusing me. Why is this making you so uneasy? Why, is he better looking than Jonathan?" she asked sarcastically. Even sick, Jonathan would be a hard act to follow.

Ivy's panicked look was replaced by the serious one she wore all the time. "You're going to have to dance with him," she stated.

"So, and . . ."

Ivy huffed, slowly shaking her head at her sister's inability to comprehend the dilemma. "How do you think it's going to look with all the other men in their tuxedos and this guy in a suit, *if* he's wearing one?"

Rose rolled her eyes and shook her head. "Have you even met the man?"

"No, not yet. Nicholas went to get him," Ivy said, patting her foot on the floor as she canvassed the room. She checked her watch then looked around some more until she spotted him. "I guess we're both about to meet him now." She pointed at Nicholas, who was walking toward them with a very tall, dark-skinned man.

Rose leaned closer to Ivy. "You should feel better now, Vee. The man has on a suit *and* it's black," she chuckled. She didn't want to laugh and make her sister angry, but she just couldn't help it. Ivy could be so melodramatic sometimes.

As the men approached, Rose noticed the small diamond winking at her from Jonathan's brother's left ear and smiled brightly. She didn't want to stare, but this man was even finer than his brother. Of course, she thought, Jonathan was a great specimen, but *his* brother . . . Rose wondered if there were more Damon brothers she didn't know about.

"Umph, umph, umph," Rose said under her breath as she watched the dark Adonis step toward her. He was taller than Jonathan and his hard, muscular body filled his black double-breasted suit oh so deliciously. The man had shoulders a woman could hold on to forever. His black hair, which he wore in a tiny Afro, was lined and trimmed to perfection. Rose had to make sure she kept herself together. Immediately, she smoothed the wrinkles from her dress and sucked in her tummy even further.

"Ivy and Rose, this is my cousin, Marc Damon," Nicholas began. "Marc, meet Ivy and Rose Hart."

Marc extended his hand to Rose, assessing her striking, round, dark brown face. Her seductive light brown eyes spoke volumes to him. "Let me guess, you must be Rose," he said lifting her extended hand to his lips. "A rose of beauty is a joy forever."

Marc lowered her hand, but kept it in his grasp. The softness of her hands made him imagine how soft the rest of her voluptuous body would feel against him. "It's always a pleasure to meet a beautiful woman."

Rose felt her face redden when she looked into his black eyes, which sparkled like polished onyx. Her eyes dropped to the neat thin mustache above his full lips. A man had never affected her like this before.

"Yes, I'm Rose. It was nice of you to step in for your brother," she said politely.

"I'll make sure I thank him for this opportunity." Marc continued to admire Rose's beauty. Her strapless gown accented her ample bosom and wide curvaceous hips. Her skin was smooth and looked velvety soft. He wondered when, rather, *if*, he would ever get the chance to touch it. For now, he'd have to settle for a handshake.

Ivy cleared her throat, and Marc's head turned in her direction. He reluctantly released Rose's hand and offered his to Ivy.

"It seems all I've been doing this evening is meeting beautiful women," Marc said, flashing a devastating smile and exposing perfectly straight white teeth.

Rose couldn't help but notice the glint in his eyes as he spoke. She glanced at her sister to see her reaction to him. Ivy had given him a half smile as she accepted his handshake.

"Nice to meet you, Marc," she said, quickly pulling her hand back. "I'd like to go over your responsibilities, so we can get started."

I knew it, Rose thought to herself. Ivy had to find Marc attractive. She was always an ice queen when it came to handsome men.

Marc's attention went back to Rose. She was unbelievably gorgeous, and he'd found it difficult to take his eyes off of her for even a moment. He was about to strike up a conversation with her when Ivy cleared her throat again.

"Why don't we get started with our toasts?" she suggested, heading to the podium before he could give an answer.

Stepping back, Marc extended his hand. "Ladies, first," he said to Rose. As she led the way to the platform, he watched the way the fabric of her gown outlined her backside.

Rose's heart rate accelerated at the thought of Marc following her, watching her every move. She knew she looked good in her dress, so she wasn't worried that he wouldn't like what he saw; it was something else that made her uneasy. She just couldn't put her finger on what it was, though. Maybe it was the way Marc's presence seemed to command her attention, or the way the huskiness in his voice or the smoky look in his eyes made her want to swoon. If she were honest with herself, she'd admit it was the entire package that unnerved her. The man was fine, plain and simple.

Once they were at the podium, Ivy handed them both a glass of champagne and signaled for Rose to begin her speech.

"Good evening everyone. I would like you to join me in a toast to the bride and groom." Rose glanced at the bridal table, and her eyes immediately began to fill with tears. "Dez, we always talked about finding our own Prince Charming. We both knew he wouldn't look anything like the one in the fairytale, but we wanted it. I'm so glad you found him in Nicholas. May your love for each other deepen and grow in the years to come. I wish you both all the happiness your hands and hearts can hold." She lifted her glass to the audience. "To Destiny and Nicholas, here, here."

As Rose took a sip of the golden liquid, she glanced at Marc and their eyes met and held. He moved closer to her, placing his hand on the small of her back, and she shuddered. Nervous excitement swirled in the pit of her stomach.

Marc leaned forward to speak into the microphone with his eyes fixed on Rose. "Wow, what can I say after such a beautiful toast? And from the most gorgeous woman in the room . . . besides the bride," he added quickly.

The crowd laughed at his flirtations, and he smiled at Rose, waiting for her response.

She turned slightly and playfully pinched his cheek.

"He's such a sweet talker," Rose said into the microphone, giving him a teasing grin. What was it about this man that had her feeling like a schoolgirl with a crush on her teacher instead of a mature thirty-year-old woman?

The guests erupted in laughter again.

Marc winked at her, then asked her to hold his champagne glass while he pulled the slip of paper with his brother's toast written on it from his pocket. When Rose handed him his glass back to him and their fingers met, an electric spark ran up his arm. Marc stared at her a moment in stunned silence before he brought his attention back to his task.

"I'm honored to stand in for my brother, Jonathan, who couldn't be here this evening," he told the crowd. He looked over at the bride and groom and continued, "Nick, he wanted to make sure you and Dez knew exactly how he felt."

Marc glanced quickly at the paper and began to read his brother's words. "Nick, I knew from day one you'd marry Destiny. When you told me you couldn't live without her, it confirmed exactly what I'd thought. You were mesmerized by her beauty, outside and in. I'm thankful to have been a part of that special moment in your life. Keep loving her as you do today and you'll be a happy man for the rest of your life."

Marc smiled as his eyes went to the bride. "Dez, you're the best thing that ever happened to my rockhead cousin. I'm so glad you put him out of his misery by agreeing to be his wife."

Everyone chuckled at Jonathan's words. Marc glanced at Rose, who had tears in her eyes, and he raised his glass. "The only thing left to say is congratulations. Here, here."

When the toasts were completed, Marc escorted Rose back to her seat at the bridal table. After he pulled out her chair and saw that she was situated comfortably, Nicholas called out to him.

"Why don't you sit with us?" he asked as he pulled out the chair next to him.

"Sure," Marc agreed, thankful for any excuse to remain close to Rose, even if he was two seats away. He embraced his cousin before taking the offered chair.

Rose watched the exchange, and the thought of Marc caused a sparkle of excitement to return. She had never been so drawn to a man so quickly. The feelings he was stirring in her were ones she thought had been gone forever.

Destiny leaned over to Rose with her hand covering one side of her mouth. "If I didn't know any better, I would have thought you and Marc were a couple," she whispered.

Rose glanced in Marc's direction, then waved her hand at her cousin. "We were just having fun."

Destiny leaned closer. "He's the cousin I told you about a couple of weeks ago."

Rose's brows lifted in revelation. "He's the smooth-talking brotha from Boston?" she asked softly.

"The one and only," Destiny replied, smiling.

For some reason Rose felt giddy. She picked up her champagne glass and took a sip, hoping to calm her nerves. Finally she looked at Marc again and noticed his eyes were focused on her as well, but they didn't divulge his thoughts.

Quickly, she broke the magnetic trance. "Ooh, and he's Jonathan's brother. Girl, please." She waved again at Destiny just as the server placed her entrée in front of her.

As Rose began to eat, she felt as if she was being watched. She didn't have to look in Marc's direction to know he was the observer.

A few minutes later, Nicholas assisted his bride from

her chair and they walked hand in hand over to the cake. As soon as Destiny's chair was vacant, Marc filled it.

"Are you having a good time?" he asked.

"Yes, I am. How 'bout you?" Rose replied casually, hoping she appeared nonchalant even though she wasn't.

"The evening is definitely looking up. I used to think weddings were a waste of time."

"Used to think? Does that mean you've changed your mind?" she asked, trying to ignore the way his slacks strained against his muscular thighs.

"Nicholas seems happy."

"Seems? They really love each other. I'm so happy for them." There was a slight pause before Rose spoke again. "Have you checked on Jonathan since you've been here?" she asked, taking a small bite of roast beef.

Marc moved his chair closer to her. "Yes, I spoke to him on my way over. He was just pulling into the apartment complex." He smiled as he took in her feminine scent. It was a mixture of vanilla and jasmine.

His deep voice sounded so seductive, Rose slowly looked at him, giving him a dimpled grin. "I hope he feels better after he's gotten some rest."

Marc lifted Rose's left hand and stroked it as she turned toward him. Instinctively, he observed the roundness of her heavy bosom. "It's unfortunate for him that he's not feeling well, but I wouldn't have had the pleasure of your company this evening if he were better."

Rose gave him a sidelong glance. She thought he was laying on the charm pretty thick and gently pulled her hand from his. "You shouldn't glory in your brother's illness. I'm sure he wouldn't feel that way if you were the one sick."

Marc felt like he'd been struck in the face. "Oh, don't get me wrong, I'd never wish my brother any harm. I love him. I was just stating a fact."

The sound of Brian McKnight's "Love of My Life" caught Rose's attention. She looked toward the dance floor as Nicholas drew Destiny into his arms for their first dance. Rose was so lost in watching the newlyweds that she didn't see Marc stand next to her offering his hand. He lightly touched her bare shoulder to get her attention and she suppressed a shiver.

She looked up into his dark eyes and then shifted to his lips.

"They want the rest of the party to join the happy couple," he said, quoting the announcement Ivy had just made. He smiled again and the diamond in his ear twinkled.

This man is going to drive me crazy, Rose thought. She pushed her chair back and took his hand. Marc escorted her to the dance floor and pulled her into a sensual embrace, lightly rubbing his lips against her ear as they danced.

Desire pulsed through Rose's body. Now she knew how Whitney Houston felt in the movie *Waiting to Exhale*. Slowly, she released a deep breath and relaxed in Marc's arms.

"You know you almost took my breath away," he said against her ear. His voice was husky and the seductive tone had returned.

Rose felt a shiver again. Was she getting sick too? Or was it the heat from the man holding her? She wasn't lost on the fact of how well she fit in the circle of Marc's arms. He held her with such delicate caution. She felt cherished, secure, and most of all desirable.

She looked into his eyes when he pulled back from her and thought, *I want to have this man's babies*. Immediately, she wondered where the thought came from. Rose had never been a desperate woman and she'd sworn off men ever since the last guy she gave her heart to took it and shattered it. Once the pain had faded, she couldn't bear to give her heart to another man ever again. She had to try to pull her feelings together—but not until the song ended.

Rose rested her head against Marc's shoulder as they continued to sway to the music. When the song was over, she released another sigh and attempted to take a small step backward but realized he hadn't let her go just yet.

"Wait," Marc said, holding her for another moment before he stepped back so he could hold her at arm's length.

Confusion swarmed through Marc's mind. Rose Hart disturbed his calm. He'd just met her a little over an hour ago, and she already had him in knots. He was usually attracted to model-thin women, but this beautiful brown honey with her lush curves had changed all that in a matter of minutes. She was an exquisite female, but it wasn't the mere fact that she was beautiful. He'd known gorgeous women all his adult life and even fell in love with one, but there was something different about Rose. . . .

He hadn't figured out what exactly, but now he had to decide whether he wanted to take a chance and find out.

Rose slowly lifted her head. "Yes?"

"Thank you for the dance."

Rose chuckled. "Thank you," she said before attempting to step out of his embrace one more time. This time he released her. "We'd better get back to our seats." She turned and started to walk away from him only to feel his hand on her back as he followed her to the bridal table.

About the Author

Sean D. Young never imagined she would get the opportunity to write heart-touching romances filled with unforgettable characters. Young, a Gary, Indiana, native, has been a voracious reader all her life. At seven, she joined her first book club. Five years later, she combined her love of reading and her interest in writing to create several short stories for her own personal enjoyment.

Total Bliss, her first novel, incorporates elements of her professional work as a bridal consultant. Young, a graduate of National Bridal Services' Weddings Beautiful division, is a Certified Wedding Specialist. With her mother, she owns and operates Young Creations.

Young lives in Northwest Indiana with her husband and children. She can be contacted through her Web site at www.seandyoung.com or by e-mail at seandyoung@comcast.net.